CW00815720

The Black Italian

When Eve Gill's father, the tough old Commodore, flung Detective-Inspector Christopher Smith off his yacht into the sea, he started something. Of course the old man had taken to smuggling again, so Eve was not wholly sorry to see the last of Smith, but her anxiety was once more aroused when she spotted a secret watcher on the marsh, whose binoculars were trained on the yacht and from time to time on her home, Marsh House.

Eve made friends with the watcher, though she could not place him. But he too became involved in the murder which took Eve to London, and so across Europe to Genoa, then the headquarters of the southern European black market and a Mecca for every kind of crook.

Not surprisingly, Eve was soon in danger, and it took all her resourcefulness, charm and energy to track down the man behind the murder, the Black Italian.

This title was first published in the Crime Club in 1954.

SELWYN JEPSON

The Black Italian

Eve Gill investigates . . .

The Disappearing Detectives

Selected and Introduced
by H. R. F. Keating

COLLINS, 8 GRAFTON STREET, LONDON W1

William Collins Sons & Co. Ltd
London · Glasgow · Sydney · Auckland
Toronto · Johannesburg

First published in the Crime Club 1954
Reprinted in this edition 1985
Copyright reserved Selwyn Jepson
© in the Introduction, H. R. F. Keating, 1985

British Library Cataloguing in Publication Data

Jepson, Selwyn
   The Black Italian.—(Crime Club)
   I. Title
   823′.912[F]   PR6019.E55/

ISBN 0 00 231992 6

Photoset in Linotron Baskerville by
Rowland Phototypesetting Ltd
Bury St Edmunds, Suffolk
Printed in Great Britain by
William Collins Sons & Co. Ltd, Glasgow

For
Beryl and Robert Graves

INTRODUCTION
H. R. F. Keating

The last book to have Eve Gill as its fizz-full heroine appeared in 1964. She came to fictional life as long ago as 1948. Little wonder, then, that, though she was hailed with delight in her day—'The most resourceful, unscrupulous and entertaining baggage imaginable,' sang one reviewer— she is a detective, perhaps more properly an investigator, who has almost disappeared. She lives, I suppose, in a few memories here and there. Perhaps some who remember her do so even without realizing it since *Man Running*, the first book of which she was heroine, was filmed by Alfred Hitchcock under the title *Stage Fright*.

Eve, for all her resourcefulness, lack of scruple and baggagery, is in many ways a fine example of the intrepid yet foolish heroine of a whole sub-genre of suspense fiction, the Had-I-But-Known school, those books in which a pretty girl finds herself plumb bang in a situation she has been explicitly warned to avoid but into which out of feminine pig-headedness (the worst sort) or to prove herself the equal of an admirer she has plunged.

Such books have been mocked at mercilessly. But not always deservedly. Given that the foolish female is portrayed with a decent degree of realism, her idiocy can be made to seem at least momentarily perfectly sensible, an action which even a man (never other than solidly reasonable) might launch into. Stories of this kind, once your sympathies are fairly engaged, can be palpitatingly effective. It was so with the great progenitor of the school, Mary Roberts Rinehart with Rachel Innes in the splendid *The Circular Staircase*, even though Miss Rachel was not your classic pretty young thing. So it is with Eve Gill, 'perhaps the most versatile, accomplished and quick-witted heroine of modern fiction', as the thoroughly entrapped reviewer for *Time and Tide* called her at the height of her success.

7

Eve's ability not to intrude herself into the affairs of the police can, in fact, be seen, together with her deadly aim with a pistol, as a harbinger of the aggressive feminist movement that began coming to the fore only about the time her creator abandoned her. But her approach to life springs from a feminism that goes much further back. It is the feminism of books even earlier than Mrs Rinehart's gothic innovation. It goes back as far as 1794, to Mrs Radcliffe, author of *The Mysteries of Udolpho*, that chronicle of the desperate adventures of Emily de St Aubert. This is —whether Selwyn Jepson in 1948 was conscious of it or not—the instinctive protest of women, for so long often a species of domestic slave.

The lonely, risk-laden explorations of mysterious old houses and sealed chambers by your gothic heroines were no less in hidden terms than a seeking for personal freedom, an unlocking of doors in the mind. This is why, down the years, this sort of book has been so popular, despite the obvious inanities of the worst kind of the species. Eve's adventures tied to the apron-strings of her ex-Commodore father, who in spite of his wheelchair is allowed masculine freedom to the full (as witness his ineradicable penchant for smuggling), fall squarely within the tradition.

Indeed, Selwyn Jepson more or less acknowledged this. Asked for a crime-fiction encyclopedia to comment at any length he liked on his work, he said only that he had never pretended to write anything other than fairy stories for grown-ups. Yet fairy stories are myths in miniature, and Eve Gill is, for all her adult outlook, the heroine of a fairy story, a quest with an ogre at the end of it. So her adventure here appeals to us, both female and male, at a deeper level than we might suppose.

But if Selwyn Jepson was fundamentally writing simply fairy stories, he was on the surface as knowledgeable, even as knowing, a writer as you could wish. What a delighted feeling of being on the inside, of learning things your ordinary mortal wots not of, must have come over readers of this book when they were told, for instance, that Genoa had taken over from Naples as the headquarters of the southern

European black market. And if today that fact must appear to us as no more than a small nugget of historical information, it is still a pleasure to discover it. Much the same can be said of the odd items of 1950s British life that have sunk into the mire of history since the book was written: the 'tryptics' without which it was then forbidden to take a car to the Continent, that one was not allowed indeed to take more than five pounds' worth of precious sterling with one when one went, that as often as not even sophisticated travellers went there or came from America not by air but by boat.

The man who knew so well the ins and outs of life at that time had certainly earned his knowledge. Selwyn Jepson, who was born in 1899, had been educated both at prestigious old St Paul's School and at the Sorbonne. He was a soldier in the 1914–18 War and served in the SOE, the Special Operations Executive, in World War II. Many of the 29 thrillers he wrote (only six of them, alas, brought us Eve Gill) are set in exotic parts of the world.

But the easy skill with which he larded his stories with the trappings and trimmings of a life that ordinary mortals don't get to see must have come from his father, Edgar Jepson, a yet more prolific writer of novels, romances and crime stories, indeed a founder member with G. K. Chesterton, Agatha Christie and Dorothy L. Sayers of the Detection Club.

One of his heroines would appear, in fact, to be a happy go-lucky forerunner of sparkling Eve Gill. Hear what the reviewer for *The Times* in the first years of this century said about the heroine of Edgar Jepson's very successful *The Lady Noggs, Peeress*: 'The Lady Noggs has a frankness, an engaging roguery, and a delightful aplomb which will make everyone enjoy her escapades.' Well, Eve Gill has, to my mind, the frankness, the engaging cheekiness and all the happy unfazed aplomb which can hardly fail to make you, too, enjoy her adventures in the pages that follow.

CHAPTER 1

I had thought myself long past the days of wishing I had
been born of the male sex. But I wished it then, shivering
with the effects of cold creek water and plain misery. I knelt
by the gasping, half-drowned Christopher and could not
fool myself. He was loathing me. Charlie Berrington was
not improving matters by trying to use artificial respiration
on the poor man; the poor man thrust him away with
surprising strength and continued to look at me with that
awful disillusion.

'I'm all right!' he said between coughing and spluttering.

If only I could have been a man, to slap him on the back
and laugh at the craziness of what had happened. Funny?
The funniest end to a love scene you ever saw!

But it had been *our* love scene, our first love scene, and
sweet enough, but all too short to fix the notion that he
loved me really firmly in his heart and head. Our first love
scene . . .

I wanted to put my arms round him and cry, 'My love,
my love,' but dared not. Could I have known that Father
would knock him off *Peacock*'s deck and nearly drown him?
Was I to have guessed that that same deck would be loaded
with cases of contraband Burgundy and maybe a little
brandy to keep the Suffolk winter out of an old man's bones
—a cantankerous, jealous, violent old man who wouldn't
wait to tell himself that there was a world of difference
between a Custom's Preventive Officer on duty (which was
the kind he rightly feared) and a Divisional Detective-
Inspector of Police on holiday (which was what my
Christopher Smith happened by ill-chance to be). A tire-
some, impulsive, dangerous old man.

All I could do was to help him sit up on the wet sand of
the small beach and keep my mouth shut—and hope.

His face was cold through the thin stuff of my swim-suit.

But he did not want his face against my breast and turned his head away.

'I'm all right,' he said again, 'it's nothing to worry about.'

But I knew it was.

'Christopher, oh please don't look at me like that!'

'Like what?'

How could I tell him, 'as if you loathed me for having such a father'? I rounded instead on Charlie, who was still standing there and for once in his life looking as awkward as he felt. 'Go and get into dry clothes!' I said. 'You'll catch cold!'

Charlie's faded jeans, dark with water, clung to his great legs as no more than an extra skin which would dry on him along with his other skins without producing even a sneeze. 'In any case,' I added without waiting for him to take the hint, 'please *go away*!'

He grinned at me in a one-sided fashion and returned to the water from which he had carried Christopher. He began swimming as strongly against the tide as he had with it, back to the *Peacock* and my no doubt still self-satisfied father. My father? I was ready at that miserable moment to disown him out of hand. He had made my beloved look a complete damn' fool in front of me, and that was a thing no man could forgive a girl.

He sat there, supporting himself on his elbows and watched Charlie cleaving the water. 'He saved my life,' he said, and shook with a fit of coughing.

'It wasn't as bad as that.' But I knew it had been and so did he. He had been out, cold, when he hit the water.

'Your father, the Commodore—' he began with a lightness in his voice which rang very false.

'It was an unspeakable thing!' I said.

'Let's not be serious about it.'

That would be exactly what I wanted but an affronted male pride, never higher in his life than when he had stepped on to the *Peacock*'s deck, would not let him be anything else.

I watched him a moment while he tried to make himself think instead of feel. I almost wished he would seize on the subject of those wooden boxes, but things would get very tricky indeed if he suddenly decided that ethically he should stand with HM Customs and Excise and do something about a smuggler for them. It was too high a price to pay for respite from my problem and I prayed he wouldn't think that way.

He sneezed, twice, violently.

'Let's get you back to the house,' I said; it sounded as though I thought him incapable of getting himself back to the house. Also, someone had to fetch our robes from the other end of the beach where we had been sunbathing before the *Peacock* sailed into view, and I made it worse by saying that if he kept still a moment I would fetch them. 'No—'

He even resented my going along with him, but the path up the dyke wall was near where they lay. He managed to climb the dyke unaided but I could not stop the instinctive help of my hands when he stumbled. The sun shone warmly and some of the colour came back to his face although his temples remained greenish—and more hollow than usual. There was now an unmistakable bruise on the angle of his jaw.

I was still trying desperately to think of something to say which would open the barrier of silence between us before it became a permanent thing.

These wide and desolate marshes, the flat grey-green sea beyond, the big sky, all this was my world, familiar from my earliest memories. I had been born in that house to which we were returning, its tall chimneys twisting higher than the trees which sheltered it. Ten generations of Gills had lived there and I was of their blood and this corner of the earth was my heritage and a solid anchorage for my heart.

I stole a look at Christopher's face—that gloomy disillusion in it—that must be driven out with all the cunning I could muster. He must be kept aware of me, physically, sensually aware of me. All the time. This was Saturday and not yet noon. I had until Monday—call it Sunday night, since he would have to catch the early train back to London on Monday morning. Even so it was a lifetime of opportunity. If I couldn't re-establish this thing between us by then I deserved to lose him.

I put him with a decanter of whisky, soda-water and a large tumbler in the guest bathroom, turned on the hot water and left him to it. He smiled at me timidly, fearing I might read too much into his polite gratitude. I pretended not to notice it and went to my own rooms to dress.

The midday mail had arrived and there were two letters on my sitting-room table, a bill for my new black suit and a large, dark blue envelope with Angela Sawyer's sprawling, emotional handwriting, its stamp showing she was home from abroad. I wondered idly what was bothering her, for she seldom wrote unless she was in some kind of difficulty. She was running to form:

Darling Eve,
    You are always so sensible about everything, and this time I really must have your advice—and *help* . . .

I put down the letter, indeed I dropped it quickly. This was not the moment for other people's troubles. Fond of her as I was, and accustomed to hearing hers, I had neither the patience nor the time now. Later, later, when I had dealt with this.

I went into the bedroom with my mind returning to practical considerations. The yellow silk? It hung well, and showed off my figure—that, with plenty of Chanson d'Amour, which was as straight seduction as a scent could be . . .

But first my hair. It had had no protecting cap when I jumped off the deck after Christopher, and Charlie's splash almost on top of me as he followed had momentarily submerged me. It was in a frightful mess.

I rinsed it thoroughly, put the electric drier to work and used a ribbon to hold it in some sort of shape. It did not quite come up to the sophistication of the rest of me, but it was the best I could do.

I reached the Long Room in time to have another drink ready for him. He came in looking peaked and his temples a more living colour. But his grey flannel suit hung from his shoulders and seemed to touch him nowhere else. His red-

14

dish hair curled darkly and damp above his bold forehead, the only unordinary thing about his face. I came as close to him as possible; and closer, to put the glass in his hand. I was not being at all a nice, modest girl. But his eyes were everywhere else.

I went quickly away. I had until tomorrow evening, hadn't I?

Mary tried to waylay me in the hall, but I went on towards the garden door. She followed me.

'Jim Crowley says the *Peacock*'s home.'

'Yes. I'm going now to fetch the Commodore,' I told her. 'The wheelchair is in the boatshed.'

'Back unexpected-like, isn't he?'

'Yes.' I knew that her shrewd old eyes under the frizz of white hair were full of uneasy comprehension.

'Everything all right, dear?'

'No,' I admitted.

'Drat that man!' she said, and she did not mean Christopher. 'You said he'd promised never again.'

'Of course he promised.'

'He'll be ashore for lunch?'

'Yes,' I said firmly. 'He'll be ashore. Mr Berrington will either stay aboard—or go straight to the cottage.' I was *not* going to have Charlie peering into my heart or watching my play.

'That'll be three,' said Mary.

'Yes,' I said even more firmly. 'Just three.'

'On the terrace?'

'On the terrace, Mary.'

'You'll want a white wine. There's lobster.'

'There are two bottles of the Anjou in the Long Room cupboard.'

'Mrs Custard says she did your fortune last night.'

I was at the garden door by then and not prepared to hear about Mrs Custard 'doing my fortune'.

'Not now Mary, please—'

'It's never been wrong, dear.'

'And never right—'

She could stop playing chaperon now the Commodore

was back and retire to her beloved kitchen. I ran along the side of the big rose bed towards the trees and the track beyond them, the salt breeze in my face with the marsh mud below the dyke wall oozing and steaming in the sun.

After a little I realized I was setting myself a ridiculously fast pace and forced myself to stop and lie down on my face to get my breath. The hay-like sweetness of the grass mingling reluctantly with Chanson d'Amour, quarrelled with it indeed, and I saw some kind of symbolism in the fact. This Kessingland world was my place; my roots were as much in it as were those of the scented grass. Was I being a fool to want Christopher, a man whose life had been in the crowded, peopled places and intimately concerned with the complications of human relationships in their most subtle and twisted aspects . . .?

. . . I raised my head, startled, my eyes focusing on the line of low hills which lifted themselves from the marshes half a mile to the west. A small spot of brilliant light had flickered for a moment and vanished, so that I was not sure I had really seen it. I thought it might have been some small but highly polished surface, a fragment of broken glass perhaps on the top of the bluff which for a brief moment had caught the sun at the exact angle of refraction for my own position.

To test this I shifted my head a few inches this way and that, asking myself why I was bothering about it; but I knew that a moment like this, when the *Peacock* was just in from one of her nefarious voyages, the slightest thing out of the ordinary always set me on edge with suspicion: a boy on a bicycle, a wandering hiker, a barking dog—even a piece of glass flashing in the sun half a mile away. He always laughed at my warnings and broke his promises, and each time I felt more keenly the inevitability of disaster. He was sixty-three. If, at best, they fined him, it would be so heavily that we should lose Marsh House and the lands of our forefathers; if they put him in prison he would die. 'Fun,' as he called it. You could pay a high price for fun when the Law called it something else.

I could not find the angle of refraction again and was

16

further disquieted by the thought that it was the object, not I, which had moved. The road, our private road, was away to the right by several hundred yards; beyond that point on the bluff lay the wildest part of the heath. What could reflect the sun as brightly as that? I lifted myself higher on my hands, slowly, to avoid sudden movement, and as I did so it came again, a pin-point of very white light, flashing briefly.

Binoculars! I pushed myself backwards off the bank and rolled down its steepness to the edge of the mud. The man would have seen me a few moments ago when I was running, outlined against the sky. That his interest, his chief object of observation, might be in the *Peacock* held no comfort, at all. He could see her clearly from the slight elevation of the bluff.

I dared not speculate. I must act on the most likely assumption that he was a Customs officer with a roving commission—or worse, working on a tip-off from an agent in Dunkirk—that he was squatting there in the gorse on the edge of the bluff watching the ketch and all that went on ... yes, might even have seen Christopher's ignominious dismissal from her deck.

There was no fixed drill for this sort of eventuality; Father had wanted to arrange one and I had refused even to discuss such a thing, saying that if his promises meant anything, there was no need for it.

But now he must be warned. I stood up precariously on the narrow verge of the mudflat, and began to move back to the house as fast as the uneven ground at the foot of the dyke would let me. The long tufted grass whipped my legs and now and again tried to throw me into the waiting mud. But I came at last to where the going was easier and the trees of the home wood took over my concealment from the watcher. I hoped he thought I was still lying in the grass on the dyke wall, and although chiefly interested in the *Peacock*, my presence there might fox him a little. I was clutching at any straw in prayer that he would stay where he was for the time being. I hurried across the garden with a plan shaping into detail.

I would have avoided Christopher but the things I needed

were in the Long Room. I could see him through the open french windows, still hunched in the chair, the empty glass in his hand. I stood on the threshold for several frustrating but necessary moments to get my breath, remembering his trained observation and relying on his unhappy preoccupation to save me from it.

He got up from the chair and smiled half-heartedly. He had not the slightest idea of how to handle the situation and was relieved when I assumed responsibility.

'The jays are at the raspberries again,' I said, and ran to the drawer under Father's bunk, built in the alcove to the left of the big fireplace. I rummaged amongst the odds and ends and came up with what I wanted, the pistol and a signal flag, neatly tied in a small bundle with its own lanyard.

At the sight of the huge revolver, a silver-plated long .45 Colt with which in his youth Father had liberated Iraquay, Christopher's eyes widened. I kept the muzzle well down, however, and went past him towards the door. 'Come along if you like,' I said and heard him following me.

Jays in the raspberries was not a problem to arouse further emotional conflicts and he was prepared to welcome it as a safe return road to some kind of normal relationship. When I arrived at the flagstaff on the flat roof over the west wing, he was close behind, climbing the skylight ladder. I unwrapped the small flag, attached it to the halyard of the mast and ran it up. Christopher looked at it.

'House flag? Meaning that the owner is in residence,' he said. 'There's something attractive about these traditions.'

I went across to the parapet and saw with relief that as usual there were at least two jays moving secretly in the birch trees beyond the fruit garden, their fawn and white plumage flickering in the frothy green above the raspberries.

'A hundred yards,' Christopher said doubtfully.

'But it makes a tremendous bang and frightens them.' I lifted the Colt with both hands, and paused. 'It also kicks like eighteen mules,' I said.

He reached out and took it from me.

18

I had no excuse, of course—unless in a resentment, almost unconscious, that he could not love me enough to take me as I was, with the sort of Father I had. I laid the trap for him with only a small twinge of conscience. Had I held the pistol in one hand and made no mention of its recoil, he would not have fired it for me and thus participated in my effort to make a fool of his god the Law.

But fire it he did. Three times, rapidly. Leaves and twigs showered out of the birch trees, but no jays; they merely vanished, instantly and unharmed in the way jays do at such times. However, my main concern was the sound of the shots. This was even more considerable than I had anticipated and I listened with guilty satisfaction to the echoes reverberating across the gardens to the marshes beyond, in a moment to reach the creek, and be heard on board the *Peacock*. A telescope would turn towards the house and read the signal flying from our mast-head, clearly visible from the water but hidden by the tall pines on the landward side; no one on the heath could see it.

Christopher peered at the birch trees, revolver still poised. A countryman would have known that every jay in the neighbourhood had left for the day and a sailor would have recognized that flag. But Christopher, the townsman, was neither. The square of yellow bunting stood out in the breeze. He did not look at it again. But now that I had sprung the trap, anxiety gripped me.

'Christopher,' I said desperately, 'I think it would be better for both of us—just now—if you went back to London and left me to deal with Father alone.'

He swung round to look at me, and said a shade too quickly: 'I had been thinking it might be easier for you without me. I—well, I'm not much use in—in—"situations". I've led such a sheltered life.'

We both laughed falsely. We were talking about it now, at last. I wished to God we weren't.

'Everything,' I said tritely and with the same falsity, 'is going to be all right if we give it time.'

'Of course it is,' he agreed with relief. 'I know he didn't meant to go off half-cock like that.'

'I'm sure he didn't. I'll explain it all to him. He'll see things differently.'

Christopher nodded.

'But it will be easier if you're not here—'

He nodded again, eagerly.

'Oh Christopher—'

I stopped myself. To have been held in his arms at that moment, to know with physical certainty that we wanted one another would have been a very sweet comfort. But it would have frightened and embarrassed him.

'It'll be all right,' I said again.

'Of course. And don't worry, my dear. There's all the time in the world.'

I tried to think that for him in the unaccustomed idiom of the affections, 'my dear' meant 'darling' and that 'all the time in the world' was merely careless use of a cliché. Time, even a little of it, was dangerous to a love so young. But time was being forced on me; I heard the distant sound of the *Peacock*'s winch, chugging and rattling at the anchor chain. How long would it take Father to land his cargo, bury it somewhere up the estuary or dump it at sea—which was more than I dared hope? A week? And after that, days of argument each of which would bring the absent Christopher a new good reason why he should not complicate his life with a girl like me.

He loved his work and it returned his love with success and reputation while he was still young. What more could a man ask for? A wife? An Eve Gill devoted to a jealous, stubborn old pirate who would fight him every inch of the way for her, while she looked constantly over her shoulder, ready to sacrifice herself to that devotion at the drop of a hat?

At this critical moment I must send him from me because of that same devotion ... and send him from me with nothing but one brief kiss already regretted by him, the only physical memory to thwart his common-sense thoughts of social expediency? What sort of chance had I?

I asked him to let me off taking him to Halesworth station;

I would ring up Kessingland Car-Hire which if it hadn't gone fishing would be here with its cab in ten minutes. He almost ran across the roof to the skylight ladder. He would pack his bag at once.

Fate was with him. Joe Greenway was not away fishing. The gentleman would catch the one-fifteen if they hurried a bit, his cab was outside the garage with the engine running.

I heard the cab arrive in the courtyard. At the slam of its door and the growl of gears as it drove away, the tears ran down my cheeks in a flurry, as though they were a power unto themselves, beyond my will to hold back.

Then, as suddenly, they dried as a new fear came to me.

Our private road crossed the heath for the first three-quarters of a mile. The binoculars had been perhaps two hundred yards south of it but there was no certainty that the man had not moved since then. Or if he had others with him, they might very reasonably be watching the road.

If they stopped the cab . . .

Christopher would not hide his identity after they had revealed theirs. And then . . .

Those shots, the sudden departure of the ketch, every-thing. . . Father would be finished and I would have lost Christopher for ever. The end of my world. . .

I tore down the stairs.

The Lagonda was in Norwich being decarbonized. Charlie's old Austin was my only hope.

I pushed back the coach-house doors and in a moment had the little engine spitting at me as I gave it more accelerator than it could digest with a cold inside. The car bucked across the courtyard and down the drive in a series of protesting leaps before it settled down. I thanked heaven Charlie wasn't there to see.

I had no clear idea of what sort of intervention I could devise, but I must do the talking; Christopher must not take any kind of responsibility, even unwittingly.

I watched the narrow curving road ahead, expecting at any moment to see Joe's cab with a man at the open door, a man in uniform perhaps, or more than one. The picture was so clear I had difficulty in realizing that I had overshot

21

the danger point and Christopher was safely gone.

I stopped the car, found a packet of cigarettes in the door-pocket and told myself to relax. The world seemed peaceful under the sun, the warm smell of gorse was all-pervading. I relaxed a little.

But I must report to Father on the extent of the danger. To be able to do so I must carry the war into the enemy's camp, find the man, know what he proposed to do about the *Peacock*'s change of mind and even perhaps distract him at the critical moment when she reached the mouth of the creek and revealed her direction—seawards or inland. It would complicate things for him if he did not know who should deal with her, a patrol cutter or those on shore.

I left the car where it was, making it into a road block of sorts by removing the ignition key, and struck off at an angle across the heath.

I was surprised he was not younger, but his grey, thinning hair and the sparse flesh of body and hands were contradicted by a noticeable vitality and alertness of movement even though just now they were no more than he needed to write in a little notebook. He was sitting on one of the small rocks which here and there thrust up from the igneous sub-strata of the heath; the binoculars hung round his neck, long powerful glasses of a service type.

I stood partially hidden by a gorse bush and took a careful look at him, this enemy in our midst.

He was certainly not in uniform, unless the faded khaki bush shirt and frayed shorts could be called one. His linen shoes were dirty and worn; a small canvas satchel lay in the grass by his side. He remained unaware of me, and I ventured closer, still keeping behind the gorse until I was near enough to see the fine wrinkles of his forehead and deeper lines splaying outward from his eyes, either from suns too bright for them or the humour of his mind. His face, arms and bare legs were very bronzed, and I realized that one way and another he looked quite unlike my preconceived idea of a Customs officer. But that, of course, made him the more dangerous.

22

I cut myself short in this uncomfortable speculation, put a bold face on my uncertainties and moved out from behind the bush.

'I suppose you know,' I said sharply, 'that this is private land?'

He raised his head, unstartled, to look at me. His eyes were an extraordinarily bright blue, bluer, they seemed, than Father's but perhaps because the surrounding sun-tan was deeper.

'Ah yes,' he said, as his astonishing eyes focused on me. 'Good morning. I suppose it wasn't you, was it? Hardly likely. A slip of a girl—'

I had not, to the best of my recollection, been called a slip of a girl before by anybody. Not to my face. It made me feel about ten years old.

'Wasn't me what?' I asked before I could stop myself.

'Fired off that gun and frightened him off?'

'No,' I said, forgivably. 'Why—off . . .?'

'Well, some fool did. He was sitting as quiet as you please, not knowing I was there and then, dammit—' he scowled— 'people shouldn't be allowed to *have* guns, let alone shoot them off. If I had my way all this—' he made a wide gesture with his arm— 'would be a sanctuary.'

'It is,' I said, puzzled but thinking it was he who had come and stopped it being one.

His eyes came back to me.

'It's not marked as a sanctuary on the map,' he said sharply.

'Why should it be? This is private land—as I tried to tell you. And you've no business—'

'They're *all* marked,' he interrupted, 'private or public. Dammit, I ought to know. I'm on the committee, aren't I? I'm responsible for the maps.'

It began to dawn on me that it was odd of him to talk to *me*, surely one of his suspects, about being on a committee which marked smuggler's sanctuaries on maps, and with such a ready air of grievance, as though I was in another department which was always criticizing his committee's failings.

'Only once before, in all these years,' he went on, 'have I got as close to one. They're all but extinct, you know.'

'What—are?' I asked, but almost able to provide my own answer. Those damned binoculars . . .!

'Reed pheasant—*panurus biarmicus*—biarmicus, a beard. Sometimes called bearded titmouse, but it's not a true titmouse, in fact, it's a pity we can't go back to "*silerella*" its original name—from *siler*, an osier.' He shook his head. 'But who'll bother, when there aren't any of him left to call him any sort of name.'

'Reed pheasant,' I said weakly, 'oh, yes—'

'Oh yes?' he repeated. 'You mean you know him—you've seen him too?' His eyes were alert, and I saw that his nose, although small, had a beak-like curve to its tip. What more natural than a bird to watch birds?

'You come here often?' he pursued me, 'you and your damned guns—'

'I told you. I didn't fire any gun. And I didn't come here —I live here.'

He stared at me in a momentary silence, as though seeing me for the first time.

'You live here? You really *have* seen him?' He sounded more friendly, anxious to have his discovery confirmed.

'I'm not sure—'

'He's one of the most beautiful of the small birds— you couldn't mistake him. Tawny-brown, predominantly— whitish borders to his wings when they're closed, under-tail black, head lavender-grey, and then, of course, the so-called beard, tufts of glossy black on either side of the bill—a yellow bill?'

'Yes,' I said. 'I think I've seen one like that—but not often.'

'Not *often*! For God's sake, girl, *once* makes you a celebrity!' He stood up, a short lean man with agile and decisive movements; then he laughed. 'And I do this sort of thing when I want to relax. Look at me! All ready to strike you to the ground because you don't know a reed pheasant when you see one—' he smiled charmingly. 'And I'm a trespasser. Please forgive me.'

'It's all right. I didn't know who you were.'

'Do you now?' He raised a wiry eyebrow at me.

'I mean I didn't know what you were doing here.'

'Came looking for a trespasser, did you, and found a crazy bird-watcher?' When he smiled he looked younger still and I found myself smiling back at him—but it was a false smile. He was after something, of that I was sure. However, so was I. How much did he know?

'I don't think it's so crazy,' I said. 'It was only that I saw the reflection of your binoculars. I was on my way to the ketch,' I added, and tried not to watch his reactions too obviously. I could have sworn he was full of secret thoughts.

'That boat—a ketch, was it? I'm not much good at ships. I'm a soldier—or was. Just retired, you see. I'm taking a day off from wondering what to do next. Are you hungry? I am. Care for a sandwich?' He opened his satchel and took out a small brown paper package. He looked at it doubtfully, weighed it in his hand and said, 'Damn the woman!' But did not, I gathered, mean me.

My suspicions began of a sudden to wear thin. Why should he not be what he claimed, and entirely appeared to be?

It could be . . .

I *must* know.

If I invited him to lunch with me at the house, it would prove nothing if he accepted and less if he refused. But the longer I kept him with me the better chance I should have of settling the thing.

So I put it up to him, making believe that I had never met anyone who really knew about birds, my chief interest in life.

'How very kind of you,' he said, 'but are you quite sure? I mean, your people—' he made a slight gesture which seemed to indicate his travel-worn bird-watching raiment —'they mightn't care—'

'My father's gone off in the ketch,' I said, 'and my mother died when I was very young. So there's only me—my name is Gill. Eve Gill.'

'Eve Gill,' he repeated, and I felt a slight quickening of

my suspicions. It was almost, I thought, as though it was not the first time he had heard my name or indeed spoken it, and that I was confirming his expectation of my identity.

'Mine is Orme,' he said. 'I should be charmed to lunch with you.'

He picked up his satchel and walked with me towards the house. When we came in sight of it he disarmed me further with an appreciation of its Elizabethan architecture, the beauty of its setting, and the general loveliness of the scene.

'Eve in her Eden,' he said. 'Where, then, is Adam?'

I came near telling him that Adam had recently left for ever and was saved by Jim Crowley on his bicycle, leaving for the lunch hour.

I gave him the key of the Austin and asked him to bring it in on his way back—he could put his bicycle in the back. He was not deceived by Mr Orme's lack of elegance for he included him respectfully when he touched his hat.

We turned into the drive and Mr Orme had a closer view of Marsh House; if he saw anything peculiar about our house flag, he did not show it, but then he was army—or so he claimed, not navy.

We came into the courtyard and passed under the kitchen windows, where I was able to tell Mary there would now be only two for lunch, although I did not explain how a change of guests had come about. She had a good look at Mr Orme and her manner echoed Jim Crowley's. Those clothes could not make him in their eyes but something else certainly did.

His appreciation of the interior of the house was not less than of the exterior; he let me see, without saying anything, that its time-grown and therefore unconscious perfection appealed to him strongly. I poured him a glass of Amontillado and he put his nose to it expertly before he drank any. I found myself saying without guile that if I had been asked to guess his profession, 'soldier' would have been the last I should have thought of.

He nodded.

'Not looking what you are expected to look like has its disadvantages. But also advantages. If I'd been bigger and bluffer, people might have noticed me in time to head me off. I've wriggled through, one way and another!'

'If I hadn't seen your binoculars, for instance, I'd never have known you were there.'

'And aroused your curiosity.'

'You did that.'

'I can understand. Strangers must be rare in this part of the world.'

I gave it a rest until we were in the middle of lunch when he complained I was making him drink all the Anjou. 'Not that I've resisted very hard.'

'Father says it's a wine people ought to know better, outside France, I mean. It's cheap and travels well. He imports it himself,' I added carefully, 'in the *Peacock*.'

'And I daresay saves himself the iniquitous duty,' said Mr Orme, holding his glass so that the sun shone in it with golden fire.

'I daresay,' I agreed.

'Sensible chap.'

Not a shadow of a second thought that I could see hovered behind his casual air of enjoyment. He was another English gentleman who felt that wine-drinking and bankruptcy should not be synonymous.

There had been no need whatever to send Christopher away . . . A retired soldier occupying his energies with the watching of birds.

My heart felt like a stone.

The innocent cause of it looked across the sunlit garden, at the trees and the sky above them, and then across the table and lifted his glass to me.

'And I got up this morning saying I would wither away and die in retirement. A day which was to bring me my first reed pheasant—and my first Eve.' He shook his head. 'I don't deceive myself. There will be too many days when it doesn't happen. When nothing happens.'

'You *are* talking like my father. He spends half his time being frightened of nothing happening and the other half

27

making sure that it does, and it's not always good for him.'

'The more I hear of him, the more I think I should like him.'

'You'd find him rather wearing,' I said.

'Retired?'

'Yes.'

'Army, too?'

'Navy—' I did not think it necessary to say which navy.

'Age-limit, like me, I suppose—'

Again I let it go. I was in no mood to talk about Father in any case, but to have to explain how it had come about that President Sandrana's gratitude had been tempered with caution was beyond me at the moment—the subtlety of the President's feeling that like other people even national heroes tend to become set in their habits and are best paid off on the understanding that having liberated the country they should stay out of it, was altogether too complicated for me today.

'—and he finds it difficult?' continued Mr Orme with interest.

'What?' I asked for once losing step with him.

'Being shoved on the shelf while he still has his faculties.' Mr Orme shook his narrow head and frowned. 'This morning I was really up against it.'

'A reed pheasant?'

'No. A letter asking for an answer about a job that had been put up to me.'

'I wish,' I said with greater force than I intended, 'that Father could get a letter like that.'

'In spite of making himself busy, he's unhappy, eh?'

'I know I am,' I said.

'I'm afraid I noticed that,' he said gravely. 'I'm sorry.'

'Did it show as much as that?'

'I wouldn't say it showed at all. Can't you be angry about it—whatever it is? I've found that helpful.'

'I can't even be angry.'

But I was wrong about that. The next moment proved it to me. Mary appeared with a telegram. 'It's for Mr Smith,' she said. 'I told the boy to wait, not knowing whether you

ought to open it—in case it's urgent—or give him the
address for re-directing.'

I looked at it for a moment. His rank as well as his name
was on the envelope, which made it likely to be official. I
hesitated while my resistance waned. I asked Mr Orme to
excuse me, and opened it.

DET.-INSPECTOR C. SMITH

MARSH HOUSE

KESSINGLAND, SUFFOLK

YOUR IMMEDIATE RETURN NECESSARY

FRAMLEY

I stared at it. Framley was his chief assistant in the
Chelsea Division. Detective-Sergeant Framley. Also his
friend. To whom he could appeal for help in a socially
awkward moment.

'Did Mr Smith—' I swallowed, and avoided Mary's eyes
—'did he make a telephone call this morning—?'

'He *might* have, Miss Eve.'

'The bell in the kitchen makes a slight noise if one of the
extensions is used.'

'I don't always notice—'

'Never mind. Mr Smith will know about this as soon as
he gets to London—if he doesn't already.'

Of course he knew already. He had telephoned Framley
and dictated the message he should send.

'Should I let the boy go?'

'Yes, Mary. There's nothing we need do about it.' Or
could do about it. Even to get slowly, furiously angry, red
in the face with anger, was neither necessary nor practical.
I made a great effort not to do so.

Mr Orme was watching me, of course, covertly.

'This job they're offering me,' he picked up the conversation, 'is quite a job. When I tell myself I could do it,
maybe I am over-estimating my capacity. Looking for reed
pheasants is perhaps as much as I should undertake.'

'Would you think me very rude,' I said, 'if I left you to
finish your coffee alone? I mean, don't go until you feel like

29

it—there's a chair by the lily pool. But I—I have to go to London—'

'That telegram—?'

'Yes—' I was already standing up. 'You'll forgive me—'

'Of course, my dear, of course. Don't bother about me. I'll get along—' He was frowning a little, as if disappointed.

I put out my hand. His fingers were warm and strong.

'You've been more than kind—' he hesitated. 'Are you sure—there's nothing I can do—?'

'I shall manage.' But I was still too angry to plan anything.

This meant only one thing. Christopher's discovery that he could do without me had come sooner and more strongly than I had feared. And I was meeting it with an instinctive reaction; an urgent intention to put myself without delay close to him again. That was all there was to it. When I cooled down something would occur to me about the details of handling the thing. It usually did and I must trust myself that far.

First, then, get myself to London.

'Oh damn!' I said aloud.

Mr Orme, whom I had forgotten in that moment of intense feeling, asked what the matter was. I shook my head. It was not his trouble that the Lagonda was in Norwich being decarbonized nor that in spite of Charlie's loving care the Austin would always fall to pieces at over thirty-five miles an hour. The vision of myself hurtling along the road at eighty miles an hour to battle with my fate vanished.

'I can get a train,' I said grimly.

'Let me drive you.'

'You?' I had not noticed a car.

'Why not?'

'But your holiday.'

He shook his head. 'I've seen a reed pheasant.' He explained that he had left his car at the crossroads.

'A mile and a half—but Jim Crowley won't have picked up the Austin yet.'

'Let's go!' He was grinning. These frustrated men of action! At that moment I would have ridden roughshod over anyone's plans but I felt almost as though I, not he, was doing the favour.

I told him to finish his wine while I packed a bag, and hurried up to my room, thinking that perhaps things were at last going a little better for me. A danger had dissolved in the thin air of my over-ready suspicion, and a possible enemy had turned out to be a friend.

Then, as though to point this change in fortune I found an excuse for seeing Christopher. Three sheets of dark blue paper lying on my desk caught my eye; Angela Sawyer's letter, open but unread where I had dropped it. I picked it up and deciphered the straggling handwriting—Angela at her wits' end again.

Darling Eve,

You are always so sensible about everything and this time I really must have your advice—and help. When I ran away to the Riviera to get away from Arthur I thought I was going to have some peace at last. But no! I seem to be a positive *magnet* for trouble and simply cannot escape it.

In desperation I thought of going openly to the police about this but I dare not—I'm too frightened. Then I remembered that you are friendly with that detective man Smith. I don't know whether Lincott Street is under Chelsea, but he can hand the thing over to someone he knows if it isn't. I simply can't face this alone any longer. Please darling ring up your Smith and tell him I need *police* help but privately as it were. He will understand I am sure. You couldn't like him if he was the sort of man who wouldn't. I tried to phone you yesterday but there was no reply. Please do this for me. Bless you.

Angela.

P.S. Arthur just won't give up. He must have been spying because he was at me within two hours of my getting home. Awful scenes! You would not think you could be bored with a man who terrifies and knocks you about, but I am. How could I know? I loved him like anything, but now! Oh God!

A.

I read it through again. I was ready to be sorry for her from habit as much as from anything else. I had had these cries for help before and the story differed very little. The sort of men she chose for lovers would always hit her in preference to any other method of conveying their views about her inconstancy.

But this was the first time she had been frightened enough to feel the need for police protection from the effects of it.

She could not, from my very selfish point of view, have felt it at a better moment. So I said, 'Poor dear Angela, of course I'll help her,' and put the letter in my purse with a smug feeling of having a trump in my hand.

I put on the new black suit and the little black hat with the close soft feathers which came down the side of my cheek. My smallest bag took nightdress, change of under-things, toilet necessities and the book I was reading, and I was ready. The thought struck me it was a good thing Charlie Berrington was not around; he would have delayed me with arguments, logical and otherwise, against the plan. He was probably quite happy with things the way they were now between Christopher and me.

Mr Orme was at the bottom of the stairs, satchel in hand, waiting for me. Mary appeared with her quiet ability to accept sudden events without surprise. Her glance slid momentarily towards Mr Orme and she asked mildly if I would leave any message for the Commodore.

'No,' I said firmly, 'but I'll let you know when I'm coming back.'

If Mr Orme had not already sensed a state of war between parent and child, he would now, but he seemed only too pleased to take the younger generation's part against his own. He took my bag from me and we set off to pick up the Austin for the first stage of our journey.

'Your car,' I asked, 'it doesn't mind going fast?' which I thought was a subtle way of finding out whether it could. But he only said he thought it wouldn't object to being pressed.

'If Angus is in the right mood, that is. He drives quite well but prefers horses. He's my batman—was, I mean. He

32

had to learn, of course, when the regiment was mechanized. Obligatory. Years ago, now. He's not bad with an armoured car—as long as he's in open country.'

'Perhaps if I drove—'

'I'm afraid he wouldn't let you do that. But I'll speak firmly to him. I used to be regarded as efficient. I'll see you through this.'

'You don't even know what "this" is and why you should help me—'

'But I can guess it's the basic trouble. After all, you *are* Eve.'

'Yes,' I admitted.

'This Mr Smith of the telegram?'

'This Mr Smith.'

'Got away?'

'It looks like it.'

'Papa would be pleased?'

'You're very quick.'

'We'll catch him. You're over twenty-one, eh? Parents' consent not necessary. We'll make the boy see sense.' He added with cheerful certainty. 'Hunt him down, eh?'

'We—?'

'You, I mean. Please don't think I'm trying to stick my nose into your business.' He was dying to, of course. Something to do? He paused before adding, not very distinctly: 'Never married . . . foolish fellow.'

It struck me that a man of such attractive vitality must have been either very busy or very spry, not to have married. But spry was what he was; the agile soldier.

The car was a shining new dark green Rolls. It was drawn up off the road by the birch plantation. A white-haired chauffeur in a uniform matching the car sat on a stool at a small table twenty yards from it where the trees gave a deeper shade. There was a white cloth on the table and silver glittered; there was also a tall bottle of the kind Hock comes in.

'Angus,' shouted Mr Orme, before he was out of the Austin. 'Get cracking!'

Angus stood up, took a cigar from his mouth and saluted.

'Sir-r!' He began packing up the lunch table.

Mr Orme said something about Angus making a fetish of his meals now that he was no longer obliged to eat out of a mess-tin, and hurried across to the Rolls while I parked the Austin under the trees. He collected a bundle of clothes and ran into the bushes with them, to return in a brief moment dressed in grey flannels and a light-weight fawn suede sports jacket over a grey silk polo-necked sweater. My bag, together with his bird-watching outfit, satchel, Angus's picnicking outfit and the folded table went into the boot.

'Angus,' said Mr Orme. 'This is Miss Gill. She wishes to reach Grosvenor Square in the fastest possible time. The fastest, Angus. *That's an order!*' He barked the last three words in parade-ground staccato.

'Sir-r!' Angus acknowledged and saluted again very smartly. He opened the door of the back for us and paused, looking with reproof at his master's feet and the canvas sneakers he was still wearing. But Mr Orme took no notice of him. As he stood back for me to get in I had a glimpse of a small crest on the door panel, a mailed fist holding a sword, and above it a coronet. A coronet? *Mister* Orme? Then the name 'Orme' came into my mind with a new connotation. I stole a look at him beside me on the wide side. He had leant forward so that he could see the speedo-meter now that Angus had reached the turnpike and the main road. That bird-like profile was now as familiar as the name; I had seen it often but always under the peak of a military hat. 'The Hawk', they called him; a soldier—yes, indeed a soldier.

I felt like a bad swimmer in a panic, putting down a foot and finding no bottom. There was little doubt I could do with help but this was like bringing up a battery of sixteen-inch guns to flush a rabbit out of a burrow. But I could not say so; in fact what *could* I say without hurting his feelings?

But as soon as I was in London I would tender my thanks, say goodbye, and hope for the best, for I had an uncomfortable feeling that Field-Marshal the Right Honourable Viscount Orme of Tarsus was not the sort of man to be said goodbye to if he didn't want to be.

34

Field-Marshals would not be Field-Marshals if they could easily be deflected from a purpose. I felt nervous. Christopher would not take kindly to a well-meant but dynamic stranger hunting him down in the interests of my love-life.

A voice accustomed to commanding men rasped at my side.

'Get on with it, Angus!'

I saved up my discovery of his identity until I could use it with effect, which I judged to be when we were well into London with a choice of routes to the West End. I said, 'I should be very grateful, Field-Marshal, if you could put me down at the top of Sloane Avenue. I'm afraid it means taking you past Grosvenor Square—'

This penetration of his defences took him off balance. I added that since we had made such excellent time, less than three hours, there was a good chance I might reach 'Adam's' doorstep ahead of him and be waiting there for him. 'The element of surprise,' I explained unnecessarily.

He had to agree that surprise was always tactically a good thing and did not point out that I had just used it on him with the result that much as he might wish to watch the battle he did not know how to say so.

He gave Angus the necessary instructions and smiling at me, took a card from a slim crocodile wallet. 'Here's my telephone number. The only return I ask, if it isn't presuming on our short friendship, is that you should let me know how things go with you.'

I said with all honesty that of course I would.

'Come any time—and if you want help—even if it's only transport—ask for it. Promise me that.' I promised him that.

We were there now. Angus stopped the car at the top of Sloane Avenue, got out and opened the door for me. We smiled our goodbyes the Field-Marshal and I, Angus saluted, and I began walking towards Terry House a hundred yards down on the right, a square block of flats with Christopher's small home hidden behind the unidentifiable windows of the fifth floor.

I tried to pretend that the feeling of weakness in my knees came from the long drive. I had Angela's letter in my purse but in spite of it I knew that my arrival like this was a confession of the kind a girl should never make. And was always making, whoever she might be, however independent or clever or wise in the ways of men.

When, therefore, Graham the head porter, fat and scar-faced, recognized me—not difficult for I was the only woman he had ever known to visit Mr Smith—and told me you've just missed him, Miss, there was a shade of relief in my disappointment.

Graham went into details:

'He came in from the country not ten minutes ago, went up and came down again in no time in his dark suit and was off in one of his police cars like he was going to a fire. An' quite forgot, no doubt, you was coming to see him. Too bad of him, Miss.'

'A fire—' I said stupidly.

'In a manner of speaking,' Graham said darkly, 'it was a bit more than that. I had a word with that Sergeant chap of his while he was waiting for him—' He dropped his voice. 'A very nasty murder, Miss, right on our doorstep—Lincott Street—' and he looked through the swing doors towards the corner opposite where Lincott Street began.

Lincott Street.

I also looked across at it, not with the morbid fascination of a sensation-seeker but with shock and slow rising horror.

'No!' I said aloud, and in my darkened mind thought, coincidence! Please God—it *must* be!

Graham was saying something in a slightly aggrieved tone, a hall porter who had been denied his right to know everything.

'The sergeant wouldn't tell me who—right on our door-step, too. Found this morning—'

I must have put down my bag when I began to move for I was no longer carrying it as my feet took me to the door and through it, followed by Graham's voice, alert with curiosity, 'Any message for him, Miss?'

I did not reply, and did not in fact start to think at all

clearly until I was across the road. My impulse now to get to Christopher without delay was based on a great deal more than my need to put myself right with him; indeed that was no longer in my mind.

If—if it was Angela, I had the answer for him in my purse.

CHAPTER 2

Lincott Street is a short street, perhaps seventy yards long, of small two-storey houses built at the end of the eighteenth century when Chelsea ceased to be a village and joined the town. They began in high fashion, passed gradually down the social scale to near-slumdom and were now being re-claimed to elegance by discerning house-short Londoners, a process which was going on in out-of-the-way places all over the city.

This Saturday afternoon there were enough people about for the police to have to block each end of the street. Two solid crowds faced each other five-deep across the comparatively empty seventy-yard length of the roadway, but both were oblivious of the other in their fixed and straining stare at what little they could see from that acute angle of a house which my horrified eyes confirmed could only be Number 23.

Three police cars were at the kerb; the door was closed and two constables, one at the railings, the other outside the door itself, further emphasized the Law's determination to set about its work in private. The only bystanders allowed to cluster at the railings were obviously newspaper men, for some had cameras.

I tried to find the willpower against rising waves of nausea which followed shock to force a way through the crowd to the containing police cordon, and claim the right to be taken to their inspector. I had information for him— vital information. I would show them the letter written by the victim . . .

But it was a stubborn crowd. It kept me from penetrating it with obstinate backs and ready elbows. My voice was gritty from a dry mouth and when I said, 'Let me through —please let me through,' no one took the slightest notice of my unauthoritative croaking. I gave up for a moment and stood back where I could breathe and gather my forces.

It was, I think, the young man's immobility which made me notice him, apart from the fact that, like myself, he was not attempting to join the crowd but stood at the corner withdrawn from it. I turned my head so that I could watch him less obviously.

The dark suit contrasted oddly with the ruddiness of his square face and hatless head with its woolly fair hair; it was an indoor suit on an outdoor man. He was feeling very badly. Then I had a sudden notion that I had seen him before; a sense of half-recognition, and my interest quickened.

He was lighting a cigarette now, as though in an effort to change his thoughts; he had to steady the hand holding the cigarette lighter with the other. Even so he puffed at the cigarette without knowing that he had failed to get the flame to it. His hands went back into his pockets. They were strong hands.

I was nearly sure I had met him with or in connection with Angela.

Was he 'Arthur'?

It must have been some time ago; otherwise, I should remember him better.

I had her letter in my handbag. Had I also her murderer within three yards of me?

He began to move suddenly. Where before he had been drawn to the scene, he now wanted to get away from it faster than his legs could carry him. His movement became a hurrying between walking and running, and I went after him without waiting to think beyond the fact that if he was 'Arthur' his whereabouts would be of great importance to Christopher.

He was so rapt in purpose that he did not once look back, which made keeping him in sight easy in the comparatively open spaces of Walton Street and Beauchamp Place and quite simple when he came to the Brompton Road, where the windows of the big shops, although closed, had their devotees to add to the general population of a main thoroughfare.

Since he showed no sign of wanting a cab, I deduced that he was bound for somewhere close at hand.

He turned into Yeoman's Row, which I knew was a cul-de-sac, and I stood for a moment at the corner waiting for him to go into one of the houses. But he turned off to the left. I started after him again and found a short alley called Yeoman's Passage which ran both ways behind the houses, matching the Row in length. He was no longer to be seen when I came cautiously into it, but a few minutes' exploration narrowed down the possibilities. The buildings were mostly small store-houses, lock-up garages or work-shops. At the extreme end, the south end, a circular iron stairway twisted up from the cobbles to a single floor level above the shuttered windows of a surgical instrument makers. A narrow iron gallery with an iron rail gave access to two small flats with painted doors, one green, one yellow. The yellow door was flanked by windows with boxes from which gay nasturtiums trailed; the green one was dirty, its unflowered windows curtained with sleazy lace. This man would not live behind such curtains, and the window boxes somehow went with his open air complexion.

I stood in the shelter of a doorway and was as near certain as I could be that the yellow door had recently closed on him. The narrow place was stuffily hot in the late summer evening and I watched, deciding what to do now, a puff of brown smoke which rose from one of the chimneys and became a thin but steady column, struck an unnatural, even a sinister note. It was not the weather for a fire in the grate.

The smoke settled the matter. If he was there he was busy and would not see me approaching. I walked to the circular stairway, climbed it quietly and instead of ringing the bell, stepped to the side of the yellow door and keeping my head down peered in through the nasturtiums.

There was too much light outside and too little in the room to let me see anything in detail, except bright flames in the fireplace and the man's face reflecting them as he knelt feeding them with pieces of paper. Dark blue paper.

It was a dramatic moment. But I should have been more worried about evidence being destroyed, had not there been one such letter in my handbag which was likely to be more valuable—as evidence—than any he was burning.

But the sight was sufficiently distracting for those few seconds to dull my caution. The flame-lit face turned abruptly towards the window and I knew he had seen me.

I stepped back, straightened, and put my finger on the bell. I did it quickly, knowing that the only way out for me was through that door. If I ran I hadn't a chance.

The door opened before my finger was off the bell and he stood looking at me with blank eyes, his face savage with angry suspicion.

'I'm Eve Gill,' I said instantly. 'I was afraid you mightn't be in—' and I stepped past him.

'What do you want?' His voice was heavy, thick. 'Who are you?'

'Angela introduced us—at the Ramseys' party, wasn't it —last year? She told me all about you. And now—something dreadful has happened—' I gave him his opportunity, which, after a split second of indecision, he took.

'Yes,' he said, 'I know.' He hesitated again, then added, 'I was to have taken her out this evening. I went to fetch her . . .'

'Oh, then you saw the police.'

'No. I heard the story from someone in the street.'

I was facing him in the square yard of hallway.

'It's quite appalling—I can't believe it—not with my mind. They know who did it?'

'I don't know—' I realized that he was very dazed, scarcely aware of himself.

'They'll find out—catch him—hang him!'

'Yes.'

'The brutal swine—' I moved on into the room he had come from.

'The only trouble is,' he said behind me, 'they'll think I did it.'

'*You!*' I made it as incredulous as I could manage.

He was close to me, trying to add me up in the turmoil of his mind.

I put a hand on his arm and felt hard muscles bunch under my fingers.

'Hadn't you better tell me?'

He shook off my hand and stared at me. I could hear the tinny crackle of contracting ash in the fireplace.

'We had a set-to last night,' he said finally. I knew who he was now, with certainty.

'But Arthur—may I call you Arthur—people quarrel all the time. That doesn't mean anything in itself. But you're going to be asked questions—a lot of questions.'

'And I've a damned thin story.'

'If it's the truth it will stand up.'

'And show I'm guilty! We had a hell of an argument. I landed her one—she fell down and I cleared out. Went home. At least I walked the streets for God knows how long. It was daylight long before I got in.'

'You hit her—'

'Yes. But she got up. She wasn't really hurt. Not strangled.'

'*Strangled!*' I did not have to act my horror. He seemed pleased to see it, in a bitter way.

'The woman next door found her, so the man said. The front door was open—made her suspicious. Angela was in the living-room.'

'Did anyone know you were there?'

'Half the street, I should think. It was rather noisy—the argument. But apart from that, everybody in London knew about us. That we were getting married and she wanted to call it off. I'm the first person the police will want to talk to—' A panic was breaking through his flat tone of recital —'What the hell am I going to tell them?'

'You said just now you went to fetch her on a date you'd made—before you'd quarrelled—' He nodded. 'In that case,' I went on, 'they'll want to know why you should think she'd keep it.'

'I was hoping she'd got over it. It's a point. Would I go back if I'd killed her?'

41

I did not say that that was just what he might have done, either as a covering move or because he had to know what was going on. Then I realized that the police would see it like that. I said so.

'God, yes. Just one more thing against me,' he said, 'it's silly to try—'

'But you will have to answer convincingly. So be ready for it.'

'In fact, I've got to learn my lines.'

'You're an actor?'

'Didn't you know that?'

'No.'

'If Angela didn't tell you, how would you know. From all the publicity I don't get from films they pay me too much for, or from the plays no one casts me in?'

'The phrase about learning your lines.'

'I can learn lines but I'm no good at hiding things.'

'That's as well. They'll soon know if you try. I see you've been burning her letters. You'll have to tell them that.'

'You think I did it,' he said again.

'No I don't think you did.'

I meant it even if I did not understand why; I knew only that I was not being entirely self-protective.

He was at the window, looking towards the archway, the only entrance to the alley.

'What's keeping them?' He turned to the fireplace, stared briefly at the silver grey ash, then looked at me with his perpetual frown.

'It's one thing to rehearse one's part,' he said impatiently. 'It's another to set a trap for oneself.'

'What makes you think I'm trying to get you to do that?'

'I don't know what the devil you are trying to do!'

'I'm giving you advice. It's good advice. Get your story clear, go to the police with it before they come to you, and stick to it.'

'*Clear!*' he exclaimed. 'It's so bloody mixed up! I don't know to an hour which side of midnight I left her. I don't know where I went afterwards, or what time I got in, I went to sleep in that chair—woke up at half-past four—the only

42

time I know for certain—half-past four this afternoon! I got the time from the telephone—I seem to have lost my watch. I had a bath, dressed, and went to fetch her . . .' He dropped heavily into one of the armchairs. 'She's dead. That goes on and on. Dead, *dead!* I wish I could take it in.'

He shook his head and fumbled a cigarette from a dark blue sealskin case with initials 'A.N.' in a square gold monogram. He got out a gold lighter but his hand shook so that the flame went out and I remembered how he had had the same difficulty a little earlier. I took it from him, flicked it alight, held it to his cigarette.

'Any ideas?' I said.

He kept still, trying to think.

'She'd dropped me for someone else although she swore she hadn't.'

'Someone she hadn't known very long?'

'Yes. I couldn't find out a damned thing about him from her. She swore there was nothing in it. I didn't believe it.' He caught my wrist before I could move. 'You know who he is?'

'I certainly don't. But if he's anything to do with this the police will find him.'

'How? From you?'

'No, I tell you!' I tried to pull my wrist away.

'The—!' he said.

It was a nasty word, even in jealousy. He let go my wrist and I wondered if a bone had gone, it hurt so. I struggled on with him.

'The mere fact that she met someone else doesn't make him a murderer. Less of one than they'll think you are unless you come into the open.'

'You're right!' he said. 'I'm getting out!'

This was not the reaction I had intended.

'You've a chance,' I said. 'Don't ruin it.'

Neither of us had heard their feet on the iron staircase outside. The bell was the first we knew of them. Now it was too late for him to run away. He went to open the front door.

I knew Christopher would be the other side of it but I

was not as prepared as I had thought for the sound of his voice, which struck into me like a knife.

'Mr Arthur North? I'm Detective-Inspector Smith. This is Sergeant Framley.'

'I was expecting you—in fact, I was just about to get in touch with you.'

'Indeed, sir? Then you know—' Christopher's tone was that of a man selfishly relieved of an unpleasant task. 'A shocking business. As a close friend of Miss Sawyer you must feel it deeply. Have you known her long, sir?' Christopher was off and away, nose down to a strong scent.

'I learnt only a few minutes ago.' Arthur's voice was unnecessarily raised to make sure I heard. Even the phrase itself sounded false. I realized then that he was quite incapable of helping himself and that no one else could. He was as woolly-minded as an egocentric always is.

'We're hoping you may be of help to us,' Christopher was saying, 'knowing her so well.'

'I doubt it, but please come in. Er—I have someone with me—she broke the news—'

Christopher took it better than I did. He only blinked once, while I flushed—my face and neck felt purple with it. Even Sergeant Framley, frog-faced and as deep as only a simple soul can be, merely coughed at the sight of his chief's girlfriend in the murderer's home.

'Mr North is unnatural—unnaturally worried—' I stumbled over the words. —'He doesn't understand that he has nothing to worry about. He's afraid that because he went to see Angela this afternoon and found what had happened, and came away without trying to see anyone in authority that it may seem—'

'Perhaps Mr North will tell us what happened,' Christopher cut in quietly, his expression telling me that he would deal later with the question of how I came to be involved.

I took all my eggs and threw them into the one basket which looked as if it would hold them. I spoke swiftly and at last with some command of what I wanted to say:

'I had a letter from Angela this morning saying she was unhappy about things between herself and Arthur here—'

Arthur stared at me—'I came to town to see if I could help. I arrived at Lincott Street—and saw the crowd and everything. Arthur was there. We've been discussing it—the difficult position he is in. Everyone knew about their differences. He realized he would be suspected. He agreed with me that he had nothing to fear from the truth—that he—'

'You had a letter from Miss Sawyer *this morning*?' Christopher brushed aside my effort just as it was reaching its climax.

I took the letter from my purse and gave it to him. He read it with photographic speed.

'This specifically mentions Mr North as someone of whom she—' he paused, and said: 'Had it occurred to you that you had opportunity to show this to me before?'

'I didn't read it until—afterwards.'

'Quite a situation,' he remarked and my heart rose to the faint humour in his tone. It lit up a path by which I could return to him. But it would not show often in a thing as grim as this. He folded the letter and put it in his pocket. 'Thank you,' he said. 'Most useful.'

'But her fears don't make him guilty, and he realizes that just as I do—and as you will. She was a muddled, helpless person—a bit neurotic and—'

'—and dead.'

'—and sometimes treated people badly—men. Whoever killed her, you'll find it wasn't this one.'

'Thank you,' said Arthur dully. 'Thank you for producing that letter.'

Christopher decided to let me run on. 'Shall I?' he asked. 'Why not?'

'Because he isn't quite so stupid as to have gone back this afternoon if he'd killed her. He went because he couldn't believe she had finished with him. Her letter bears that out. He would have gone on trying to get her back for the rest of his life. He couldn't and wouldn't believe that he had lost her. How could he have done the one thing which would have lost her to him irrevocably?'

'The case for the defence,' said Christopher, and again

45

the whisper of our secret apartness from this thing.

'It stands to reason,' I went on, 'that whoever did do it, would be—'

Sergeant Framley's back stopped me. He was standing on the hearthrug looking down at the grate.

'That's just another silly thing he's done,' I said. 'But I should have done the same, I think. If anyone had written *me* love letters and there was a danger of anyone else reading them—particularly strangers, the police—'

'Particularly,' said Christopher.

'Even if a policeman himself had—' I stopped.

'Had—?'

'—written them. They could be just as precious—and private.'

'What the hell are you talking about?' Arthur demanded. 'She's told you the whole thing—and put my neck in a noose. I'm through. You don't have to tell me.'

'I think I should like a statement from you, Mr North,' said Christopher formally. 'I must ask you to come to the police station with me. But before I do so it is my duty to warn you that everything taken down in writing and signed by you may be used in evidence.'

Arthur hunched his shoulders and went out, followed by Framley. I turned and went after them since there was nothing in Christopher's glance to suggest that he had anything to say or wanted to hear from me.

I was beginning to feel a reaction; I was glad the circular staircase was no longer than it was. I walked in silence by Christopher's side towards the archway, Framley and Arthur North a few yards ahead.

I knew he would have to say something and prepared myself for some scathing comment on my interference which would give me the chance I needed to explain more fully how circumstantially—and innocently—I had come to be here. But he remained silent and we were through the archway. Framley was opening the door of the police car which waited there and I realized I was going to be denied the opportunity.

'Christopher—' I began desperately.

'You're staying with your Aunt Florence?' he asked, not as a man wishing to know where he can find a girl but as a policeman wanting to know where he can lay hands on a witness.

'Yes,' I said, 'and anything written down and signed by me may be used in evidence. An accessory after the fact!'

'Actually, I don't think so,' he said quite seriously, and got into the car beside the driver. It sped away, the darkened glass of its rear window hiding even the outline of his head with its soft, unpoliceman-like hat.

'Damn you, damn you!' I cried aloud and would have stamped a foot if I could have been certain of remaining upright in my shaky state of body and mind. 'I hate you!' I said, and realized that there were people—not many, but enough to embarrass me—within earshot. I also saw at the opposite kerb a bottle-green Rolls. The chauffeur in matching uniform was holding open the coroneted door, and looking in my direction. He raised his hand in military salute and almost mechanically I crossed the road towards him. If I was to take hold of myself it would be easier in company, even that of Angus.

'He says for you to have dinner with him,' he said, relaying an order.

'Does he—'

'Yes, Miss. On account the situation has changed, he says.'

'Has it, indeed?' But I was not quite aware yet of what was happening. Angus had put a large, hard hand under my elbow and had assisted me into the wide seat at the back before I found my tongue.

'Now *what*?' I demanded.

'To tell you the tr-ruth,' said Angus with a surprising but endearing intimacy, 'I think he's been caught napping.'

'You don't say!' I commented, and asked hopefully: 'By whom?'

'The enemy it must be.' Angus shut the door on me with a firm and final click, climbed quickly behind the wheel and we were moving. The glass partition was ajar.

'Angus,' I said, 'please tell me what you're talking about. What enemy?'

Angus was obviously feeling he had already told me more than he should and several seconds passed before he half-turned his head.

'The one that did his poor niece,' he said. 'Miss Angela.'

The wheels of my mind, already clogged, seemed to stop working altogether. '*His niece*?'

Angus nodded briefly and made as though to shut himself off from temptation by closing the partition. I put out a hand and stopped it as it slid across.

'Miss Sawyer is Lord Orme's niece? I don't understand. This means that he—' I paused. I still could not straighten out these implications into an orderly pattern.

'He'll explain, Miss, I've no doubt.'

'You—he followed me to Lincott Street—'

'That was aboot it, Miss.'

'More, Angus, more *please*.'

He decided I was not going to be put off, and he was right.

'When you went into that place on Sloane Avenue, "We'll wait a bit," says he, "to make sure she's all r-right." So we sit waiting, then out you come next minute in a hurry and across to Lincott Street, and us following. "Gracious God," he says when he sees the people and the po-licemen, and whips out of the car to find out what's happened, poor fella. "Keep tracks of Miss Gill," he says, "and bring her in when you've an opportunity, but don't force her." And he'd be off home himself as soon as he'd found out what was up. So I took the fir-rst opportunity and that's the lot, Miss.'

I let him close the partition. I wanted to see his Field-Marshal no less than he wanted to see me. Why hadn't Angela told me, to whom I thought she had always told everything, that she had such an important uncle?

Nothing was clear yet, but I realized that faint light was beginning to creep in.

Reed pheasant indeed!

CHAPTER 3

My first impressions of No. 43 Grosvenor Square were vague. The manservant who opened the door to Angus's touch on the bell was large but seemed to become smaller with the immensity of the hall beyond him as he turned, asking me to come this way, please.

The floor of the hall seemed to be of white marble with a straight but intermittent pathway of dark rugs leading across it to a great branching staircase. I followed the man along it but I did not remember reaching the top of the stairs although I knew I had started up them. The thickness of the corridor carpet robbed walking of conscious effort, and the back and shoulders of the manservant still filled my horizon. Finally he came to a stop at a wide mahogany door. He opened it and I was in a large study-library room of which the curtains were already drawn.

The only light was a reading-lamp in the middle distance which shone on the profile head and shoulders of a man I had not seen before. The Field-Marshal's hand came out of the dimness beyond him and gestured at me in welcome and request to sit down and wait until he was free.

He was speaking rapidly and did not pause. I went no farther into the room but found an armchair near the door, realizing I had come in upon a scene of tension and conflict.

The face under the lamp was pale and undistinguished and normally, I thought, would show the world a concealing blandness of self-confidence. But it was nervous now, and glistening with sweat, the eyes expressionless.

'. . . of all the damned silly stories,' the Field-Marshal was saying, 'I don't believe it. Why *Jones*? Why not Smith or Robinson? And you only knew him two days! I want the truth, d'you hear!'

'That's the name he gave me—' The man had a thin, high, emasculate voice.

'All that trouble for a stranger!'

'It wasn't any trouble.'

'A hundred and fifty miles—!'

'He paid me—'

'—in the middle of the night!'

'—twenty pounds.'

'Come off it, Mr Shope.'

'You can take it or leave it! You got me here under false pretences! I'm going—and you can't stop me!' He half-stood but the crack of the Field-Marshal's voice put him back in the chair as if he had been physically thrust there. '*Sit down!* The only reason you came here was because you were offered a chance to earn fifty pounds. I am still giving you that chance.'

There was a silence broken only by the man's uneven breathing.

'Mr Turnbull—'

'Sir?' Quiet though it was, it startled me. Whoever Mr Turnbull was, he remained invisible somewhere in the half-darkness beyond the desk.

'You followed the car from the moment it picked up this gentleman at the western end of Eaton Place and followed it as far as the Oval?'

'Yes, sir. That's where I lost it. He went the wrong side of a trolley bus just beyond the cricket ground and beat me through the lights at the junction. I tried to get through after him but the cross-traffic stopped me. He was going very fast and I couldn't catch him after that.'

'Tell Mr Shope about the speedometer reading.'

'One hundred and fifty-one miles during the time the car was out of the hotel garage between midnight and seven-fifteen this morning.' The unseen Mr Turnbull had a way of stating his facts as though he lived in a witness box. They defied doubt with unshakable truth.

'Well, Mr Shope?'

'Where I went is *my* business—' there was plenty of fight in the man. In spite of his jitters he was sure of himself; he did not have to tell anybody anything if it did not suit him.

'Don't you *want* fifty pounds?' asked the Field-Marshal. 'Or is it because now you know what I want to buy, you're afraid beyond greed to sell it? I'm talking of murder. Murder in Lincott Street, Mr Shope?' The words were spaced and sharp, and although I was half-prepared for them, they stabbed even me. The man Shope quivered convulsively.

'Me—I—wasn't—I never went near the place!' he shouted.

'You were there on Friday morning, watching the house.'

'Not that night—*no!*'

'But Eaton Place is not so far away—the western end, where you waited for your friend. He came straight to you from his killing, for your help.'

'You've got no proof! No proof of any of it!'

'You were watching the house half Thursday and all Friday. Why, if you weren't preparing the way for him?'

Mr Shope was struggling to his feet.

'I swear I know nothing about it!' His pallid face disappeared upward into the half-darkness above the light as he stood up but the Field-Marshal tilted the lamp to follow it.

'You will tell me,' said the Field-Marshal with venom and determination, 'who that man was—his real name and where he came from—or by God I'll see you hanged!'

'I swear I don't know!' the man cried. 'How can I tell you something I don't know! And as for seeing me hanged, who do you think you are? You're not the police!'

'The police, Mr Shope, are going to ask the same questions and they're going to ask them longer.'

'Let 'em!' There was desperation in it. He swung away, his face at last out of reach of the persistent lamp. I heard the click of a switch; two crystal chandeliers filled the room with light and revealed Mr Shope blundering in the direction of the door. He focused wild eyes on it, pulled it open, and half-fell through it. He turned and looked back at his tormentor.

'*Jones* he said he was!' he shouted in a quavering voice. 'That's all I know!' And he used the last of his strength to slam the door.

'Let him go.' The Field-Marshal was hunched like a tired bird in a high-backed leather chair behind the desk.

Also I now saw Mr Turnbull. He had risen from a winged easy-chair which was half-turned to the carved wooden fireplace some fifteen feet beyond the desk. He was a stoutly-built middle-aged man in a blue suit with an oval, childish face under thinning hair. He held a bowler hat and his expression was unhappy.

'I'm sorry, m'lord,' he said.

'Not your fault. I made the mistake of assuming he was on his own. I should never have taken you off the house.' He rubbed his face, then looked across at me. 'My fault. No one else's. I ought to have *made* her tell me. It must have been worse than I thought, so much worse.'

'You won't want me any further, m'lord?' Turnbull spoke softly, with sorrow, a voice unaccustomed to conveying emotion. He coughed awkwardly.

'On the contrary—on the contrary—'

The Field-Marshal's youthfulness seemed to have died since I had last seen him a few hours ago, and he was very tired. He had to wait for words to say what he wanted.

'Keep after Shope. He's the only link. Don't lose him again, will you? He may shift from that hotel. The police may do better with him.'

Mr Turnbull went out quickly, softly and closed the door. There was a silence which I could not have broken had I tried. I had never seen a man's face so bleak and worn, and I could not bear to look at him.

'I shall have to talk to the police,' he said finally. 'There's little to give them, but they'll have to make do with it.'

'Well,' I said, 'I don't want to seem discouraging, but they've all but arrested a young man who must have about the thinnest story a murder suspect ever put up.'

He leant forward, his eyes cold and gimleting.

'What's all this?'

I told him about Arthur North, leaving out as not pertinent the aspect of my relationship with the policeman concerned to whom I referred merely as 'an Inspector'. He interrupted me twice; first, for a description of Arthur, which I gave him and at which he shook his head, the second time when I began to tell him about Angela's letter. He stopped me with a sharp question. 'You got it this morning! What was in it besides Arthur North?'

'Nothing else.'

'You've got it with you?'

'I had to give it to the inspector. It made very little difference to Arthur North. Half a dozen people will come forward to say she was afraid of him. And I couldn't risk concealing it. Angela almost certainly told someone she had or was going to write to me, in fact it's quite likely the idea of police protection wasn't her own. She did talk about herself a good deal—to people.'

'Not to me,' he said bitterly. 'Can you repeat it word for word as you remember it?'

'I think so.' He listened tautly and shook his head. 'She only mentioned North in the postscript. The rest—I don't know . . . it might be.' He thought a moment. 'How long had she known him?'

'At least a year, I think.'

He brought his hands down on the desk and said positively:

'North didn't kill her!'

'I had a strong feeling that he didn't. But the police—'

The Field-Marshal, however, was not listening.

'Shope—the thing behind him—it's recent, very recent. Tell me, did Angela get in touch with you, see you, talk to you or write to you after she came back from Cannes?'

'The letter this morning was the first I knew of her being back.'

'I came looking for you—'

'Yes, the reed pheasant.'

'There was a reed pheasant—' At any other time he would have shown his quick smile but he was anxious and intent on what he was saying. 'I came, knowing you were a close friend of hers, to make you betray her confidences, but I didn't know quite how to go about it. I am afraid I was guilty of some deception—and when I realized your mood —it did not seem at all normal—I had to play even more carefully. I didn't know, of course, any more than you did, how great and near the danger was.' He paused. 'Turnbull had only a glimpse of Shope's passenger—"Jones", the one who joined them and was driven away, who in every likelihood killed her. Turnbull was across the street and the nearest light was some distance. His impression is of a very dark man—probably French or Italian. That fits with the other stuff I have—' He looked at me and asked carefully: 'Did she ever—and I mean before she went to the Riviera —tell you about such a man?'

I hesitated. She *might* have told me about him somewhere in the mass of gossip which accompanied her when she was with me like a cloud of midges, buzzing about one's head on a summer evening, and I could have heard without hearing.

'I don't—I don't think so. Lately it has been about Arthur North, or the blond giant—I've forgotten his name, who went off to Iceland to start a shark fishing industry instead of marrying her—because it would be safer. He was jealous, too.'

'I didn't think you'd have any other answer, but I had to try. Something happened—she met someone at Cannes, or Juan-les-Pins. It was extremely important, to the man.'

'She was very attractive.'

'I didn't mean important as a woman.'

I was puzzled, not only because he was being rather cryptic, but also because his face had blurred and was swaying about like a balloon on a string.

'Eve! What's the matter?'

The matter, of course, was that exhaustion had finally caught up with me. His face disappeared in a misty darkness.

I was in a narrow four-poster bed, under a soft sheet and a patchwork coverlet which smelt of lavender. Behind the lavender was a faint background smell of something else which I thought must be brandy. Then full consciousness returned, and apart from being in a bed, in a smaller room than the one in which I had passed out, things seemed to be much as they had been at the moment of leaving them. Even the Field-Marshal's face was there, close to me, and still so tired and drawn that he looked an old man compared to the one who had come looking for me under the guise of a bird-watcher.

'Thank God!' he said.

'Nothing wrong with her that something to eat and a night's sleep won't put right,' said a deep voice from the other side of the bed, and turning my head I saw a red-haired man with a stethoscope clasped about his neck. He looked too young for that voice, but it was indubitably a doctor's voice. I took a look round the room; ancestral walnut furniture, flowered silk curtains which matched the hangings of the four-poster, and my coat, skirt and underthings neatly folded over a chair. It dawned on me that I really was properly in bed in large scratchy pyjamas. The doctor was packing away a hypodermic outfit in his bag. The Field-Marshal saw him to the door saying, 'Thanks, Billy, for coming so quickly. See yourself out all right?' To which Billy replied that he was glad 'he had been in, that the B-Twelve would begin to take effect very soon, but if it woke her up too much she could have one of the yellow capsules to make her sleep.'

My fingers found a small needle bruise on my left arm; I was relieved he had gone, although doctors, even young ones, think nothing of taking off people's clothes when they are unconscious.

'There is food on the way,' said the Field-Marshal, sitting down at the bedside and taking my hand, which he patted with clumsy reassurance. 'You're not to talk until you've eaten.'

'I can't understand,' I said, 'why Angela never told me she had an uncle.'

He did not say anything to that for a moment and I saw that he was making a decision. Finally he said:

'It may sound odd, but I think because I am not—was not—her uncle. She was my daughter.'

I was still only half-there. 'But her name was Sawyer, not Orme.'

'Sawyer was her mother's name. Customary, when the parents are not married.' His dry tone was brittle. 'A long while ago—only time in my life I ran away. Except in battle,

55

of course. Always running away then—made me a good field officer, knowing when to—' He broke off and reverted: 'Apart from Angela, marriage would have been a mistake. Another chap she couldn't get out of her heart—lost him, you see, and tried to forget him with me. Never works. She was happy enough,' he said slowly, 'as happy as she could be, that is. The child was everything. But she resented me and disliked me for being the wrong father. Trouble was, she didn't put it right with Angela when she was old enough to be told. Left it too late, and died—Angela fifteen or so, then. Had to tell her myself—she'd have had to know sooner or later. It was a considerable shock and the fact her mother had seen fit to hide it from her made her think the situation had been far worse—even sinister. She was very suspicious of me. But she'd have come round in time. And now—this . . .'

He paused. 'There is something I have to know about her now. Then you must rest and get food and drink into you—' He paused again. 'Tell me, was she what they call a bad girl?'

It was a difficult question, not only because he was so embarrassed in asking it. What, by his standards, was a bad girl? He clarified and made it worse by adding: 'What they used to call a bad girl.'

I tried to wriggle out of it, tried to avoid those sharp, shrewd eyes.

'You mean, do I think the way she died was something to do with the way she lived?'

'That is what it comes to.'

'People will say so if it turns out that Arthur North did it.'

'He didn't.'

'I don't think he did either. But they'll have to have a cast-iron alternative.'

'Will they believe she was murdered for a reason quite remote from the apparent motive—a crime of passion?'

'Of course. If there's proof—'

'You mean, they won't see it easily.'

'Not easily,' I had to admit.

56

'Proof,' he said. 'There's so little to start on.'

'I can't even judge the chances. I don't know much about this Shope-Jones thing.'

'There's not much to know. But it will *have* to be that . . .'

I saw what was driving him. He had had little enough of his daughter while she was alive. Now she was dead, perhaps because he had failed to get her to confide in him. And he had nothing left but a hope of saving her good name. It was beginning to drive me also.

'Before I passed out,' I began, 'you were going to tell me—' and was interrupted by a tap on the door. The large manservant came in with a bed tray; I pulled myself higher up the bed while the Field-Marshal tried to arrange the pillows; he was not very good at it. More efficiently he lifted the lids of silver dishes and frowned into them. The manservant, fresh-faced, shaven-headed, almost stood at attention, his eyes fixed on a point on the wall three feet above his master's head.

'I said *Sole Colbert*, Harris—not grilled sole. I suppose Mrs Harris had her reasons as usual.'

'Yes, m'lord. She thought the butter might be too rich.'

'You will tell her that there's nothing wrong with Miss Gill's stomach.'

'Nothing wrong with Miss Gill's stomach,' repeated Harris. 'Very good, m'lord.'

I felt it would have been less personal, somehow, if they had still been in army uniform, but their simple gravity was disarming.

Harris's next words, however, made my knees jerk in reflex and the dishes rattle.

'Detective-Inspector Smith is here, m'lord. He asked me to say he was able to come a little earlier than you suggested, but will, of course, be happy to wait should you be engaged.'

'I'll be down in a moment. Where did you put him?'

'In the morning-room, m'lord. Angus is still here.'

'Don't think I shall want him again.'

'To report at O-eight-hundred hours as usual?'

'Yes.'

Harris imperceptibly clicked his heels and at last went;

my anxiety had to wait until the door was shut.

'This Detective-Inspector,' I said. 'He doesn't know I'm here—that you and I know one another—that I—?'

Calm as I tried to be, it was a poor effort; and the eyes-which-missed nothing were on me.

'I am struck,' he said, 'by the coincidence of the name "Smith". But of course there are quite a number of them.'

It was a time of heart-deep confidences; he was entitled to know about Christopher. So I told him quickly, not waiting to see if he was taking it all in. But he seemed to, for he said: 'So he was "Adam". Funny I should have thought there ought to be one . . . But it *is* a coincidence.'

'Not really. He was, of course, the "policeman friend" Angela talked about in her letter. The only coincidence was in his being at Marsh House—but even so, where else at a weekend should he be, seeing we were fond of one another?'

'Yes, of course. And so you quarrelled about something.'

'We quarrelled, and he went home. I was using Angela's letter as an excuse to follow and make it up with him. But it was only an excuse. As I told you, I didn't take it very seriously. Although in point of fact, it was too late. Even before her letter reached me she was . . .'

He nodded, and asked what the quarrel had been about.

'He misunderstood something.' I was ready to swop secrets, but not Father's.

'The man,' said the Field-Marshal, of Christopher, 'must be a fool.'

He opened the half-bottle of champagne expertly, filled the hollow-stemmed glass, sniffed at it and passed it. He put it in my hand.

'Don't worry, I shan't let him know you're here or that I've ever heard of you.'

'But he'll guess if you show him you know about Arthur North, that I—'

'I shan't. Drink that.'

'I can't just lie here!'

'Drink.'

I drank a little of it.

'Just a minute,' he said. He left the room and returned a

moment later with a box-like thing which had a length of flex attached to it. He plugged it into a socket by the bed-head and made room for it on the tray; I saw that it was one of those house telephones incorporating a small loudspeaker—an intercom. He pushed down one of the switches. 'It's now connected to the one on my desk in the library. I shall open the circuit there. You will be able to hear us without being heard yourself, so don't worry about making a noise. Reverse this switch should you want to join in.'

'I shan't—' Reassurance was slow. 'You asked him to come—it wasn't the other way about?'

'Of course not.'

'You asked for him by name?'

'I didn't know it until I rang up the police-station and said I had information which might help the investigation; and could I speak to the officer in charge. He came on the line and announced himself by name. Satisfied?' He smiled again.

'Y-yes,' I said.

'Cheer up. I don't suppose he's brought a search warrant.'

Neither did I, but my feeling of insecurity remained for several moments after their voices began to reach me from the small box beside the champagne bottle.

The conversation had well begun by the time they were within range of the desk intercom, but the Field-Marshal did his best to recapitulate the gist of it for my benefit. He was saying: '. . . that's why I did not try to see you in person when I came to Lincott Street this afternoon. I felt it might be useful to get hold of the man as quickly as possible— make sure, anyway, that he could be found when the police wanted him . . . cigar?'

'Thank you, sir, no. Somehow I haven't had time to eat today, and it might be a little heavy . . .'

'In that case I don't suppose a drink—no?' There was no discomfort in his voice because he had himself eaten the lunch Christopher had missed. He plunged straight into his story.

'I propose to give you everything I know,' he said. 'You

59

may think it slight and scrappy but there's enough to justify investigation and you will find your answer in it—' He paused, thinking perhaps that out of habit he was being too authoritative.

'I want to make it clear,' he went on, 'that the only reason I have not the complete story is because my niece and I were not as close to each other as I could have wished. She was naturally independent. She had to live in her own house and go her own way. Briefly then, she went off early this summer to the South of France for two months. She took a return rail-ticket from London to Cannes. She returned ten days ago by air from Nice three weeks before the two months were up. That was on the tenth of June. She rang me up and came round to see me the evening of the day she arrived home. In the first few minutes I knew there was something very much on her mind. I thought she had come to tell me about it and ask advice and help. But I realized after a bit that she was limiting my role to being the sort of person who might, by mere contact as it were, restore her self-confidence. Am I making myself clear . . .? It's difficult to point to any specific thing, such as anything she said, or any subject she avoided, but I knew that she had very recently come up against something unpleasant and quite outside her normal experience. I gave her every opportunity to talk about it, but she stuck to people and events obviously unconnected with her main preoccupation. But I got this much in the course of it. Her five weeks out there had been divided roughly into two halves, the first a stay at the Grey-Albion in Cannes, the second with a small party of people on a yacht—the *Norse Girl*—belonging to an American called Gordon Chester whom she had met casually. I pretended I had heard of Chester and by drawing her out while discussing him, learnt that he had made several million dollars as a building contractor in Kansas City and had been married unhappily several times. But she did not like talking about this part of the holiday and it struck me forcibly that it was on the yacht that this something had happened. I continued to worry and dropped in on her a couple of days later. I found her no less haunted. I couldn't stand it any longer and came out into the open. What was worrying her? She said, rather quickly, nothing—perhaps she was letting one of her young men bother her unnecessarily. But she could deal with him.'

'Did she mention his name?' Christopher's voice was casual.

'No, and I didn't ask for it. He was obviously not the real reason for her jitters. I asked her point-blank why she had cut short her trip. She'd been bored, she said. I told her that wouldn't wash with me. She fought back even harder than I had expected, which told me I was right. Something had happened out there. I went on at her and finally she lost her temper with me—it was a very unhappy leave-taking. But I wasn't giving up. I came straight back here and cabled a friend of mine in a British bank at Cannes, asking him to check on Gordon Chester's whereabouts. I proposed to go over myself and ask questions—Chester or someone in his party might answer them if Angela wouldn't. Egerton sent me this reply . . . you see? Gordon Chester returned to the States about the eleventh—the day Angela flew to London. The coincidence did not make the thing any less vague, but it fixed the certainty of it in my mind. I asked Angela to dinner the day I got that telegram. She was sorry, but she had a date—and for the next night. She was avoiding me because she was afraid I would chase her about her trouble. She sounded more on edge than ever. I wanted to keep close to her, protect her somehow. I couldn't do much about it myself so I called in Turnbull of the Turnbull Agency—'

'I know him,' Christopher said quietly, 'a good man in his way.'

And the Field-Marshal went on to tell him the rest of the story as it had emerged during the interrogation of Shope, ending with Shope's drive with the dark stranger to Folke-stone—or Dover—late last night and his refusal to admit any knowledge of the crime or more of his passenger than that he had known him two days and that his name was Jones. 'Turnbull will give you a vague description of the man. The point is, he sounds like a native of the part of the world where my niece had been. You don't need me, Inspector, to show where all this leads. It's obvious. She saw or heard something which was extremely dangerous to somebody, so dangerous that there was no safety for him while she lived. It may sound far-fetched but it is a situation which has happened before and been solved before—by murder. The far-fetched-ness is only in the fact that it has happened in one's own circle, to one's own relative—a very close relative.'

'Yes,' I heard Christopher say gently. 'I found Miss Sawyer's birth certificate amongst her papers—' and he broke the brief, awkward silence by adding with the subtlest tact, for which I loved him: 'You must rest assured, sir, that the person responsible for your niece's death will not escape.'

I heard the Field-Marshal sigh, taking comfort for what it was now worth, in the knowledge that his secret, which had also been Angela's, was safe in this policeman's hands.

'He will not escape,' agreed the Field-Marshal, and the microphone's distortion did not disguise his grimness. 'Not if I can help it.'

'It's our job,' Christopher said, without emphasis on the 'our'. But the word was there.

'You will want Turnbull. You know all about him but here's his telephone number. Scotland Yard will be your channel to *Interpol*. I know the Americans have resigned, although I don't suppose their cooperation is any less active when a crime crosses national boundaries.'

'Scotland Yard,' replied Christopher, 'hasn't, in point of fact, been called in. I am making an immediate report through my Chief to the Director of Public Prosecutions. The need for central investigation has not arisen.'

'It hasn't? Please don't think I'm doubting either your powers or your capacity. It's only that what I've brought you surely widens the horizon. *Interpol* exists for just such an eventuality. You—'

'I should like, sir, to go back to a point you made. About Miss Sawyer's admission that one of her young men was bothering her.'

'Not an admission. An excuse.'

'That was your impression, sir.'

'I told you—a very strong one. She may have been having trouble with whoever he was but that was not what was frightening her. I use the word as the mildest description of her state of mind. What are you getting at—?' The Field-Marshal was prepared to play ignorant, if only to hide me.

'We know, sir, there was a situation of that kind which was troubling her to the extent of fright.'

' "Know"?'

'She wrote a letter to a friend of hers—a woman—to that effect,' said Christopher carefully.

'Indeed. But, all the same—'

'We already have the letter. It names the man.'

'Nevertheless—'

'And he admits that he quarrelled with her last night.'

'And that he killed her?' asked the Field-Marshal sharply.

'No sir.'

'Well, then.'

'He's not the type—in my opinion—to admit anything. At this stage, anyway, before he's had time to think it over. I am not of course relying on a confession. There is ample concrete evidence on which to bring a charge. Factual evidence.'

'You're telling me politely,' said the Field-Marshal coldly, 'that none of what I've told you is of the slightest interest.'

Christopher cleared his throat slightly and allowed silence to answer his Lordship in the affirmative.

'You don't look like a man,' said the Field-Marshal, 'who would take the easy way out at the expense of truth.'

'But neither, I hope, sir, one who ignores physical evidence.'

'So you've arrested this chap North?'

There was another and even more awkward silence at his use of the name. I found my hand within an inch of the switch that would have reversed the circuit before taking it hastily away. I could almost see them; Christopher masking his recognition of the slip, the Field-Marshal equally poker-faced, calling upon his wits.

'Yes, sir,' said Christopher. 'And charged him.'

Wasn't he going to ask how the Field-Marshal knew the young man's name—if Angela had not mentioned it? The Field-Marshal would be wondering the same thing. The fact that he did not ask only made it more certain, to me at all events, that he had a damned good idea. After all, I had been Angela's best friend.

Then, as I waited on tenterhooks, I realized that I had heard or half-heard a sound which had come from some source other than the intercom. Awareness came too late to define it but not to know its direction. Somewhere near the door. I turned my head slowly to it. The bedside light barely reached that far, but I was as near sure as I could be that it was open at least two inches. I strained my eyes and ears at it, but although I heard nothing some other sense or senses told me someone stood the other side of it.

Harris? Angus? I doubted it. Discipline was strict and honesty in such men their very souls.

Who then?

Christopher must have just made his delayed pounce but I had missed it in my sudden change of focus; I heard only the Field-Marshal's explanatory reply.

'. . . Well, I assumed it must be North. I had heard about him.'

'From whom, sir?'

'Mrs Alfred Sawyer—Angela's aunt, you know. She thought him "unsuitable" and hoped Angela would discover it sooner or later—' The Field-Marshal was putting up a good front.

'I see,' said Christopher, and he saw nothing of the kind; he was seeing *me* somewhere in the background of the Field-Marshal's up-to-the-minute intelligence service.

By this time I was out of the bed, the rustle of my first clumsy movement—the sudden change to the upright position and the unnatural length of the pyjama legs—was hidden by their voices. I held up the pyjamas and went softly to the door.

'. . . where I can get in touch with Mrs Alfred Sawyer?' Christopher was saying.

'Maine House, Guildford—telephone eight-three-one-two. Oh God, I'd forgotten she'll have to be told.'

. . . Whoever was outside the door his breathing, now that I was close to him, was just audible, an obstructed breathing punctuated by a faint but regular whistle.

'It's all right,' I heard the Field-Marshal, sharp with irritation which in any other circumstances he would have been at pains to hide. 'I won't prejudice any evidence she may have for you by telling her you've caught the wrong man. It's merely more seemly that *I* should tell her.'

'Of course, sir. I'm being over zealous.'

'And I have your assurance that you will get in touch with Turnbull about Shope? At once?'

'Yes—'

The breathing beyond the door panel quickened perceptibly, shortening the intervals between the whistle.

But by then I had not needed this turn in conversation in the library back to Shope to confirm that *he* was sharing my eavesdropping.

I pulled open the door and spoke at the same moment.

'They'll find you, Mr Shope, if you hang around like this.'

He let out a strangled gasp. He must have turned out the passage lights for his white face was the only distinguishable part of him. I was almost sorry for the man. He was having a horrid time in this house to which he had come so trustfully at the thought of picking up fifty pounds without asking himself in exchange for what. But why hadn't he cleared off when he could?

'There are thick window curtains in here,' I said reassuringly, 'you can hide behind them until this nonsense is finished and the house is quiet—when we can talk.'

That was my mistake, 'when we can talk.' But for those four words he might have fallen for the implied suggestion that I was on his side. To have to talk, even with a sympathizer, was something he did not want. He backed away, turned and made off down the passage.

'There's a police car outside!' I whispered loudly enough to reach and momentarily halt him, his pale face glimmering back at me. 'If you have decided to leave, at last,' I kept at

65

him, 'for Heaven's sake stay out of the way until they've gone. Good night, Mr Shope—' And I shut the door. I had done what I could to prove that I was taking his part.

If he followed my advice it would give me a few moments. Turnbull had lost him. And he must not be lost. He was the only lead we had.

I zipped up my skirt; grabbed my handbag, picked up my shoes and barefooted—there was no time for the nicety of stockings—went after him.

The passage was still unlit but there were lights on the staircase and in the vastness of the hall below. I saw now, which I had not noticed when I came in, that double doors of frosted glass and ornate grills now half-open, cut off the street door from the main hall when closed and formed a small outer lobby. There was an unobtrusive door in this lobby which I guessed was that of a small cloakroom. It would be a normal place for one.

I was guessing that Shope was in there. He would have seen the police car about which he had been warned and its waiting driver, a uniformed and trained policeman in spite of his chauffeuring whose observation you could not cheat if you left this house while he was sitting there.

Also Shope would have seen, as I had, Christopher's dark brown hat rather lonely in the otherwise deserted wastes of the twelve-foot Louis XIV table which did little to furnish the hall. He might not have recognized that hat as intimately as I did but he would still assume it belonged to the inspector. The safe thing to do would be to stay until he had gone, the police car with him, and the cloakroom was handy and close to the street door. There would be a closet in it for complete hiding.

I went back through the inner doors seeking a hiding place of my own. I tried the first door on the right in the hall, opening it cautiously. The room was quite dark. It smelt odd, unlike an ordinary room—dining-room, drawing-room, whatever it might normally be expected to be. A kind of zoo smell. Then there was a sudden chirping of small birds, many birds it seemed to me, and flustered flutterings.

66

It was easier, of course, to watch them if they lived under the same roof with you.

I closed the door hastily.

I found a small telephone cubby-hole under the staircase in which the light went on when you opened the door. I solved this disadvantage by loosening the bulb and stood there in the safety of darkness with the door ajar to hear, calming myself.

'. . . it comes to this,' the Field-Marshal's voice grew louder and angrier as he descended the stairs over my head. 'I understand very well what you are thinking. That I am a grief-torn parent refusing to believe that her death resulted directly or indirectly from that sort of thing. That I am chasing any kind of alternative wild goose to put the blame on.'

'No, sir—' Christopher was hating this.

'You think I've invented the thing.'

'Perhaps you've been encouraged—'

'Encouraged! What the hell do you mean?'

'Someone could have come to you with the same view,' said Christopher. 'It helps to have that kind of sympathy, constructive sympathy, and—'

'I don't know what you're talking about,' said the Field-Marshal flatly. 'I don't need to be told what to think.'

'No, sir.' Their voices echoed through the high spaces of the hall as they crossed to the lobby and the street door.

'I consider myself at liberty to take this to a higher level!'

'As you see fit, sir.'

'Dammit, I do!'

The front door closed with a definite snap and I heard the Field-Marshal's footsteps, punctuated by short silences, as he passed from marble to rug and rug to marble on his way back to the stairs, I heard the police car start up and drive away. Then there was a longer silence from the Field-Marshal; footsteps indicating that he had paused; his voice ended it with an explosive: 'Damned dull-witted obstinate bastard! She's well rid of him!' This was followed by an inexplicable thud, and his footsteps again and the faint vibration over my head as he mounted the stairs.

I came quickly out of the cupboard to stand in the shadows where I could see the distant lobby and the cloakroom door. I hoped to heaven Shope would leave at once, before the Field-Marshal had time to discover I was no longer in bed and my clothes gone. He would come down again straight away after that and I should have no time for explanations. I pressed against the well of the staircase as the cloakroom door opened. Shope came out and waddled across the ten feet which separated him from the street door. The next moment he had gone, leaving the door against the latch to avoid the sound of it closing.

I ran half the length of the hall, and pulled up. In his disturbed state Christopher had forgotten his hat; it was no longer on the table, however, but on the floor near it, squashed almost flat. That thud must have been the Field-Marshal jumping on it, which showed that Field-Marshals were human like anybody else and lost their tempers. But in this instance it seemed a little unreasonable.

Cross as I had been with Christopher and crosser than ever now at his mean suggestion that to spite him I had encouraged the Field-Marshal to cook up his theory, I was still not so angry as to be blind to his right to a point of view. Arthur North had everything a policeman needed— motive, temperament, opportunity.

I gave up a precious second or so to his poor hat, pushing and patting it back into some sort of shape, and returned it to the table.

At the street door I put on my shoes and went out into the warm night. Shope was thirty yards away, walking east towards Bond Street, making a fair pace with his unwieldy shape and fallen arches.

Our only lead. I went after him praying that if he took a cab there would be another one at the same time for me. If there wasn't, I should have to chance everything and share his. It was an awful risk. He was in no condition to be rushed.

CHAPTER 4

It happened as I had feared; a cab with its 'free' sign lit up passed me without another in sight. Twenty yards ahead Shope saw it and raised his arm. I sprinted, debouching into the road for the outside door. He had opened the other, given the driver his direction, which I was too far away to hear, and was settling himself in the seat when I reached the cab. The driver looked round at me.

'I saw it first—!' I began and then affected to recognize his passenger. '*Mr Shope*! Oh, thank heavens!' I threw myself on to the seat beside him, pulling the door shut, caught his hand and told the suspicious face looking back at me through the partition that it was all right, we were together. The driver shrugged his shoulders and put his engine into gear. To Shope I said quickly:

'I got away too! But only just!' And I gasped noisily for breath.

'What's all this *about*?' Shope was grappling with the instinct to have none of me crossed by a curiosity as to my game.

'He's done this to us and he's got to get us out of it!' I said, and twisted my head to look through the small window in the back, as though afraid we might be followed. 'He *must*!' I hurried on, clutching his clammy toad-like hand more tightly. 'I've done my job, you've done yours—and now look at us! Left holding the can! *Murder*—' I dropped my voice. 'He didn't say it was going to be *that*!'

Shope was going into one of his shakes. I forced the pace. 'I see now, you didn't know I was in it any more than I knew you were. He's too sharp, of course, to work any other way. If it hadn't been for that Orme man we shouldn't ever have known until we stood in the dock together. Thank God Orme chose to have us in at the same time!'

'Who the hell *are* you?' He was almost shrill.

'I was a friend of hers. Or so they thought. But I didn't

know—I swear I didn't know what he meant to do.'

He was steadying himself; it might be a good sign or bad.

'You may know his real name but I don't,' I went on, bitterly now, the underling who resents his employer's sensible mistrust. 'This "Jones" stuff! What *is* his name—anyway?' I neither expected nor waited for an answer. I plugged away at him: 'He got us into this and it's up to him to get us out. I'm not anybody's sucker, see?' It was the only line of attack I could devise, and like any other, success lay in repetition. 'Don't tell me, Mr Shope, that you like being a top suspect in a killing. Because I don't. Are you going to let him get away with it? *I'm* not. Give it some thought, Mr Shope.'

'For God's sake let me be!' he said.

'You handle it any way you like,' I told him, 'but I know my limitations. The police don't like me but I'd chance that rather than let him get away with it.'

It worked, it pushed him over the edge. He swung round on me, thrusting his face into mine. His breath was nasty and the words came out with it in a slobber of anxiety.

'You'd squeal?'

It was a professionalism which put him at once in his category, and I hastened to join him in it.

'I'd sing until they put their hands to their ears.'

'You'd never dare—' he whispered. 'You know who they are, don't you?'

'Yes,' I said, because to have said 'no' would have stopped him before he had properly started. 'Yes—and I'm out of their class.'

'What's your class when you're in it?' he asked, but mechanically, trying to assess how serious was my talk of squealing.

'This and that,' I said, 'but not murder. I leave that to fools.'

'There's no proof—'

'You'd be surprised.'

'Not against *me*. I didn't know! That's the truth, that's what I told that toff back there and that's what I'll tell anybody—the truth!'

I laughed. 'As if that matters. Do you think I knew either? Haven't I told you that's the whole *point*!'

'All right, all right!' he whispered fiercely. 'Take it easy. It's worth talking over.'

He was looking out of the window, as though we were approaching his destination.

'Got any money?' Mr Shope mumbled at me as he climbed out of the cab. 'Saves a bit to walk the rest—apart from anything else.' Apart, I thought, from the principle that it was wiser to approach the cave cautiously.

'No,' I said. 'He didn't give *me* enough to ride in cabs either.'

He counted coins into the driver's hand while I stood back and waited and tried to orientate. The journey had taken about fifteen minutes and I had been able to keep track of it only now and again; I thought this long, slightly curving street of small depressed Georgian houses must be somewhere in that unhappy area between Camden Town and Primrose Hill which had sunk steadily in social esteem beneath the unending sootfall until only the choiceless poor lived there.

Angela's death was uglier than ever. This place, this dreadful man staring after the taxi as it turned and drove away from such an unprofitable hunting ground, this was filth and decay breeding evil, nourishing hate and greed and all beastliness; murder born here would be as dark as the sooty counterpane which covered it. Death from jealousy gone mad would have been a clean and shining thing by comparison.

Shope waited, watching the street to satisfy himself that he had not been followed. There were four or five lighted windows to be seen from where we stood, but each was completely curtained. Passengers from cabs might be rare, but minding your own business was not; it was the only common ground in the fight for survival.

He nodded and shuffled off. I kept by his side. He did not speak and I would leave well alone for the moment.

We came to a street on the right, narrower and darker

with a name on the corner house, Pawley Road. He paused again to make finally sure no one was behind us before turning down it.

'I'm trusting you, see?'

'We're trusting one another,' I said. 'We have to.'

A street lamp on the other side made it possible to distinguish details of the house at which he came to an uneasy halt, as though now that he was here he was uncertain of the wisdom of coming to it at all.

It had two storeys above the ground floor and a semi-basement of which the one window on street level was protected by a wire screen so thickened by a patina of dust that its mesh was scarcely visible. Three steep steps of worn stone led up to a slab of cracked paint of unrecognizable colour which was the door. It had neither bell nor knocker and the keyhole might have been made by a desperate rat; a narrow letter-box yawned in its blind face.

The figures Three, followed by half a Five in once white china told you its number. No light shone behind curtains as close drawn as the neighbours'.

Shope was searching himself for a key which he failed to find. This troubled him sorely, a last straw in the burden of a bad day. He swore very profanely and after nerving himself, went up the steps and banged lightly on the door with the side of his fist, hollow thumps—two, then a pause followed by two more, an obvious signal of identification. Nothing happened.

'Where the hell'd she be, this time of night?' he asked himself irritably. He came apprehensively down the steps the better to see the secretive windows, but the dark curtains did not move. He went up the steps again and put his shoulder to the door without belief that it would open, and it did not.

He was peering futilely through the black slit of the letter-box when a dark saloon car without lights came quickly round the shadowy corner. It came to a standstill before he had time to see it and having seen it, decide its significance. His expression as he turned was half expectancy, half doubt. Was this, thank God, the guardian of his secret lair, home at last to open it for him?

He seemed to know at once, however, that it was not, and his doubts multiplied.

There was only the man behind the wheel; he was thin and red-faced as if freshly sunburnt, hatless, and seemed to have sandy hair. He kept the motor running and leant out of the window.

Shope said: 'Why, Sammy—' in a tone of surprise.

'Jump in,' said Sammy. 'Not the girl. Business before pleasure.'

'I *am* business,' I put in quickly.

'Maybe,' said the man, 'but ours isn't that kind. Get in, Shopie.' The back door of the saloon swung open as the man put his hand over the seat and released the catch. Shope's surprise had become something else; perhaps he recognized, as I did, a firmness behind Sammy's comparatively light manner. It became a little deadly under the lightness when he added: 'Or do I have to fetch you?'

Shope looked wildly over his shoulder at the denying door of the house.

'What's the idea, Sammy? I'm busy. I can't leave just now.'

'Don't be silly. Get in.'

'I'm tired. I've had a full day. I—'

'I said get in, Shopie.'

'It's all right,' I said, realizing it was very far from that, 'I'm coming with you.'

'If you know what's good for you, you'll get the hell out of this, quick,' Sammy commented.

'Mr Shope and I—'

'Mr Shope and you will have to put it off for another night. Kiss him goodbye and let's get going.'

Shope looked at me with glazed eyes, then at Sammy.

'You're not in this,' he said, but there was an element of question in it. Suddenly he was thinking that maybe Sammy was in it, and this shook him like a knock-out blow. All his defences fell away and he took a faltering step towards the open door of the car.

'Where's he taking you?' I asked under my breath. 'You

don't have to go with him if you don't want to.'

Sammy had sharp ears to match his fox-like air. 'Oh yes, he does.'

Shope began to climb awkwardly into the back seat. He paused to look back at me. His fear was naked in his pale moon face.

'Unfinished business—you and me,' he muttered. 'Maybe you're on your own now.'

'Not her kind, for long,' said Sammy. 'Shut the door and let's go, for crissake.'

He fumbled at the instrument board, blazed the head-lamps briefly before he found the switch for the sidelights. It occurred to me that he was unaccustomed to the car— that it was probably a stolen one, stolen just for this trip. He glanced out at me with a leer on his red face as he released the clutch and I heard him say, 'Mizzie losing her grip—letting you bring them to her place?'

Then the car was moving. Twenty seconds later it turned at the end of the street and was gone as quickly and decisively as it had come.

I stood there helplessly, faced with the probability that Shope had been taken away in the most permanent meaning of it.

Confirmation came startlingly in a taut whisper from the door of the house.

'The poor—damn'—fool! I told him it would end like this.'

The street lamp scarcely reached her—a white face, a gap of dark frock against the black rectangle of the open doorway, and below it pallid legs glimmering. I peered at her. The inner planes of her face were heavily shadowed making her head a skull.

She seemed to be extraordinarily thin, and her hands emerging in a spasmodic gesture of distress were fleshless claws. She had put my heart, already unsteady, into a startled quaver.

'And as for you—' There was a glitter in the recesses of the large eye sockets. 'You've helped him to it!'

By now I was up to the steps and closer. Her hair caught

the light and the skeletal hollows of her face shallowed; she might even be young and pretty.

'Get away from me!' she said, and tried to shut the door. I held it back with the weight of my body behind my hands, urging her to listen, to realize that something had to be done about Shope and immediately. 'Have you a telephone—?' She was only half listening, as though she could hear other voices in argument against me.

'No—' She was glaring at me. 'You're not that yellow-skinned bitch. Who are you?'

'Where's the nearest—I can help him—'

'No one can.'

'The police—'

'Don't be silly. What would they care?'

'He's in trouble.'

'You're telling me!'

'He wanted help—anybody's, mine for that matter.'

'You nor anyone can give it to him. It's too late—will be —even for the police.' She spoke with the same finality and looked nervously past me into the street.

'You'd better come in—' She suddenly relaxed her pressure on the door before I realized her invitation, and I stumbled across the threshold into the darkness of the narrow hall. She pushed me aside with a thin sharp shoulder to slam the door. It was as black as pitch with the door shut, a velvet, absolute darkness and I was glad to be in it. She obviously knew something, even if it was only a little.

'I warned him!' her voice came out of it. 'He wouldn't listen. I *knew*!'

'Knew what?'

'That it'd come to this—that they'd be the finish of him . . .' She was having difficulty with her breathing as her violence spent, leaving her tremulous.

'Who?' I asked, holding my own breath.

'Bloody foreigners of some kind,' she whispered.

I let out my held breath slowly. I had not after all lost the only lead.

'I want to know all about them—I want—'

'You don't!' It came out desperately. 'I've nothing to tell you. See? Nothing!'

That had been Shope's refrain with the Field-Marshal.

'All the same,' she added with a return of suspicion, 'I still don't figure you.'

'Mr Shope was bringing me here, where we could talk. So that I could help him. He was going to tell me the whole thing.'

I wished I could see her face. It was like talking to the air.

'Was he?' There was a feline snarl behind it. 'He was, was he? Why? If I couldn't help him, how could you?'

'We can't talk here in the dark,' I said.

She was beginning to give way but her instinct for security through secrecy still demanded flight from me and every-thing else to do with Shope. She did not want to talk and not even to listen if listening would add to knowledge she already regretted having. But I felt there was another thought in her mind, bringing hesitancy. Loyalty to Shope? I wondered about their relationship.

'All right,' she said reluctantly. 'Mind you, I don't know Mr Shope's business and never did. He only lodges here—sometimes.'

She came to my side and shot a bolt on the door below the lock, turned and went down a passage. I was aware of her perfume, cheap but used lightly and therefore inoffensively.

I felt my way after her, touching wallpaper slimy with moisture. There was linoleum on the floor, which clutched at my shoe heels with fibrous cracks of age and wear. She opened a door and went on into a darkened room, turning on a light.

It was a small room which although cluttered with in-numerable small objects was less squalid than its approaches had promised.

There were many photographs, interspersed with odds and ends of pictures cut out of magazines, tacked on the walls and standing on a thin mantelpiece.

She had a disdainful air as she faced me which did not come altogether from suspicion. The slender, poised body in its thin frock was strong and functional. Showgirl, or even dancer, I thought.

I gave her a moment for a longer look at me; she might find some reassurance if she saw me to be as unglamorous as I felt. The pause allowed me time to decide that direct methods, even brutal, would work with her.

'Someone killed a friend of mine,' I said. 'Girl. Mr Shope knew about it.'

She reacted strongly.

'Bertie! He wouldn't kill anyone! He hadn't the guts for one thing! He—was—it was his being a bit soft made me—' She stopped, and I took it up again.

'He knew about it only as a witness, an indirect witness. And that put him in trouble with the man who did kill her. I want to find that man. I could have found some money for him—if he would help me by telling me who the man was.'

She relaxed a little, stared at me. At least I wasn't his girlfriend and now I was claiming to have wanted to help him.

'And now he's gone and he can't tell you,' she said. 'No one can. I can't. I know nothing, nothing at all!'

'You talk as if he'd never come back.'

Her eyes were huge but tearless as she shook her head.

'He won't.'

'You knew he was in trouble—you wouldn't open the door to him.'

'Because you were with him and I thought you were—'

'It wasn't that. You were afraid.'

'Why should I be afraid?'

'Because you know why he was afraid—both of you afraid of the same thing.' I eased into details. 'He lives here?'

'Rents a room from me on the first floor. Comes and goes. Lives in hotels—moves about.'

'What's his job?'

'He hasn't one. At least, I don't know what it is. I tell you he doesn't talk about things. Really uses this place for having time off. Used—' she paused. 'Funny I don't seem to mind. He was all right. But awfully wet, really. Not tough, like he acted. Poor Bertie—' she sighed. 'But I've got the others, so I'm all right.'

She saw my expression and went on to explain that three students rented the other three rooms and 'paid regular'. 'It's my house—'proudly—'I own it. No mortgage. It's a living when I'm resting.' 'Resting' confirmed the theatre background but she did not say how she had acquired the house.

It was time to press again.

'All the same, you knew about this latest job of his—'

'I didn't!' she snapped.

'Then what did you mean "bloody foreigners"?'

Her large eyes moved away from me. 'Did I say that?' But she knew she had.

'I think it was an Italian—a foreigner—who murdered this girl.'

'I don't know anything!' The denial was beginning to hamper my mind with irritation.

'You won't save yourself by sticking your head in the sand!'

'Save myself? From what?'

'Car rides with Sammy, for instance.'

'Sammy's nothing to do with them.'

'So you know Sammy?'

'*No!*'

'You used his name easily.'

'Bertie'd mentioned him—a friend of his!'

'And you also said he was nothing to do with "them". The foreigners. After all, Sammy's a crook,' I said. 'If Italians can pay him in pounds, that's all he cares. He's no nationalist, from the look of him.'

She stared at me. Nationalist? What was I talking about?

'Who *are* you?' she said. 'All these questions!'

'If I gave you a name would you know whether it was false or real? All you know—all I know—is that I'm trying to catch up with a murderer.'

'A ruddy silly thing to do,' she retorted, and it came to me that she was quite right.

'That's my lookout,' I said.

'Why should I make it mine?'

'Don't you owe Bertie Shope anything at all?'

'No!' But I had got under her guard. 'No,' she repeated. 'He was close-fisted and selfish and talked about marrying me—as if he would. Just a line.'

'You said you'd marry him and he didn't do anything about it?'

'I said I wouldn't marry him if he was the last man on earth. You *saw* him, didn't you?'

'Then how do you know he didn't mean it?'

'I think,' she said after a pause, 'I think maybe he did.'

'Then he loved you.'

'That still doesn't mean I owe him anything!'

'Doesn't it?'

'Men falling for you . . . what's it got to do with a girl? They just want . . .' She paused again. She could not get away from the fact that Bertie, with all his faults, had wanted something more. I let her think about it. The house was quiet, and I wondered where the students were; perhaps in a pub somewhere, talking about Marx. She sat down in one of the armchairs and stared at her fingernails. Finally she spoke.

'I really don't know anything—much.'

'However little, it may be quite a lot.'

She got up and went to the door, opened it and stood listening. Satisfied that we were quite alone, but still reluctant, she came back to the chair. I ought to have sat down also, to take some of the tension out of the atmosphere, but could not.

'He said—' she frowned, if she was going to tell me she might as well get it right—'I had asked him for something, it didn't cost much and he said, yes, I could have it "when they pay me off" and I asked who was "they" and he said, "the foreign end of it". When I asked what foreigners had to do with him he said it was no business of mine—but it was a good thing and that was all that mattered. I said for him to be careful. But he laughed and said it was easy money and wouldn't take long. That was about a week ago. I saw him Wednesday night. He looked like he was short

on his sleep. I asked him what was up and he hit the ceiling
—I could keep my nose out. I tried to keep quiet. I wanted
what it was he was going to give me too bad to risk a row.
But it looked as though the money wasn't being quite as
easy as he'd expected and I said again for him to be careful.
I felt kind of responsible. It might have been through me
he'd got mixed up in whatever it was. You see, I was in a
piece that did a tour of Italy. Bertie came out for a holiday,
and a nuisance he was, too.'

'Italy?' I asked. 'And France as well? The Riviera?'

She shook her head. 'Only Italy.'

'When was this?'

'This spring.'

'Where did you go?'

'All over. Milan, Turin, Genoa, Florence—not Naples.
That fell through. Six weeks in all.'

'And Shope with you all the time?'

'Yes.'

'Who did he meet—anyone in particular? Anybody you
remember who might—'

'No. I've tried to think. But there isn't anyone. He had a
lot of time to himself. We did three shows a night—didn't
finish until one in the morning. They never go to bed, those
people.'

'You said he was a nuisance?'

'About the food. It gave him a belly ache.' She looked at
me expectantly. Beyond confirmation of the Italian *motif* she
had contributed only the name of four cities; had she said
Nice or Cannes or Antibes or one of those places already in
the pattern of the Field-Marshal's theory, it would have
been more encouraging. But she hadn't.

'That's all?' I said glumly.

'I swear it is—' But she had hesitated.

'For God's sake,' I said. 'I must have everything.'

'It's nothing to do with it—'

I waited. Her face screwed up like a child's and her
knuckles whitened.

'I was scared,' she said. 'I—didn't want to get mixed up
in it whatever it was—and I *didn't* know what it was. So—

I pinched his key—so he could only get in if I let him . . . maybe if I hadn't—'

'It wouldn't have made any difference,' I said.

'You think not?'

'Sammy didn't look as though he would be stopped by anything. Not tonight.'

She shivered. 'I don't like him. Creepy.'

'So you do know him.'

'Bertie introduced him once, in the street. But like everything else, he didn't talk about him. Tell you the truth, I didn't particularly want him to.'

In the quiet came the unmistakable sound of knocking on the front door, clear-cut, as though something hard was being used to save the caller's hand.

The girl was motionless like a pointing dog.

'One of your lodgers?'

She hushed me swiftly, shaking her head.

'They've all got keys.' I did not remind her that she had shot her bolt. She flicked down the switch, putting us in darkness except for a slight luminosity from the upper part of the window. The knock on the street door was repeated and became a rapid tattoo of insistence, then paused, the silence emphasizing impatience.

'It doesn't follow—' I began but again she stopped me with a frightened 'ssh!', and I realized what the trouble was. A friendly visitor would be using the identifying knock.

'I've nothing to be afraid of,' I heard her say fiercely under her breath but she still made no move to go to the street door.

'Couldn't you see from one of the front windows?'

'Oh God,' she whispered, 'I'm frightened!'

I found I was in much the same state. I looked at the window. It was not difficult to imagine a couple of scalable walls, a side alley between houses in a parallel street, and freedom. But also I saw Shope's room upstairs, with a desk, and neat files, each appropriate to its subject, and one of them marked *Italy* in large letters one could read across the room.

'I can't stand this,' I heard her voice. 'I'll be screaming in a minute!'

'Surely it's better to take a look than stand here, frightening ourselves,' I said. 'Perhaps he's gone away.'

Another repetitive series of knocks, harder and angrier, told the falseness of the hope.

'You're in this more than I am,' she whispered fiercely. 'You can tell them I don't know anything! Wait here.' I heard a soft scrape as she got out of the chair and then the creak of the door handle as she went into the dark passage.

I stepped out of my shoes, picked them up and went through the door after her. I judged by the sounds that she was entering a room on the left. No lights went on and I guessed she was making for the window and a chink between the curtains. Then unmistakably I heard a voice the other side of the street door; it was pitched low but I thought it was Sammy's. He had someone with him. Shope? I did not think so. I advanced into the passage, groping desperately for a break in the left-hand wall; I had hugged the other one on the way in and knew therefore that the staircase must be on this side. It was nearer the street door than I expected. I felt my way up it as fast as the darkness would let me; my distance between the door and the men who waited there felt like scanty inches which did not increase as I climbed away from them. First floor back, hadn't she said?

I would have given a great deal for a flashlamp; but I had a cigarette lighter somewhere in my handbag. I put down my shoes and searched for it. It would have been easier to find it with less shaky fingers . . . unless, of course, in my hurry I had forgotten it. Then I found the lighter, sighed with relief, which went instantly as the knocking on the street door began again. They would pass it even if they had to break it down.

I flicked the lighter and in its glimmer saw a small landing with three doors. The room facing me would be Shope's. The lighter went out but I felt for the door handle; it was locked but the back of my hand touched the key. I turned it, stepped inside and realized by the complete darkness that the window was totally obscured and I could use the light. The switch eluded me for a moment but I found it with the lighter. I pressed it down. It clicked but that was all; either there was no bulb or it was broken. Or there was another switch somewhere. The lighter flame was feeble and consumed the fuel in the top of the wick faster than it rose; it went out three times before I had established even the shape of the room, apart from any search for another light switch.

But there was a desk, just as I had hoped. My dream of orderly files vanished; a litter of papers covered every inch of it and overflowed on to a table jutting out at right angles from one end. My lighter was good now only for a brief and microscopic gleam. I put on my shoes, gripped my handbag under my arm, picked up the nearest piece of paper and held it close to the lighter. It was a pencilled list of racehorses with the odds marked against them, so was the second; the third was a double-page Form Sheet. Then the lighter merely threw sparks when I pressed its lever. I stumbled to the window and pulled aside heavy plush curtains which smelt of soot. The window was moderately clean but it let in very little light from the night sky, certainly not enough to read by. I heard a splintering noise downstairs and knew that Sammy and his companion had resorted to force at last, perhaps with a jemmy, which in this neighbourhood would not be as great a risk as it might seem. Legitimate householders forgetting their latchkeys might carry them.

I went back to the door, changed the key to the inside and turned it; a waste of time, probably, but for a moment it gave me a slight sense of security, even though it did not lift the feeling of nightmare, as though my feet were stuck in heavy mud as I fled from nameless horror.

There were voices in the hall below, the girl shrill and protesting and Sammy growling back at her. I shook the lighter downwards to force the fuel and tried it again. It burned long enough for me to see more of the room, still hoping for those files. Shope playing the horses might be a matter of frenzy and therefore untidiness from which his more serious business interests did not suffer.

But I could not see a filing cabinet, or even a cupboard in which files might be kept.

There was a large studio bed which filled the right side of the room and on the left a bookshelf, half given to its proper use and half to bottles and a few glasses. Beyond it was a fireplace, and beyond that a potted fern on a thin-legged stand. A row of little flat white objects on the mantelpiece, not all the same size but all rectangular, caught the last of the flame and continued to show as dim ghosts against the dark background.

I went over to them and realized by the feel of one that they were calling cards, a whole collection of them. There was nothing else on the mantelpiece and this, apart from the number of them—I guessed there must be thirty or forty —gave them significance. Had he collected and treasured them, given them a place of display all their own, mementoes of people he had met—or done business with—as another man might collect ashtrays or those small crested china ornaments as a record of places he had seen? Or done business with . . .

I slipped the useless lighter in my pocket and ran my fingers from both ends of the mantelpiece to the centre, gathering up the cards into an uneven pack which I put in my handbag.

. . . Sammy was on the stairs by now, still growling. I could hear the words now.

'. . . Okay, Mizzie—I believe you. You don't know a thing. So leave it to me, will you.'

She was below in the hall, and all but screaming.

'There's nothing there— he didn't use the room, scarcely! You've got him, haven't you? He'll tell you!'

Sammy was not alone on the stairs for he said: 'She's probably right, like I said. Anyway, he was cagey. I tell you he'd not keep anything—'

With an effort of will I went over to the door and took the key out. To have found it in the lock when they broke in would have had but one answer, and I did not want them to supply it—not while I had the smallest chance of getting out of this somehow.

The noise they were making enabled me to reach the window and on the way to collide with the table—my hip always seemed nearer the surface than any other bone I had —without their realizing I was there.

The door handle rattled; Sammy called out: 'Come on, Mizzie—where's the bloody key?'

I looked down on a flat roof four feet below the window sill—the roof, probably, of the kitchen—and somehow opened the lower half of the window.

Mizzie's reply to the question about the key must have been delayed, for Sammy demanded it again. She was puzzled, of course. She knew what went on in her house and the key should have been in the lock—outside. But she did not tell him so. I hoped she wasn't jumping to any accurate conclusions. I climbed out on to the roof, reached back and closed the curtains. I pulled down the window, leaving an inch crack at the bottom for my fingertips to find purchase when the time came to open it again. If someone did not open it from inside, first, and find me. I was in the girl's hands. But I was hopeful, realizing that she had not told Sammy I was in the house, in her sitting-room, as she thought. It looked as though her loyalty to Shope was upholding her in spite of her fear.

Sammy and his silent friend settled the matter of the key by breaking the lock, which must have put up even less resistance than the one on the street door; there was a protest from the girl about it, 'smashing up the place, you swine.' I sat on my haunches close to the wall below the window and kept my face down, the only part of me light enough to be seen from the window; my stockingless legs were hidden by the upper part of my crouching body. They would not see me unless they knew I was there. And if by chance they did, I should have to risk a broken bone in dropping off the roof into the black pit of the yard.

I thought unexpectedly of Charlie Berrington. It would be nice to have had him waiting in the yard below; he was the only person I knew who was strong enough to catch a young woman jumping off a roof.

A thin line of light from between the curtains struck the

roof and remained steady. The girl would have known, of course, where to find the right switch.

'For crissake look at that!' Sammy's voice was clear and close and for a horrible moment I thought he was talking about me, but I realized that the line of light had not widened. He meant the desk. 'Didn't he ever throw anything away?'

The past tense was not lost on me.

'As a matter of interest,' came the girl's voice and I could hear the attempt at casualness, 'where is he? I haven't seen him for a week.'

'Busy,' said Sammy. 'The only thing to do is to take the lot. You can't go through it here.'

'You' was his companion who was still managing to keep out of the conversation, whatever else he may have been active in. Sammy told the girl to find a suitcase.

'You can't take his stuff without him saying so—'

'He says so.'

'*You* say—'

'That's right. *I* say. I also said get a suitcase. Don't stand there arguing! *Get one!*' And he hit her, violently. She cried out and I heard her stumble; she must have gone at once to obey him.

The second man now spoke for the first time, but so softly that his voice reached me only as a wordless murmur. I was surprised to detect a puzzling familiarity in it. Sammy answered him reassuringly: 'He wasn't anything in her young life much. She's all right.'

The past tense for Shope chilled me again. The other man said something, the words still inaudible. I was certain I neither knew him nor should expect to recognize him by his voice but its tonal characteristics remained familiar. I relaxed conscious effort in the hope that memory would move automatically and listened with all my attention to Sammy. At least he did not mumble and every little word could be important in our state of groping ignorance.

'One letter in all this . . . what sort of letter? I tell you, *no*. . . And if you'd let me in on what's behind it, I'd know better what to do . . . okay, okay, have it your own way.

But this is England. They don't beat us up just for the fun of it, and not a woman—besides, I tell you she's all right. I know the type. . . *Type*! This is beginning to get me down. I thought you said you'd been to school in England for crissake.'

I felt a tremor of excitement. He had given me the clue. The other man had a foreign accent. I could hear it in the cadences, and now recognized it as Italian in the rise of key at the end of the sentences. Had he been speaking his own tongue I should have known it at once but his unaccustomed English had disguised it. Even so, I had been slow; after French, it was the one language in which I could manage competently, provided I was not expected to write it.

Was he—*the* Italian?

If he was, why Shope's drive to the coast? But after all, we were only guessing it had been to the coast, to one of the cross-Channel ports. But if it hadn't been, what and where its purpose?

I steadied myself. There could be two Italians—or more. Mizzie had referred to 'them', in the plural. But unless she had been very clever with me she knew that as a feeling, nothing more.

'. . . You can borrow this,' came her voice. 'I said borrow. It's the only good one I've got.'

'Why should you care? You're not going anywhere—unless you insist,' Sammy said tersely.

I heard the suitcase lid being opened, followed by rustling of papers as they gathered them up. Sammy was doubting whether the case was large enough; the Italian had returned to silence, his uneasiness about the girl either satisfied or suspended while she was present.

I was beginning to think that he was probably someone who had stayed behind to tidy up after the actual murderer rather than the murderer himself. Stayed behind? That impression came from Sammy's reference to the man's schooling in England; he would have said it differently had he been a resident in this country. It also explained Sammy and his attitude. He did not know as much about the background of this business as he would have liked, which sounded as though he had come into it in the same sort of way as Shope, either to work with him or to watch him, friends to be divided and ruled by their Italian masters. It made sense. It also made certain of the likelihood that they knew all about Turnbull and therefore the Field-Marshal, and the latter's interest in Angela after her return from the Riviera. They had known obviously about Shope's visit to Grosvenor Square, and Christopher's shortly afterwards. Their anxiety was well-founded.

The only thing they did not know about was me. At least I did not think so. Sammy had dismissed me easily, without hesitation, when he came upon me outside with Shope. Shope's reputation as a womanizer had saved me. But I was safe only as long as Sammy never set eyes on me again. At all costs that must not happen. In the meanwhile I was a chink, the only chink, in their armour, a tactical position which I thought might suit my kind of effectiveness.

Apart from that I wanted to live.

Mizzie broke the silence.

'. . . for God's sake what's he looking at me like that for?' It was an explosive cry but there was fright in her indignation. Sammy did not make it any better. 'Mr Morelli doesn't trust you. Perhaps he's right at that.'

If no less sinister with his long silences, soft voice and way of looking at girls he did not trust, he was now a shade less anonymous. Morelli. It would be no effort to remember his name for the short time before I reached Christopher with these vital developments.

Mizzie said with commendable but weakly bravado that he could do what he liked about it.

'Unless you're bloody careful,' Sammy assured her, 'he will. I've gone bail for you. Can't think why. But I have. See . . .?'

I might have been in the room so strong was the smell of her fear.

'Of course I see,' she said in a voice she could scarcely control. 'It's—it's okay by me. . .' And I had not the slightest doubt that it was. The loss of her Bertie and this outrage of her rights as a householder were forgotten; she wanted only to make them believe she would cooperate.

'I've got some of his clothes in my room,' she said. 'Nothing much—a couple of shirts and things, a pair of slippers.'

'Thanks,' said Sammy. 'We'll take them along.'

'He—he may need them,' she said more steadily, sealing the unspoken bargain, immunity for her silence.

'So he may. Let's clear this lot first.' Sammy's voice was light again.

It occurred to me I had neither given her sex-appeal the credit it deserved nor remembered she had said that Sammy 'made eyes' the only time she met him. Perhaps he was thinking of taking over Shope's room sometime. It would kill two birds with one stone that way—or rather keep one bird alive . . .

They were leaving the room. Sounds ceased and the light went out. I stood up carefully, easing my back, and leaned against the wall by the window.

It seemed a long time but could have been only a few minutes before I heard a car start up a little way down the street. Its engine had an older noise than the one which had taken Shope away. It would have been natural, also, for Sammy to have parked away from the house. He had been in a hurry before, but with Shope out of the way the worst was over and he could afford discretion.

And so could I now, which was a luxury. Tomorrow was Sunday. Christopher could not bring Arthur North before a police magistrate before Monday morning. A few extra minutes, another hour or so if need be, before I saw him, would not matter against the importance of being careful.

I raised the window slowly. Where before I had been able to close it without being heard, the silence now made every creak a pistol shot. I forced myself to pause when it was wide enough. I had no idea which part of the house Mizzie was now in, whether she was still downstairs or had gone to bed. But even if she had, fear was on her pillow to keep her awake.

I seemed constantly to be taking off my shoes, putting them on, taking them off again.

I climbed back into the room and kept a decent gap between the table and my hip as I crossed blindly to the door. It was open, as I had expected; I brushed against the lock hanging from the splintered wood.

There was still no sound that I could hear from the landing and I made the descent of the stairs a cautious step at a time.

Mizzie had propped a chair against the lower panel of the street door so that the curve of its top was wedged in the letter-box. I pulled it away and since I could not replace it from outside I did the next best thing by lowering it on to its back close to the door so that she might assume it had slipped and fallen with its own weight.

. . . I put on my shoes at the bottom of the steps and began at once to feel the relief of moving and walking without fear.

The street lamp showed me my watch, a few minutes past midnight. Time had not, in fact, flown as fast as I had expected. But I was reluctant to waste any finding a call-box from which to reassure the Field-Marshal. My chief concern was to find Christopher.

I came to an area of wider but still decrepit streets of dark shops with late pedestrians here and there. This was Camden Town and being on one of the main north–south routes I should meet a cab returning to the centre from an outward trip to Hampstead or Highgate.

One came in sight almost at once and I hailed it. I gave the Terry House address. If Christopher was home and in bed he would have to get up. If he was not home yet, I still had to collect my bag. Graham would be off-duty but there would be a night porter to give it to me.

But the nearer I came to Sloane Avenue the more I began to reflect. It was all very well to know that what I had to tell Christopher was extremely important, but the thought of facing him was infinitely more difficult than it had been when I had chased after him with Angela's letter as an excuse to mend our love. It had been bad enough then, but now I was coming to tell him that I was right and he was wrong about Arthur North, and had made a fool of himself with Lord Orme. That one way and another he did not know his job.

I was in a panic about it by the time the cab turned into the Avenue. I would not even try to see him. Whatever unpleasantness might be in store for his ego it must be administered by anyone in the world rather than by me. The Field-Marshal was the obvious and ideal person.

The cab stopped at the entrance of Terry House with its illuminated porch and I sat for a moment telling myself I could even manage without my bag. I pulled myself together. No man because I loved him could be allowed to reduce me to such cowardice!

I got out, told the driver to wait and went through the revolving door into the empty lobby. The porter's door was shut but I was honest enough to remind myself that after midnight, when the operator had gone, the lift became one of the night porter's duties. I looked across and checked that the lift was in fact being used. I could wait two minutes, couldn't I?

It was quiet and reassuringly peaceful in the lobby. The indicator lights went on and off as they recorded the climbing lift, it could go no higher than the top floor. In a moment it would stop, the porter would let out the passenger and bring it down at once. A moment after that I should have my bag and be gone.

I heard the revolving door creaking behind me and deliberately kept my back to it, ignoring the sensation between my shoulder-blades which crawled up to the nape of my neck and stiffened the small hairs there.

'Hello,' said Christopher, 'what's happened?'

'. . . Happened?' I stuttered, 'I couldn't remember where I'd left my bag.'

'You left it *here*?'

'This afternoon—oh, it's all right,' I said. 'I wasn't eloping to you—I was on my way to see Angela—about that letter—before bringing it to you, if I thought she really was in some kind of danger. And this was a handy place to leave my bag. Graham took it in—the night man—' I gestured at the lift gates as words ran out. He stood looking down at me with his rumpled hat on the back of his head, a man as weary as death itself.

'Guilty conscience?' he asked amiably.

'About what?' I was surprised at the amount of resistance left in me.

'You know Lord Orme, of course.'

I waited.

'Yes,' he said. 'Seen him lately? Today for instance?'

'And if I have—what's strange about that. Angela's—'

'—Uncle,' he took it up. 'Look, Eve, leave the poor chap alone. You're not helping him, not in the end.'

'He's not a fool, Christopher. He's shocked with grief, but he is still a thinking man.'

'Championing the down-trodden, Robin Hooding— what's the feminine equivalent of Robin?—Robin Hooding at the drop of a hat. You can't help it, I suppose. But your loyalty does you credit.'

'Oh, don't be sarcastic!' I cried out. 'If I appear disloyal to you it's only because I don't want you to do the wrong thing!'

He looked worried and said he had not meant it sarcastically. I was glad to see it bothered him to be misunderstood by me. 'I meant your loyalty to Angela,' he explained, 'convincing yourself she wasn't a messy sort of person and encouraging him—Lord Orme—in his fantasies. Loyalty, even if misguided and time-wasting. And I don't mean *your* time . . . but that's enough of that. I daresay he would have started something in any case. But I've just spent an hour and a half at the Yard, and I'm not at my brightest.'

'Oh, Christopher—'

'I'm all right.' He did not want anyone's sympathy, mine least of anyone's.

'Then about Shope—'

'If anybody says that name again I shall hit them over the head with the nearest chair!' he said. 'Damn Shope! He doesn't exist.'

'That's probably true,' I began. 'You see he—'

'Then for God's sake why did Orme invent him?'

He scowled at me venomously.

The lift gates opened and the night porter appeared.

'I think you ought to know,' said Christopher, 'that Arthur North has given up trying.'

I stared at him. His drop in tension was as sudden as the explosion had been.

'His legal advisers may even have difficulty in getting him to plead "not guilty".'

'Oh?' It seemed the only word left in my vocabulary. He had turned to the night porter.

'Miss Gill left her bag with Graham.'

'Yes, sir. It's here.'

'That's your cab outside, Eve?'

I nodded.

He took the bag, escorted me to the taxi, opened the door, helped me in and put the bag at my feet.

'Sergeant Framley will take that statement from you in the morning.'

'But surely—'

'You can substantiate Angela Sawyer writing to you for help, and explain how you followed North from Lincott Street and saw him burn those letters. No need for you to come to the Station. Framley will call on you, officially. Good night.' He smiled, an attempt at friendliness for old times' sake, and closed the cab door on me. 'Fifteen, Thurloe Square,' he told the driver.

He looked at me once again, without the smile, but with an expression which although indefinable nevertheless went sharply to my heart.

The taxi moved off and his face was gone.

I slid back the glass panel and told the driver, not Thurloe Square, but Grosvenor—Number Forty-three.

CHAPTER 5

The Field-Marshal in a purple silk dressing-gown opened the door.

'You damnable girl!' His tone was angry, relieved and

93

affectionate, and more to his own surprise than mine he clasped me briefly but hard against his small, muscular chest. He continued to hold me by the shoulders as he searched my face with lively eyes. I think if he hadn't held me I should have fallen down. He satisfied himself that I was all in one piece and helped me upstairs. He walked the corridor outside the bathroom and waited while I got into bed, this time in my own nightgown and with face cream and tissues within reach.

I did not hurry over any of these preparations, knowing that until I had revived a little, even temporarily, I could not have put words together coherently.

The Field-Marshal put himself in the chair he had sat in before, when I had made my first effort to end the day, and made me promise to stop if I needed a rest.

'If I stop I shan't be able to start again . . .'

But once I was well into the story the effort became easier than I had expected.

The Field-Marshal was silent for an appreciable passage of seconds after I had finished. Then he let out a slow, audible sigh of relief. 'It was well done. You might have ruined it by trying to do too much. You were right not to force the girl. You would have made a good soldier if you'd been born a male.'

When he had gone I lay still on my back letting weariness have its way. In a last flicker of energy I pulled my handbag on to the bed and went through the cards I had taken from Shope's mantelpiece. It was a varied collection, a mixture of private and business names, many of them yellowed and grimy. Amongst the fresher only one seemed to have a remotely possible connection with anything we knew, and even then suggested only an ill-defined by-path on the direct road offered by Mizzie and Sammy. I put it back in the handbag and the remainder in the drawer of the bedside table. Almost before my arm was back in bed with me I fell off the brink on which I had been teetering into a deep well of sleep.

Climbing out of the well to see sunlight edging the curtains

94

was a slow business, and it took me a little while to identify unaccustomed sounds of traffic as coming from Grosvenor Square and not from the garden below my windows at home. Still half-awake I got out of bed to pull the curtains and a sheet of writing paper which was propped against the intercom box on the bedside table caught my eye.

The message written on it brought me sharply to reality:

Eve,
  Please ring 8 when you wake up. That young idiot has foozled it.

D. O.

I pressed down the switch marked '8' on the intercom, knowing that I need not ask which young idiot had foozled what. Nor what 'foozled' meant. I seemed to remember it as the term used in golf when one failed to put down an easy shot. The buzzing ended with a click and his voice came over: 'Ah! you're awake. You slept well?' I told him like a log and that I felt almost normal again.

'Then you can stand a set-back. I called up Smith as soon as I left you—got his home number from his station after a tussle—gave him the salient points of the story as if from Turnbull—just the facts of what he would have seen if he'd followed Shope, watched him go with "Sammy", and seen the girl afterwards. I called him up immediately afterwards and briefed him on it just in case your young man checked with him. Your young man! I'll credit him with the diplomacy of an elder statesman. Not a hint he was so done he could scarcely speak—it took five minutes of telephone bell to wake him. No reproach, when he could have told me to go to hell—I've no authority over him. He listened very politely and said it was "interesting", and then pulled out the same old suggestion he had put up originally—' The Field-Marshal seemed to be containing his emotions with difficulty, and only because the odious Smith was my young man—'that it certainly was very clear that some kind of nonsense had been going on in Lincott Street, and that the people concerned fell out with one another in the course of it and perhaps because of the murder. They would not know until Monday morning's papers that someone had been arrested who was nothing to do with them, but in the meantime they had dealt with Shope for jeopardizing them. If that car ride of his was what it sounded like. The picture wasn't changed merely because the Shope thing had been painted in with more detail. It was still coincidental—and unnecessary to the picture. Arthur North was quite sufficient for him. But he had given his assurance, had he not, that the Shope angle would be examined, and had confirmed this to Scotland Yard—who "seemed to have got on to it". He knew perfectly well how they'd got on to it but he'd be damned if he'd let me know he knew. Are you still there?'

I said I was. 'So he won't do anything about it fast enough?'

'Oh, he took action all right. He sent a sergeant and a detective to Pawley Road, but they didn't get there until somewhere about three o'clock this morning. And couldn't make anyone hear. Although the door appeared to have been forced at some time it would not open under "normal pressure". I suppose the girl put the chair against it again. Anyway, they gave up and came away. They did not feel justified in "effecting an entry" without a search warrant. And Smith backs them up. The evidence that a crime had been committed wasn't strong enough for drastic action, but he's applied for a warrant and will use it as soon as it's in his hands. It doesn't take much intelligence to guess what will have happened in the meantime.'

'She'll have gone.'

'Wouldn't you?'

I realized that I should have told Christopher the story, the whole story, myself. Getting it first-hand, from me, he would have believed it and handled the thing differently. I said so, and that I felt guilty at having shirked it.

'Don't,' said the Field-Marshal. 'He believed it all right. But Ananias's worst enemy couldn't have made him believe that it had any significance in Angela's death.'

He went on to say that he proposed to accompany the police party and was leaving in a few minutes. He would

96

come straight back. I would be here? Yes, I said, of course. He told me to ask Harris for anything I needed. I could either have breakfast in bed or in the morning-room if I felt like getting up.

I had not forgotten Christopher's official warning that he was sending Framley to Thurloe Square to take a statement from me. It was now nearly half-past nine and I set about dealing with it before ringing for Harris and breakfast. But there was no external telephone in my room; I knew about the one under the main stairs but it seemed sensible to look for a nearer one. I found it almost at once in a room two doors away which proclaimed itself beyond doubt as the Field-Marshal's bedroom.

It was as near a 'state' bedroom as I had ever seen, with a huge carved Elizabethan four-poster hung with magnificent contemporary brocade of rich golden-yellow. Its vast cover-let of the same material, however, was smooth and flat without bedclothes or pillows under it, and a narrow camp bed crouching by its side explained its purely symbolic function. An ancestral bed, if ever there was one, and I wondered what family tree supported the new earldom; a large, well-grown one, I felt, for he was neither the man to have acquired the material trappings of the old elite to go with a young one nor to sleep in a humble camp bed because it became his true station in life. Obviously he had convinced himself when he was young—and in the Service where such things were experienced—that it was the only comfortable form of bed, and had stuck to it. It was too low to justify a bedside table and the telephone, an antiquated up-and-down type with separate earpiece, stood on the floor at its head beside a large gold presentation cigarette box, a bat-tered tobacco tin with a label scrawled 'Sleeping Pills', and a photograph of a young girl in a small, oval ebony frame. I recognized her—Angela as she had been when we were at High School together; and with a little shock of personal relationship I saw that it was a picture I had taken of her myself, on the first negative of the first spool in my first camera.

I squatted on my heels and rang up Aunt Florence to

make sure that the Sergeant had not already come looking for me; I did not seriously think he had, with the Field-Marshal spoiling his sleep with the Pawley Road investigation.

Aunt Florence at once wanted to know where I was and what I was up to and in the same breath said that my young man had called up twice since nine o'clock but luckily she had kept her head and told him I was asleep and mustn't be woken because I was so bad-tempered when I wasn't allowed to wake up in my own time. 'Such a *useful* reputation, darling—and remember to thank me for it when you're married. Men like your young man are *so* energetic in the mornings. I said you'd probably get in touch with him when you felt like it. I do hope that was right?'

I said it was, perfectly, and then had to break the news to her about Angela, and that I was staying with her uncle because he needed someone to see him through the first awfulness of it. I did not give the 'uncle' a name but told her the telephone number, for her own information, no one else's—particularly Christopher's. She had only met Angela two or three times and her grief was for me rather than for herself. She would be very careful to keep my young man at bay.

My young man. It hurt every time.

I rang up his police station and asked for the CID. I was put through, and of the voice which answered, asked for a message to be given to Inspector Smith. But when I began by saying who I was the man interrupted politely. The Inspector wanted to speak to me urgently. My heart in hope skipped a beat. And when he came on the line there was a note in his greeting which I thought I recognized, in my hopefulness, as affection uncertain of itself.

'This is very good of you, after my boorishness last night,' he said. 'I was tired—'

'Of course, Christopher—that's all right. I was in a bad mood too.' I checked myself as I was about to say that perhaps the whole of yesterday might be written off for similar reasons.

'Sweet of you to forgive me—' He paused, and I gave

him time by saying that it would be easier for me, if it was all right with him, if I came to the station to give my statement.

'Certainly. As a matter of fact Framley is out on a job. This afternoon will do.' He went straight on, without making the suggestion, obvious to anyone seeking reconciliation, that we should lunch together: 'Eve, there's something you can help me in, I think. How well do you know Lord Orme?'

My heart subsided, dully.

'I told you yesterday—he's a close relative of Angela's.'

'I know. Very close. You probably know I saw him last night, and had a bit of a scene with him. He seemed to be using rank to push this theory of his. He can't see it as separate from the murder. He's been on to my Higher-ups about it. They wouldn't play but it hasn't stopped him. He's ferreting around for evidence to support himself and his notion and unfortunately getting it. It's the wrong time for me. I haven't an inexhaustible staff and he's got it running its feet off on a wild goose chase when we've never been so busy. This particular case—terrible as it is—isn't the only one on our plate. Can you persuade Orme to stop this thrashing about?'

It was for Christopher a long speech but it was also a personal appeal. I could have asked him why he should expect me to come to his rescue when he had finished with me. But I didn't. I said I was sorry, but I did not know Lord Orme well enough to change his mind when he had made it up. Nor, I thought, did anyone.

'Wouldn't it help,' he said, 'if you admitted to him that your support for North's innocence is emotional rather than sensible?'

I clamped my mouth tight shut for fear of what might come out of it. He had not finished.

'Can't you see your wanting to save Angela's reputation has—'

'—blinded me to the truth?' I suggested. 'Let's stick to our clichés.'

'Unkind,' he said. 'I'm not very good with words—or with subtleties.'

'You,' I said, 'can pretend anything you like to me, but not that you're lacking in subtlety. Or words for anything you want to say. Except perhaps to me.'

I instantly regretted that.

'I daresay not,' he said emptily. 'Never mind, I'll manage.' And he rang off.

I had breakfast, brought me by Harris; dressed and went downstairs. It was just after half-past ten.

The door of the room which I had opened and hastily closed when I was seeking cover from Shope last night was open now, and the Field-Marshal standing on its threshold. I saw that an inner door of wire-netting restrained the otherwise free flight of the numerous small birds who had startled me in the darkness. They were active now, chirping, fluttering, darting, a mixed and busy colony. I wondered if the early craftsmen who had carved the ebullient designs of flowers and foliage on cornice and ceiling of that huge room had ever imagined them as nesting places for living *aves*. The floor was thickly carpeted not with Aubusson but with straw, and a large stone bird bath occupied the central position where a state dining-table had no doubt once supported the elegant feasts of the fashionable mighty.

The Field-Marshal turned from calming himself with the watching of the birds and said gloomily:

'Of course she'd gone. But not a piece of paper, not a letter, not even the signed photographs you mentioned. Nothing. The cleanest sweep you ever saw. From the state she was in when you left she must have pulled herself together quite remarkably after hearing the police at the door the first time. Search warrants!' He was almost snarling.

It sounded as though Sammy had lent her a hand. I said so, and made the point that although she had been frightened of him she might easily have been more frightened of the police.

'But you were sure she didn't know anything.'

'Not of what they could get out of her but of the mere fact that she might be known to have been anywhere near them, however unwillingly.'

'Fear—'

'Yes, but an enormous fear.'

'Angela—'

'And Shope, and Mizzie, even Sammy, who hid it fairly well. I could feel it everywhere, a solid, real thing,' I said.

'This Morelli?'

'He was the one who used it, yes, held the weapon at their throats. But I think it had a double edge for him. As if he held it by proxy.'

'Shope was as scared as anyone I've ever seen.'

'He could have been a coward at the end or a brave man baring his chest to it, accepting the inevitable. He knew he would never make them believe he could hold his tongue. They wouldn't even bother to listen as long as it was simpler to kill him.'

'Bound hands but standing at attention.' The Field-Marshal nodded slowly, seeing something in his long past. 'You're saying that with a fear as big as this, the police will have a job finding the girl—and Sammy if he's with her. They can't identify him, by the way. He's new, they think.'

'He didn't sound, or act, new.' I added in afterthought: 'But he did seem a bit over-drawn, now I look back at it. He might have been trying too hard.'

The Field-Marshal came out of the aviary, closing the outer door.

'It would be easy to let it go,' he said. 'The thing's at the top of a damned difficult tree which seems determined to stop anyone shinning up it. Much easier than hoping.' He looked at me, and I wondered whether he was seeking rebuttal or agreement.

I could have given him agreement. Christopher had a murderer who was content to be one, and even if we began to climb again and by some miracle of luck reached somewhere, the only sure thing I knew we should find was danger.

The Field-Marshal had doubtless made his own arrangements with fear by now, but I was afraid of it, more afraid of it than anything in life, including death.

'They are so convinced about Arthur North,' he said.

'I'm not!'

I came out with it more quickly and sharply than my thoughts of surrender would have seemed easily to allow.

'You're not?' He was eager. 'So we carry on, but with somewhat empty hands.'

'Very empty,' I agreed. 'I think we've only this.'

I fished out the card I had selected from Shope's collection and gave it him.

He read it aloud:

BERNARDINO, S.A.
Via Gambino, 17   Importazione
Genova   Generale

I told him where I had found it. There was a light in his eyes again, perhaps the light of battle.

'That is the only comparatively new one which doesn't seem in keeping with the rest which are all English names and only one or two with addresses. Mostly women with phoney, tarty-sounding names. But we'll look at them again.'

'Genoa?' The Field-Marshal frowned doubtfully.

'One of the places Mizzie went to with Shope—or rather Shope with Mizzie.'

'Yes, yes—' His frown was impatient, a scowl of thought. Then he turned abruptly, crossed the hall to the lobby and went out of the street door so quickly that I wondered with concern what had happened, and ran after him. The Rolls was at the door and Angus jumped out and also started after him, infected by his master's urgency.

We were close behind him when he pulled up at a post box on the corner of Mount Street. He stood swearing under his breath and looking at it as if he wanted to tear it apart.

'Damn, damn, damn!' he said more loudly, then swung about and strode past us back to the house. I went with him, half a pace behind. Angus got back into the car with a glance at me, which said clearly, it's all yours, chum.

The Field-Marshal hurried down the hall to the telephone under the stairs and once again came to a stop. He put out a hand to pick up the receiver and drew it back. He was still holding the card in the other. He read it again and became aware of me. His eyes were an angry soldier's looking upon a failure in duty.

'Why the devil didn't you give me this before?'

I reminded myself that I had not taken the Queen's shilling and told him a little shortly that I had not regarded it as of any importance while Mizzie was available, in short, until this moment, and even now only as a straw.

'Don't you see, I've posted the letter! I've posted it—the thing's done—not a thing a man can have second thoughts about. Not after a month to decide. Can't ring him up and say, sorry old boy, disregard it—tear it up—can't do it. He'd think I'd gone crackers, a stuffed shirt like that. He *is* a stuffed shirt.'

'Who?' I ventured.

'Home Secretary,' he muttered. 'But even if he wasn't, I don't think I could stop myself now.'

'You—you've complained to him—' I was in a panic, seeing Christopher carpeted into demotion or resignation.

'Complained?' he said more quietly. 'No. I've accepted that job.'

He stared into his thoughts and I had to ask him, what job?

'Commissioner of Police,' he said, and there was a silence in which I began to realize the implications of this astonishing announcement. *Commissioner of Police!* Head man over all policemen, a man to whom important creatures like Divisional Detective-Inspectors were as dust beneath the feet! My panic on Christopher's account rose to breathlessness.

'Isn't—isn't there something,' I said jerkily, 'about taking a sledge-hammer to crack a nut . . .'

Commissioner of Police! Where was my little bird-watcher?

'I wasn't looking at it like that,' he set out at last to explain. 'You see what happened. I wrote that letter last night on the strict understanding that I would post it as soon as I knew which way the Pawley Road business turned out. We were afraid it would go wrong, and it did.'

'Strict understanding with whom?'

'With myself, of course. Who else?'

Who else indeed.

'And taking the job wasn't just another way round of dealing with these policemen. You are not thinking that?'

I admitted I had, guiltily.

'You know me better, surely?'

I nodded affirmatively. I couldn't explain that knowing him better was a thing which might reasonably take anyone a little time, including Solomon.

'You see, the thing that stuck out like a sore thumb was the apparent boneheadedness of chaps like your young man, when obviously they aren't by nature anything of the sort. The Scotland Yard people seemed the same way—worse almost, because they were more polite than he was. It dawned on me in the middle of the night what was the matter with them. They are too busy, too damnably overworked to think further than "thank God for a straight answer." There just aren't enough of them to do the tremendous amount of crime prevention and crime solution called for in this over-populated country, particularly in its vast cities. They're thirty per cent under strength and therefore only something less than seventy per cent effective in it.'

'I see,' I said, beginning to see, and to breathe again.

'Of course you do.' His voice and eyes were themselves again. 'Hardy is retiring. He's done a wonderful job. When it was put to me to take it over I was uncertain. I hadn't any great feeling about it. But now—well, I'm a soldier. I think I know a bit about recruiting and there are magnificent men coming out of their National Service every day who can be steered into the police. I suddenly saw myself at it,' he added shyly.

'So do I,' I said. 'You couldn't do a more useful job.'

'I'm glad you see it. But now this—' He held up the card. 'I can't do anything about this. From tomorrow morning, when the Home Secretary's P-S opens my letter, I'm tied hand and foot. I can't go rampaging about like a distraught and ill-used citizen, yelling for *Interpol* to be brought in to solve a murder that's already solved. And for at least a month while I play myself in I've got to sit at the Yard twiddling my thumbs like a good boy. And after that, too, although probably I could do quite a lot within my terms of reference. But late, perhaps too late.' He looked at me.

I took the card from him, and he went on:

'Can you keep the ball rolling until I can do something? You can have Turnbull and anyone else you want to work through,' he said. 'Anyone—and anything. Languages will be important.'

'I was nearly bilingual in Italian as a child.'

'Useful,' he said, 'but you'll have to keep out of the firing line yourself, of course.'

'Of course,' I agreed. This was going to be difficult. I was beginning to feel my hunch about Genoa even more strongly. And I knew that when things got into the hunch department, I was always better on my own.

My mind reverted to something else. I began to give it words, then stopped. There was no need to ask him to go easily with Christopher when he became dust beneath a Commissioner's feet. He had already shown that he did not blame him, only the handicap under which he did his job.

'There's a good deal to do,' I said instead.

'Indeed there is. But before anything, breakfast. Could you eat a second one?'

'Easily.'

'There's some Hymettus honey,' he said. 'Have you noticed, Eve, how carefully you have avoided calling me by my baptismal name?'

'No,' I said, 'have I?'

'You have. It bothers me. Put it right, will you. *That* is an order.' He smiled at me.

'Yes, Douglas.'

'You know, your papa is going to have some difficulty in getting you away from me.'

'Oh!' I said. 'I'd forgotten. I *must* telephone. I've got to get that signal down!'

'Ah, yes,' his smile was a grin as I grabbed the telephone and dialled.

'The Gill house-flag—' he added, '*Plague aboard, keep away.*'

If the long-distance operator had not answered at that moment, I might have turned on him. But then who would want a Commissioner of Police who did not notice little things?

CHAPTER 6

I was taken aback for a moment when instead of Mary a man answered, a voice which was certainly not Father's with its booming roar to set the receiver buzzing, for he refused to treat the telephone as anything but a ship's speaking-tube. I asked sharply who the voice was.

'My name is Berrington,' said Charlie. 'Who is speaking please?' I told him not to be silly, that I hadn't recognized him since I could not remember in all these years having heard his voice on the telephone, except of course on the internal line from Marsh House to his cottage.

'But that's quite different.'

'In what way?'

'It always sounds as if the person at the other end is talking under six feet of water,' I explained, and remembered too late that he had himself installed this amenity, using scrap from his workshop floor, or at least that was what the bits had looked like. He was naturally very proud of it.

'Talking of people under water—' he began in his slowest, most irritating way.

'I don't think we will,' I cut him short. 'Is Father there?'

'He's down in the wine cellar, mixing mortar. We're doing some subtle brickwork.'

'Oh.' I felt a little sick. 'I thought my signal might have frightened him and—'

'It didn't. I'll fetch him if you'll hold on.'

'No. Don't bother. I was only ringing up to say that everything was all right. But you seem to have discovered that for yourselves.'

'Yes. I landed at Oyster Soup Bay and reconnoitred. Three miles of mud in the middle of the night.'

'I'm sorry. But I was in such a hurry.'

'As long as you've made it up with your young man.'

'He's *not* my young man!'

'Oh!' he said cheerfully.

The Field-Marshal was still there behind me, listening with interest and the ghost of a return of his characteristic youthfulness. Charlie asked if there was anything else.

I turned my head slightly and managed to convey that I wanted to be left alone with my domestic problems; the Field-Marshal muttered an insincere apology and went away. I felt unkind to have robbed him of even the smallest diversion but it would have lost its value had he stayed.

'Charlie,' I said. 'Angela Sawyer . . .'

The note in my voice stopped him playing.

'Yes?'

I told him the bare outlines very briefly, leaving out the Field-Marshal and my night's adventures, but going on to say that Christopher seemed to have made up his mind about Arthur North rather too quickly. Charlie, momentarily shocked into silence, paused before asking if he could help in any way at all.

'I don't think so.' It would never do to have him on my hands, organizing me for my own good. 'You can't leave Father. Not just now. He *may* have got away with it again, but you can't be certain. In spite of your brickwork.'

'I suppose not—'

It was usually safe to bet on his loyalty to the Commodore. Charlie stood by his side always, being a man who betrays country rather than friend if faced with the alternative. And in this case Father was more than friend and Charlie all but son. Indeed from Father's point of view a better son than I was a daughter if to give him his own way was filial.

Charlie knew his own weakness and was as ready as I to leave the subject. 'Did I understand you to say that your ex-young man has caught the wrong man?' I told him that was so but through no fault of his own.

'So you're trying to put him right?'

'I'm doing nothing of the sort. He'd hate me if I did.'

'Oh, I don't think so,' he said falsely. 'He'll understand.'

'All the same I'm not risking it. I'm going to Italy.'

It was a deceitful inference to put into his straightforward mind, but he shouldn't have tried even indirectly to auto-suggest me into ruining what was left of my chances with Christopher.

'*Italy?*' He sounded startled for once. 'That's rather a long way to run, isn't it?'

'So, please, you'll look after things—according to your lights? I'll let you know where I am when I know where myself.'

'Just a moment!' His guess that the receiver had already left my ear for its cradle was as sure as if he were with me. '*Eve!*' His voice filled the cupboard. I returned the receiver to my ear reluctantly. Again as clearly he knew that I had done so for his tone was normal. 'All the same, it's to do with Angela?'

I lied to no one, much, and never to Charlie successfully.

'In a way, yes.'

'I don't like the sound of this.'

'And from the sound of you, you've got that "now-listen-to-me" look I hate so much.'

'Let's not be personal.'

'I can't help it when people start interfering. I've promised to send you my address. Goodbye.'

I hung up quickly on a speech beginning, 'For your own good, Eve,' and which would have gone on forever. It was a nuisance; this meant I should have to ring up again hoping to get Mary and ask her to put a suitcase of clothes on a passenger train at Halesworth for me to pick up at Liverpool Street.

The Field-Marshal was standing at the bottom of the stairs out of earshot for anyone hard of hearing, which he was not. His eyes were full of lively curiosity: 'Another Adam?'

'Charlie?' I laughed. 'Why, I've known him all my life. Besides, he's years and years older.'

He asked how many. 'At least ten,' I said.

'The wrong side of thirty, poor ancient fellow.'

'And anyway, he's a kind of brother.'

'Half or step?'

'Well—' I began.

'Not related and older than the stones. Starts at a disadvantage, doesn't he?'

He was leading the way up the stairs to the library.

'Things are difficult enough without Charlie's problems,' I said. 'We have a lot to do.'

'We have indeed. Conferences, that's the next thing. In the rarefied air I breathe, a mere "talk" isn't good enough.'

In the library he went straight to a Chippendale piece of which the top was a cupboard containing a large ice-bucket with champagne growing out of it in a lush blooming of golden heads; there were wine-glasses on shelves above. He chose a bottle, unwired the cork and eased it out with a gentle pop.

'In fact,' he said, 'he sounds quite fascinating.'

I realized he was still talking about Charlie.

'He isn't,' I said. 'Not in the least.'

'Very nice for a girl, I should have thought. Someone who wants to look after her. Not like some chap who'd walk out on her because her father doesn't care for him. Rather see him drowned, in fact.'

'What *didn't* you see?'

'Soldier's job, keeping his eyes open.'

'I've been thinking,' I said. 'Is Mr Turnbull the right kind of man for us now?'

'I'm doubtful whether he ever was. Reminds me, I suppose he's still looking for Shope. Daren't report he lost him again. However, you're right. You've got to have first-class help. Absolutely expert help—in the field.'

'There's a man called George Wick,' I said.

He handed me a glass, saying, 'Well, here's to Charlie's jolly good health. Who is he?'

I found myself unwillingly drinking the toast with him.

'He helped us in a thing once.* Also he was one of the best secret agents the sabotage people put into France during

* *The Golden Dart.*

109

the Occupation. He knows the Continent thoroughly—from underneath, as it were.'

I went on to explain I had been thinking about George for the Riviera end of things, for Cannes or Nice or wherever the Chester yacht had been at the time of the incident from which all this had sprung. It could have left repercussions of which the echoes might still be heard by an expert listener.

'How do we get hold of him?'

'If he's not away on a job, he'll be at his flat in Curzon Street.'

'Round the corner. In the book?' He pulled out the appropriate volume from the stand beside the desk. He found the number and looked at me over the receiver after he had dialled.

'Wick, you say?'

I nodded. 'George Augustus Wick.' The call signal buzzed rhythmically half a dozen times and was then broken. I heard George's voice, small but clear, announce briefly: 'Wick.'

'Daudet?' suggested the Field-Marshal, and held the receiver away from his ear so that I could listen in.

There was an infinitesimal pause before George said he thought this must be the wrong number rather than answer to his ill-famed *nom de guerre*. But the pause had been long enough.

'Major Wick. My name is Douglas Orme. I daresay you remember me?'

'I don't think I—'

'Come now. I once ordered you to be shot.'

'Did you?' George became defensively imperturbable. 'There were several orders of that kind in the air at one time. I gather you were fighting on the other side?'

The Field-Marshal snorted, recovered. 'No. I was merely unable to believe you had five thousand armed men hidden on the Raspaille ridge slap across the Boche communication lines.'

'Oh, *that* Orme,' said George. 'High brass on a Sunday. Whatever next? Yessir?' I could see him pushing his free hand through his untameable red-yellow hair. Douglas handed me the receiver.

'George. This is Eve Gill.'

'Oh—I see.' There was a sigh in his voice but no surprise. 'Got yourself into bad company? Don't come to me to get you out of it on my day of rest. Unless of course you've changed your mind? I'm still in bed.'

'Poor Nerinda.'

'She took me for better or worse, knowing the worst. Besides she's in Buenos Aires inheriting a fortune for me to spend.'

'Stop being licentious, George dear. Put on your shoes and walk round to forty-three Grosvenor Square.'

'I don't think so.'

'Please, George. It's a job.'

'Not with that fellow Orme mixed up in it. He's one of the things I wake up sweating about. I'm gradually getting rid of them. No, darling Eve.'

'Do you remember a girl called Angela you met at Ciro's at my birthday party?'

George did, with very great pleasure, and added that however richly I baited the trap he did not propose to step into it. I told him the gist of the story. He listened without a comment or question. I also told him, the Field-Marshal nodding permission as I came to it, about her being his daughter. There was complete silence when I finished.

'George? Are you still there?' I said.

'Sorry. Yes. I was putting on my shoes.' He hung up.

The Field-Marshal nodded slowly at me. 'I think you've had a very good idea.' After a pause in which he replenished my glass and his own he asked whether Charlie had ever made any trouble about George Wick.

'Oh, Douglas, for Heaven's sake!'

He smiled. I knew what he meant. It was typical, in his view, that the first time I used his baptismal name of my own accord should be when I was cross rather than pleased with him.

'We'd better get on with things,' he said. He went to the open window and shouted 'Angus!' in the direction of the

Rolls at the kerb below. 'He's in charge of transport,' he explained when he came back, 'and in any case knows more or less what's going on.'

A moment later Angus arrived, saluted, and was told to sit down.

'Conference,' said his master, an announcement which Angus acknowledged with his usual 'Sir-r!'

'Miss Gill and perhaps two other people. Italy immediately. How? Remembering mobility when she gets there will be essential? Reminds me, Eve, I suppose Wick will be able to find suitable chaps to go with you?'

'You'll not be going yourself, sir?' asked Angus.

'Would have said, wouldn't I? Nor are you. So put the Rolls out of your head. Too noticeable. Anyway they have seen it and will connect with me. If she's to be any use on this mission she must not, repeat *not*, be spotted.'

Angus did not ask who 'they' were or what my mission might be. He merely wrinkled his long Celtic nose.

'Air would be fast to get her ther-re, but she'd have only her own two feet after that, for I wouldn't fancy the young lady in a hired car. Not in Italy, the way they drive, like madmen with only the day to live.'

Douglas snapped impatient fingers at him, asking how many times had he told him to keep his thinking to himself until he had the answers. 'Never let the other chap see the wheels go round. Secret of leadership.'

This seemed a little harsh when manifestly to lead was not amongst Angus's ambitions; as long as he had his beloved Field-Marshal to order him about he was quite content to be led. He acknowledged the rebuke with another 'Sir-r!' but his jaw muscles twitched. A craftiness came into his eyes.

'In that case, sir-r, I'll get on with it, with your permission.' He stood up, clicked his heels and made for the door which as he reached it was opened by Harris ushering in George Wick. At the sight of George, Angus let out an informal 'Cor stone me!' and shook hands with him warmly. 'Major Wick, sir-r!' He looked back at the Field-Marshal and nodded approval—but not forgiveness. He went out

112

with Harris, and George came easily across the room, smiling faintly and saying that Angus was one of the few really kind men he had known. He had offered to cook his last breakfast on that awkward occasion when the Field-Marshal had been so suspicious. 'But of course, sir, you were only a General then.'

Apart from this naughtiness, he maintained a respectful junior-to-senior-officer attitude towards him during our 'conference'; and if occasionally he looked to me to confirm some conclusion the Field-Marshal put forward, the circumstances of their original meeting perhaps justified his doubt.

He listened but with frequent questions as we passed the story back and forth between us.

'Christopher Smith?' he said when that name first came into it. 'Oh, dear me.'

'Yes,' I said. 'Oh, dear me.'

But that was all on that aspect of our problem. He knew without being told how necessary it was to prevent Christopher from hanging the wrong man—quite apart from the wrong man's point of view, which could be said to be not unimportant.

There was only one reticence; the Field-Marshal held back mention for the moment of his Commissionership. It did not affect the issue now and indeed might have complicated it for George, who was highly individual, and therefore unpredictable.

When we had threshed out the thing for him to the limit of every grain of fact and supposition, the Field-Marshal asked him a question he had to ask and which we must also ask ourselves until we had more proof.

Did it really stand up? Were we convincing ourselves out of prejudice, out of love and affection for Angela, that this was not what it seemed, the *crime passionel*?

George hesitated. He could have made the Field-Marshal happier by removing his last doubts, but honesty stepped in.

'Everything you've told me, sir—you and Eve—is obviously true as you see it,' he said, 'and I am sure you haven't exaggerated Angela's state of mind when she came back to

England. But Smith's interpretation is as good as most people—and all policemen—could ask. Even if Arthur North comes to his senses and puts up a fight—' He paused. 'Self-preservation is a hell of a thing to ignore in oneself. But he's got damn' little if anything to fight with. Looking at it from here, sir, I could agree with most people.'

The Field-Marshal fastened on the 'could'. 'But you don't?'

George picked up the 'Bernardino' visiting card.

'Genoa is a very tough city. Practically any sort of skul-duggery could come out of it. For one thing it's taken over from Naples as GHQ Black Market, South European Region. Tangiers is still the chief centre for currency games, of course, but goods, no.'

'I thought of smuggling, or something like it,' said the Field-Marshal. 'I've heard that those small Riviera yacht harbours are used for that sort of thing.'

George shook his head. 'The French have cracked down. Fast *vedettes*—boats which could make circles round the kind of craft fellows were using to bring the stuff in from North Africa. And they infiltrated a few smart *agents*, also encour-aged squealers to the extent of rewarding them. Business is very poor indeed, and so are the types in it. They're sitting in the sun talking about the good old days without the francs for Pernod to comfort them. Small men with small souls, lazy except when fat profits look easy. Even when business was booming, they weren't organized enough to reach out all the way to tie off a loose end. But as I say, it folded months ago. No, sir. If this isn't a complete wild-goose it's a lot bigger.'

'What then? How could Angela—?'

'How could anyone? The innocent bystander on the cor-ner gets three bullets in him, just for standing there.'

George glanced at his watch. 'Would you mind if I put through a few telephone calls?'

The Field-Marshal pushed the instrument across the desk to him, and glanced across at me. I nodded. George was with us. George caught our interchange and grinned. 'It's my sort of meat,' he said, and about to dial, paused, saying

Angus seemed to be on the line, on an extension somewhere. The Field-Marshal took the receiver from him, listened frowning and then broke into the conversation: 'Good God, man! Is it made of platinum . . .?' He listened again and reddened visibly. 'I beg your pardon, Angus. Yes, I did. Do it your way. But plug in the other line here, would you. I'm much obliged.' He gave the receiver back to George.

'What's a Bristol?' he asked, and George, dialling, told him that it could be a piece of ruby-red glassware, one of several types of aeroplane or just a motor car. A car? In that case Angus was talking about a very fine sort of car indeed.

'At thirty-one hundred pounds,' said the Field-Marshal grimly, 'it had better be.' He took a cheque book from the middle drawer of the desk and began writing in it, growling a little.

'Look,' I said, 'I have a perfectly good car at home—at least it's being decarbonized, but in a few days—'

'We can't wait a few days for anything. Besides, I know when I'm being taught a lesson. Least I can do is to put a good face on it. But why the hell should he buy it from the Duke? Just because he loves it, doesn't want to part with it and rightly makes a steep price. That's why!' Then he laughed. 'How could I live without Angus?'

George was speaking to Transatlantic Service.

He wanted New York City. Circle three-two-four-eight; person to person . . . Mr Haken. 'Thank you—' He pressed down the bar and released it, dialled CON and while he waited said: 'This Gordon Chester. I think I want to know more. Competition is very keen in a place like Kansas City. A chap might have to cut his corners on the way to becoming a millionaire there. Haken will know or soon get to know—' He broke off to place three calls with Continental service to Paris, Cannes and the third to Portofino. 'Charming little place, Portofino. Protected as a national monument, hills, olive trees, pink and yellow houses, even film stars and ex-kings look the right size in it . . .' He broke off to speak into the telephone. '. . . yes, please. I have a call booked to New York but interrupt any other. Thank you.' He cradled the receiver and looked at me. 'I suppose you're not letting anyone keep you out of this?'

'I am not.'

'Disposition of forces,' said the Field-Marshal, who had been watching George with approval. 'I propose to look after our base here in London, deal with planning and co-ordination including, of course, supplies and services, and leave field operations to you two and anyone else it may be necessary to recruit. Any comments?'

'No, sir.' These military sounds had made George a little restless but he accepted them as inevitable.

'It is thought,' the Field-Marshal went on, 'that you should see if you can pick up anything on the Riviera—'

'I had the same notion. I know a chap at Cannes—' George nodded at the telephone. 'He's well-informed, in certain ways. I've a strong feeling that it's there we'll find our best lead.'

'I'm inclined to agree with you.'

'I can catch the morning plane—'

'—and I'll make straight for Genoa,' I said.

'You'll need someone to go with you,' the Field-Marshal said firmly, and George nodded. They both looked at me with the 'we-know-what's best for you' expression I knew so well.

'I shall be less noticeable alone,' I said, and added: 'After all, I'm only going to explore—on the off-chance.'

'As you were doing last night?' asked George.

'I couldn't have been more careful!'

'Or nearer coming unstuck.'

'Nonsense! Besides, how else would we have got hold of this?' I smacked my hand down on the visiting card more loudly than I intended.

'There you are. Emotional. Impulsive. Other words for trouble-prone.'

'Oh, don't nag.'

'All the same, you should have someone with you.'

'Of course she should,' said the Field-Marshal briskly.

The argument was stopped by the return of Angus. He made a good showing of casualness.

'Sir-r, in this matter of transport for the Italian party—'

His master had his revenge for what it was worth by cutting him short with the cheque he had written; he handed it across the desk to him. 'Have the thing round here in ten minutes. May as well see what we've bought. I expect it's possible to get a tryptic in emergency. Try the AA. Book car-space on the first Lympne–Le Touquet plane ferry. Tonight if there is one. Don't stand there!'

Angus gulped and left the room with the cheque. Then the telephone rang with the first of George's calls and there was no more talk for a while of a bodyguard for me in Genoa.

George spoke to someone called Bill in Cannes, saying he would be glad to know his old friend Wick proposed to be with him sometime within the next twenty-four hours. Then the New York call came in and George dealt with it no less speedily. He would be much obliged for a full personal and confidential report by cable soonest on Mr Gordon Chester of Kansas City. But in the meantime did Haken happen to have any gossip about the gentleman? Seemingly he had. After listening a few moments George thanked him and gave him 43 Grosvenor Square, care of Orme, as the address for the cable. He dropped the receiver on its bar with a precise gesture of satisfaction.

'I thought the name was familiar,' he said. 'Gordon Chester gave evidence before the Kefauver Committee sometime in the fall of nineteen-fifty.'

'The Commission set up by the Senate to investigate interstate crime,' the Field-Marshal commented, then added slowly: 'Very nearly a thousand people appeared as witnesses, the majority willing to help Kefauver to get at the truth—'

'—and who did not wait for a subpœna. But Gordon Chester did. And successfully escaped service of it for weeks.'

'Even so his reluctance may have been reasonable. There was a lot of dirt flying about.'

I understood his attitude; having reached our main conclusion by the jumping method, he was now leaning over backwards to avoid making a habit of it.

'I quite agree,' George said. 'It's only that I like it as a bit of atmosphere.'

117

He next spoke to Paris, explaining to someone that he would be passing through very shortly and would need two hundred pamphlets, if that would be convenient. I guessed he had remembered about currency restrictions and that 'pamphlet' was probably the code name for a thousand-franc note, for at the end of the call he turned and remarked there was no time for me to buy Travellers' Cheques and my five-pounds limit of English money would have to get me to Portofino. But once there I should be able to pick up all the *lire* I might need. From Fig.

'What is Fig?' I asked, getting up from my chair with an uncomfortable thought which I took with me towards the nearest window.

'Two "g's". Figge.' George explained. 'She lives in a castle on the headland beyond the harbour. A great girl. A born fixer, knows everyone, knows Italy, Genoa included. Mad as a hatter. You'll like her. My fear is she may be in Rome or somewhere. She gets about so.'

My uncomfortable thought was becoming more insistent. It had not come entirely from intuition. I reached the window from the side.

How had Mizzie reacted to that middle-of-the-night attempt by the police to get in to her, apart from deciding to leave before they came back? If she had managed that alone, it was all right. But the Field-Marshal thought from the suddenness and finality of her going that she must have called in Sammy to help her. If it was a correct assumption, and I realized I had accepted it as one, it meant that she had overcome her fear of Sammy's ready fist for women who irritated him in the greater fear she had had from the beginning—of what Sammy's friends might do to her if she turned stool-pigeon. It would be no more than natural, then, that she should have gone the whole hog and told him about me in order to convince him whose side she was on.

What would Sammy make of it—of *me*?

Would he, after further and exacting questions, decide I must be the girl Shope had brought home with him—not a pick-up to take his mind off his tangle with Lord Orme but someone quite different.

118

He would be shaken by it, perhaps quite badly. Would he try to work it out on his own, or go to his masters with it? Not, I thought, that. Not at first. He would want to make sure he could not find and deal with me himself before revealing to them what was in effect, a piece of slovenly work on his part.

He could be down there now in the Square, watching this house, waiting for a glimpse of me—for an opportunity to . . .

I went to the nearest window and looked out, cautiously.

'What's the matter?' asked the Field-Marshal from the desk. I nearly told him. So very nearly. I was glad George's attention was distracted at the same moment by the telephone bell.

'I thought I heard a car stop,' I said.

'Angus can work fast, but I doubt if as fast as that.'

I surveyed the scene anxiously and in vain during the few seconds I could stay at the window. If I told them what I was really doing there they would never in a thousand years allow me to go to Genoa alone.

I was 'blown', as George would have worded it professionally. The enemy knew I existed. That was quite enough.

I listened mechanically to George's one-sided telephone conversation and gathered that Figge would be delighted to welcome any friend of his. Eve Gill—yes, that's her name —would not be entirely on holiday; she would explain when she arrived. 'Bless you, Figge, you're an angel.'

'Friend of all the world,' he said as he put down the receiver.

'I like all this,' the Field-Marshal told him. 'Now what about fees? You can't take a hand just for the fun of it.'

I lost their voices as I faced this new trouble. I mustn't panic. How badly was I 'blown'? Only Mizzie had fully seen me. Sammy had had only a bare moment or so to look at me in the uncertain light of a street lamp at least thirty feet away, and at a time when he had been concentrating on Shope. But it did not mean that he would fail to recognize me if he saw me anywhere near this house. If I could avoid that, my loss of anonymity would be limited. I might reach

Genoa with only Mizzie's description of me in their hands.

'I think,' I said, 'we're being a little careless. Wouldn't it be safer if I picked up the car wherever it is than have Angus bring it here—to this house. He didn't go in the Rolls—it's still at the door.'

The Field-Marshal reached for the telephone with one hand and a desk address-book with the other. 'I should have thought of that. I'm not used to undercover stuff.' And George nodded approvingly at me. Neither of them had seen further than the thought I had put in their heads, that if the Rolls was known, the Bristol would immediately become so if it appeared here, particularly with Angus in it. I had managed to get away with something and in a perverse way I felt good about it.

'. . . Dickie? Douglas here. I gather I've bought a car from you. Would you mind keeping it in your garage a few hours—tell my man that I've changed my mind about his collecting it. Thanks. Yes, indeed. Very good of you to let me have it.'

As soon as he had finished I rang up Mary and told her what I wanted packed and put on the train at Halesworth, using not more than a light-weight bag and a small hat-box; she would find my passport in the middle drawer of my bureau and also a flat leather case at the back of the bottom right-hand drawer. She wanted to protest at this final item but realized perhaps that she ought not to know what it contained. She could not keep anxiety out of her voice; I assured her that Mr Berrington knew I was going abroad and would have told the Commodore. . . I bade her good-bye, promised to write. I hoped she would not let them know I had thought it necessary to take a .32 automatic pistol with me.

The conference now got down to the details of methods; communication, contact points and so forth; George would stay at the Grey-Albion Hotel in Cannes, and I was to let him know the moment I checked into a suitable hotel at Genoa.

He searched my handbag for objects which would identify me, and urged me to get rid of passport and car papers in a safe hiding-place as soon as I possibly could after entering Italy. He briefed me thoroughly on the necessity for keeping in touch both with the Field-Marshal and himself, daily touch. He began to sound like an old hen, and I did not need his constant watch on me lest I go too near a window, or in any way risk being seen before I left.

Dusk was falling when I stood with the Field-Marshal in a narrow passage at the back of the house behind a door which opened on to Adam's Row.

Angus had gone out by the front door fifteen minutes earlier to make an unobtrusive tour of the immediate neighbourhood of the house to spot any watchers there might be. George had also left the house, but by taxi, as though after a casual visit, but he would come back on foot to cover my exit via Adam's Row after checking with Angus at an arranged meeting place that the coast was clear.

All this expertise from George was something the Field-Marshal could appreciate with confidence, but I could have wished for some of it for myself; George's attitude towards me had robbed me of credit for a capacity to survive which I had shown—so I thought— last night. I was on tenter-hooks lest something should happen at this final moment to sway them completely against my project. I knew they were permitting it because they believed Cannes to be the real starting point and my 'Bernardino' chase unlikely to prove anything but of the wild-goose kind. The slightest sign of the enemy at this moment would turn them into a couple of fuss-pots who would rush into alliance against me.

The small transom above the door admitted just enough light to see the Field-Marshal's watch and the approach of zero hour, as he termed it. The usual noises of work-day activity in the mews were absent in the Sunday quiet; there were no chauffeurs washing their cars or tuning motors, and we should have no difficulty in hearing George and Angus as they approached. The Field-Marshal strained his ears and fidgeted. The minute-hand crept up to the hour, moved past it and seemed to increase its pace as it left it behind.

'A few minutes more or less doesn't mean anything,' I said.

'But we allowed longer than they really needed.'

We whispered rather than spoke, as people listening are inclined to do, and this made George's voice even more startling for it came suddenly, unheralded by any other sound, from immediately the other side of the door.

'Got a match, chum?' He spoke loudly to make sure we should hear him.

Before there was time to do more than get my hand on the door knob to stop the Field-Marshal opening it, which might not have suited George at all, there was a single smacking sound, a shuddering grunt and a thud as something fell heavily against the door.

'All right,' said George in a conversational voice, and I pulled open the door. If he had not been holding the man by his shirt high up at the collar, he would have completed his fall into my arms. I shut the door quickly.

'Well, I'm damned!' said the Field-Marshal several times.

George lowered the man to the ground. He rubbed his fist tenderly with the other hand and took out a flash lamp.

We looked at his victim. He was small, thin and nondescript; his sweat-dirty hat lay on the floor by his head, his clothes were dark and worn, his tie an elderly blue with a tight knot; his hard white collar was the only thing clean about him—his Sunday collar. And he was out, cold.

'Found him leaning against the wall a yard from the door. He looked as though he'd been there for days—' George opened the door for Angus, who tapped on it three times.

The Field-Marshal had by now adjusted himself to this indecorous episode and asked what was to be done with the man.

'Nothing,' said George. 'He won't know anything we don't know already, and he'd be an encumbrance to keep even for a short time. We'll put him back where we found him as soon as Eve is away.'

'He was here because of Shope?'

George, transferring things from the man's pockets to his own, said that was so; they would be uneasy because Shope had had dealings with this house; they would want to know all they could about it. For a while anyway.

'He won't have learnt much. And I doubt if he'll tell them about this. They weren't paying him to be careless. You expect to wake up without your wallet after an opening gambit as corny as that one—asking for a light.'

'He certainly wasn't here because of me,' I said, and took the opportunity to step over the victim and open the door. 'I'd better be going,' I explained, and started off.

The Field-Marshal called to me to wait but I continued to walk fast. 'There isn't a lot of time,' I said over my shoulder, 'if I'm to pick up the Bristol and be at Lympne for that plane.'

'All the same,' he said, catching up with me, 'I'm thinking you should not go at all after this bit of nonsense. And certainly not alone.'

'It doesn't prove more than what we knew—that because Shope talked to you they're uneasy.'

'And damn' dangerous.'

'Murder's always inclined to be that—beforehand. This is after,' I said, not convincing myself; I could see that after murder might be much worse in that way.

'Hell!' said the Field-Marshal. 'All right, all *right*! I know what it feels like—to have a notion how to fight a battle and all the brass against you because it isn't in the book!'

I slackened pace and we proceeded without further argument.

There was time for little more than a fitful doze during the flight across the Channel and I left Le Touquet as the red sun was rising in its haze over the Flanders plain. Two cars were unloaded before the Bristol and were away ahead of me, large and fast-looking cars, but I overtook both of them in the first twenty-five miles. I drove for two and a half hours before pausing for breakfast of omelette and coffee at a café on the edge of the great road. I was in Dijon by noon, having averaged nearly sixty for three hundred and thirty-odd miles. I had never driven at these consistently high speeds and I knew that to feel so little strain must be a remarkable tribute to the car. It sat down on the road at eighty miles an hour with the same solid yet delicate feeling of confident balance as it did at forty, and my sense of affinity with it might have come from years of driving it.

Dijon. I massaged the slight stiffness from my neck, the only ill-effect I could find, and avoided *Les Trois Faisans* with its promise of *Coq à lie de Chambertin*, but also of a bill to suit its reputation; I had not all that money and the car's need for fuel was more vital than mine. However, I found a Michelin one-fork restaurant in the Place Republique and ate very well, so well indeed that I was helplessly overcome with sleep and I parted reluctantly with two gallons of fuel's worth of francs for a room at a small hotel. But I knew as soon as my head reached the hard, rustling pillow that it was well spent. Indeed, it was evening when I woke up, terrified at the waste of time.

It was a waste which I recovered, however, as I drove steadily southward, refreshed and in much better spirits and this helped me in the feeling of being the only person left on earth in the long climb to the top of the Mont Cenis pass, the mountain crouching over it like a great black cat against the empty desert of the moonlit sky.

I was a little nervous about the Customs examination at the Italian frontier on account of that flat leather case wrapped in my lavender silk nightdress, but the officials were wholly concerned with my lonely status in such an elegant car at such dead of night. No husband, no lover? Never mind. Italy, la bella Italia would soon remedy my unfortunate predicament. They tried to kiss my hand in prophecy and waved me through the barriers.

I came down into the townlet of Bardonecchia and found it still awake and cheerful with Italian faces and sounds in the late night. I found a hotel and slept without dreaming until the inevitable church bells awoke me to the equally inevitable peach-jam breakfast. The map told me that I was now only a hundred and fifty miles from Genoa.

It took an effort to drive through that city without stopping but I had to establish a base and collect some money before I could begin work. Portofino was less than thirty miles farther on, and so I felt better about it.

The clock on the village church tower pointed to a few

minutes past one when I parked the car in the open space where the promontory's twisting coast-road ended. I left all my things in it and walked the fifty yards past the stalls of the lace-makers to the piazza, coming into it through the narrow gap between the houses where a low chain hung across it to stop all but foot traffic.

I realized afterwards that to ask anyone in Portofino did he know a Signora Figge was like asking a policeman in Trafalgar Square if he knew of a monument to Nelson thereabouts. A wrinkled fisherman looked at me as if I were a fool and waved a thumbless hand at one of the tables set out on the cobble stones in front of a café ten yards away. There could be no doubt which was she of the seven or eight people talking and laughing over pre-luncheon drinks but I could not have said exactly why I was so sure.

When I sat down two tables away, ordered a *cinzanino* and waited for a less public moment to introduce myself, she glanced at me twice, casually, but I knew at once that she had spotted me as the young woman about whom George had called her from London. It was the sort of quickness which would have appealed to him in the first place and kept him as her friend for as long as she chose.

She was only a year or so older than I, and attractive without being pretty with the surer, more enduring attraction of vivid personality. She wore a wide-sleeved black linen blouse and a calf-length circular skirt in clear yellow; she was eating fried prawns from a large communal dish with slender fingers which now and again she wiped delicately on a crimson handkerchief hanging from the hip pocket of the young man sitting next to her. But she was more than merely decorative as a star in an extravagantly mounted stage-show; the way she got rid of her party without incurring its ill-will, particularly since it was under the impression it was lunching with her, was as neat a piece of manoeuvring as I had ever seen. Furthermore, no one realized that she did it in order to lunch alone with me in a hole-in-the-wall restaurant on the eastern and less social arm of the harbour, so that we were seen together only by the proprietor and the one girl who was serving.

When I left her an hour later I took with me everything I could at the moment think I might need, from a thick bundle of thousand-lire notes which she ran out of the door to borrow from a seedy old woman with a fish barrow, to a short list of three people in Genoa who might be 'useful', not least of whom was Taglioni, *Capo di Polizia*, although she felt that until his dyspepsia improved it was unlikely he would be any use to anyone. She had given him absolutely the right pills for it, of course, but doubted if he was sensible enough to take them regularly.

She wanted more than anything in the world to know what was behind all this but she limited her curiosity's demand to: 'You tell me someday, eh?'

'Of course.'

'George is terribly cloak and dagger, isn't he, what?'

It was now two o'clock and I set off for the car knowing that I had established an advance post as solid and reliable as I could wish. Figge had, in fact, without a word of promise or assurance, given me the extra fillip I needed to face the issue in Genoa.

Twenty yards from the car, even while I was looking at it, I stopped short.

I had seen something a moment ago which now registered itself in my mind with an almost audible click, as though its significance had been building up against my obstinate consciousness and had at last broken through into it.

A sailor . . . old, with rounded back and bare feet, ragged jeans, and a dark blue jersey—it was that jersey, much newer than the jeans and several sizes too large for him, which hit me. It had a ship's name across the chest in embroidered red letters and I could still see it in my mind's eye. . . *Norse Girl*!

Could it have been a trick of subconscious transposing of letters, some similarity to set up an uncensored image?

But it was silly to stand there trying to decide. I turned and hurried back towards the harbour.

I caught up with him at the far end of the piazza where it narrowed to become the western side of the harbour. He carried a large chianti flask by its straw handle and an ancient canvas holdall from which a long loaf sprouted in a miscellany of small parcels. I passed him, turned, pretending to become interested in a small boy fishing with a piece of string.

It was *Norse Girl* all right and a moment later I was a few feet from him while he pulled in a dinghy at the stone steps opposite the larger of the two motor yachts moored in mid-harbour. She was perhaps thirty yards out and I had no difficulty at all in reading her name on the rounded white stern. *Norse Girl*, and under it the initials F.Y.C.

I stared at her. The air above the low flat funnel was still; no pennant hung at the short mast-head, no ensign or national flag from the taffrail staff. No one moved on her. The old man clambered down into the dinghy, his bare feet scuffing the wood, and turned to take the wine and the bag of food from the edge. I handed them to him.

'*Grazie, signorina* . . .' His voice was as sandpapery as the soles of his feet, and ten thousand days of sun and wind had wizened his face and neck and arms to the colour and texture of dried coconut shell.

The superior but oversize jersey sagged from his bent shoulders and it was this garment which told the rest of the story. Discarded by a burlier man it was merely the outward symbol of his authority as caretaker. I should have liked to think he had been a member of the crew, but obviously he had not.

I asked him when Signor Chester was expected to return.

He didn't know. *Chi sa?* The movements of millionaire *Americani* were beyond the knowledge—and comprehension—of ordinary man. The day was beautiful, was it not? He grinned toothlessly at me, crinkling lids over faded blue eyes.

I said I was disappointed to have missed the *Signore*. I had hoped to see him here in beautiful Portofino, even to visit his beautiful ship of which I had heard the marvels.

His idea that the second half of this disappointment at least might be remedied sprang immediately to a mind already receptive to the thought of separating me from a few lire—a thought which had come into it, of course, the first moment I had spoken to him.

That I was a friend of the yacht's owner sanctified a proposal which in any case was quite in order since I came under the heading, like practically everything else in sight, of '*bellissima*'. And in any case the chromium fittings were firmly screwed down. His name, he told me, was Giuseppi, and it would delight him to show me over the ship.

'*S'accomoda, signorina*—' and I got into the dinghy with him.

I stood in *Norse Girl*'s main saloon and disliked its pale wood, blue paint work, and spiky modern furniture.

But somewhere here Angela had seen or heard a secret for which she had to die. This starkness now, a sterile atmosphere in which no emotion stirred except the old man's hope of a tip from me, robbed the moment of its significance.

The mounting expectancy with which I had climbed the ladder had subsided into a dull certainty that I had gained nothing further than the knowledge that Gordon Chester had laid up his yacht at Portofino instead of the other side of the Gulf somewhere. There was not even coincidence in finding her here. If, as I was committed to believe, Genoa was the focal point of his other than social activities, there was not another place in the two hundred miles of coast enclosing the Gulf which combined safe harbourage with the cover of a tourist background.

Committed to believe—yes; and after all it was yet another pointer to the truth of it. I felt a little happier and began to ask Giuseppi about the kind of crew the ship carried. But although he was ready to talk his head off about anything in the world, it was soon clear that he knew nothing whatever about *Norse Girl* before his caretaking began. He had been given the job by an officer whose name he could not remember who had immediately gone off in the bus to Genoa—a 'foreigner' he was, which meant only that he was not Portofinese. The crew, also strangers, and an unfriendly lot, had departed two days before that. The officer had been the last man to leave.

I said I hóped his wages were being paid regularly. So far, yes, although he hastened to add, they were considerably less than the bare minimum on which life could be sustained. But, I asked, wasn't even the smallest sum in dollars a fortune?

He sighed and shook his withered head. No dollars. Just lire from the *signore*'s agents in Genoa.

I seized on this but did not use it until he was sculling me back to the steps. Then I said that if he would give me the address of the agents I would perhaps write to Signor Chester through them to assure him his beautiful yacht was being scrupulously guarded. I took a thousand-lire bill from my handbag; Giuseppi bowed low over my hand and took the bill from it. He would be much, much pleased if I should do that, and the firm was *Bernardino—via Gambino, numero diciassette* . . .

I was able to repeat it, as though making sure I had it right, without a quiver of surprise. It was rather like drawing one card to a flush on a strong hunch that it was coming up.

Three-quarters of an hour later in Genoa I was putting the car discreetly away in a lock-up 'box' in a garage near the de luxe *Grande Savoie*, to which I humped my suitcase.

I took a fourth-floor room with private bathroom in my own name; indeed I could not have used another in view of the universal habit of reception desks in this kind of hotel using your passport particulars as a basis in filling up the police registration form; also of including your permanent address for good measure.

My first move was to spend a refreshing half an hour in a tubful of tepid water while the maid pressed a black cotton frock, which I had asked Mary to include as the one really indigenous-looking Italian garment I possessed.

I put it on, left off my stockings, wore no hat and went down by the stairs instead of the elevator, and returning to the garage, put passport and car papers in the glove compartment of the Bristol; at least I would not be held up by the need of them if I had to leave Genoa in a hurry.

This insurance effected and feeling more comfortable because of it, I set about losing myself in the teeming crowds which filled the streets of the over-populated city.

On the assumption that my leaving London had been noticed by the other side, which I doubted, and my arrival here observed, which I doubted even more, I made believe I was being followed. I entered a café by one door, for instance, and went out by another, then watching the exit in a shop window reflection to check on who came out; I boarded a tram without previous indication of intention and got off it with the same suddenness at the next stop.

I shopped for half an hour in a square filled with market stalls of every description, buying first a very second-hand fibre suitcase into which I put further purchases of cheap clothing and cheaper toilet articles. Thus prepared, I made a tour of the low-life district which crawled in dank decrepitude up the hill to blossom into the lusher area of palaces and grand avenues at the top.

In *via Santa Madre* I found the kind of place I needed, a street—if a passage too narrow for wheeled traffic could be called a street—deep in a canyon of perpetual shadow which wound its way from the heights of Piazza de Ferrari down eventually to the open water front near the Porto Vecchio. The heat in it was almost worse than that of the outer sunshine, sticky and still with the unchanged air of centuries. But it had all the advantages of a burrow and the particular hole in it was as secret as I could wish.

A fly-spotted glass sign '*Albergo*' hung over its greasy entrance, a hotel, but so anonymous that it avoided any means of identification beyond that generic name.

A dirty fat man in a dirty shirt dozing in the gloom behind a rickety desk half-opened his eyes as I came in, then opened them wider with cynical appreciation and glanced beyond me to the doorway for a man companion. He was even more puzzled when I said I was looking for a room for as long as a week. But I explained briefly, clipping the ends of my words in the slovenly Neapolitan fashion, that I was an actress in a visiting *compagnia teatrale*. I also opened my handbag and said I would pay in advance for a suitable room.

130

When he had recovered from his surprise at my mistaken belief that his house was really a hotel he groaned his way up to the second floor to show me a small room filled by a bed so large that it barely allowed space for a small wardrobe and an old-fashioned, bowl-and-pitcher toilet table side by side opposite the curtainless windows, into which the people on the other side of the street could see with ease—and indeed reach, if they cared to lean out a little. I fought back my distaste, took heart in the fact that the coverlet on the bed was quite clean, said the room might do and haggled about the price lest his surprise become suspicion. Having beaten him down to three hundred a day, I agreed to take it if he would accept an even two thousand for the week. This strained his cupidity but satisfied his doubts; obviously I was from the thieving South. He took the money and showed me that the lock on the door was not only strong but also worked.

In exchange for this courtesy I told him my name was Flavia Sardoni and my home town Amalfi; he nodded, with no intention of bothering to make out a *fiche* for police registration and left me. I was content if somewhat nauseated. I now had what George had recommended in his secret agent vocabulary as 'a safe house', a place and identity removed from my own in which to take refuge if necessary. I locked the door of my home from home and kept the key in my handbag.

I returned to the *Grande Savoie* by a roundabout route, and once in my room relaxed deliberately, trying to keep my mind as quiet as my body while I had another bath to wash off the smells of the *via Santa Madre*. Afterwards, in a dressing-gown, I ate an excellent dinner sent up from the restaurant. It would have been easier not to think, or rather to think of something else, had I not been alone. However, I drank a little more of the good Barolo than was quite sensible, which blurred the mental outlines and enabled me to sleep for ten hours, which would have been as long again if the town below had roared less early and less clamorously, insisting that I should join the merry fight for survival.

Strong coffee revived me, and my plan for the day came into focus.

The pale yellow silk suit, the one good thing I had brought with me and which the maid had pressed last night, had cost a lot of money at Jacques Fath's earlier in the summer, and looked it. In spite of its gay colour it had a serious air, but its own small hat's soft grey feather framing one side of the face lightened the effect without being frivolous about it. Grey handbag, gloves and shoes completed the whole. I was ready.

I hesitated several moments on whether to take the pistol with me and decided that I would, and put it in my handbag —although this was to be a behind-the-lines reconnaissance in the guise of a sweet young thing and innocence would perhaps be a better weapon if things went wrong. Father would have disagreed, and for once I felt like easing my conscience by doing something of which he would approve, even if his views were coloured by his pride in the accuracy with which he had taught me to shoot.

Father . . .

I wondered what was happening at Marsh House. They would have finished bricking up the brandy by now . . .

I left my suitcase open but I dropped the pistol case and Flavia Sardoni's black cotton frock in the hollow top of the wardrobe, and set out, first calling at the Central Post Office. It was a little soon to expect anything but it was sensible to make sure.

There was, however, a cable from the Field-Marshal. I took it into the shelter of a cubicle to read. After my name and the *Post Restante* address came the strictly professional text:

FOLLOWING FROM NEW YORK QUOTE SUBJECT RETURNED EX-EUROPE MID JUNE DISAPPEARED SAME WEEK STOP IN-FORMED SOURCES AGREE PROBABILITY TROUBLE THIEVES OUTFALL UNQUOTE ACK ONE TWO.

Which, being translated, meant George's friend Haken had learnt that Gordon Chester had gone to earth when he reached home on account of disagreements with his crooked associates, and that I was to acknowledge the cable to the Field-Marshal (one) at home and George (two) at Cannes to indicate that I had arrived in good order.

The point, and it seemed significant, lay in the fact that Gordon Chester had gone into precautionary hiding so soon after his arrival; he had scarcely had time, surely, to meet his friends, let alone to fall out with them, and to my eye his flight from Europe and disappearance in the States looked like one movement. It suggested that the falling out had been here in Europe and that he considered the consequent peril as powerful enough to reach after him to the other side of the Atlantic.

It was logical to suppose, furthermore, that he had found himself in the same jeopardy as had Angela, *and perhaps for the same reason.*

This important news would not materially change my plan, but it gave me an extra and powerful lever with which to set it moving. That it also increased its danger could not be helped.

Later would do for sending the Field-Marshal an acknowledging message; in the meantime I tore his cable to small pieces which I let trickle from my fingers from the open window of the cab which took me to *via Gambino.*

CHAPTER 7

'For Heaven's sake!' I said pettishly, 'aren't I making myself clear? I am here on behalf of a friend. She wouldn't have asked me to break my journey for nothing. It's important.'

The hatchet-faced gentleman in charge of '*Informazione*' frowned at me.

'Say again, madame, please—'

I went over it again, at a shout, in the accepted manner of an Anglo-Saxon trying to get a foreigner to understand.

'A friend of mine left her diary—you know what a diary is?—on a yacht belonging to a client of this firm. A *yacht*—'

'Yes, please?' His expression was still blank.

'She left her diary in a drawer next to her bed!'

'Bed?' He brightened a little.

'In her cabin!' I stamped my foot at him.

'Ah! *Cabine*,' he cried. 'You desire the Department of Ships.' He was very relieved and signalled to a boy. '*Ragazzo! Accompagna la Signorina sopra—al numero trent' uno.*'

'Bernardino' was a bigger concern than I had expected; it seemed to occupy the whole of this great medieval fortress-palace in *via Gambino*, a street of such houses, built by the merchant kings in the great days when Genoa was the foremost trading city of the world.

Its stone walls enclosed a central courtyard in which a militant Neptune stood on a plinth of pink marble, trident raised to hurl at anyone who ventured through the elaborate iron-work gates, the only break in the four-square, hollow box.

When I had entered them a few minutes ago I felt a wavering in my belief that our answer was here. The impression not only of this firm's size and importance but of its respectability was a little shaking.

The *Direttore* of the shipping department on the second floor wore a black jacket, striped trousers and a pair of spectacles with square, heavily tortoiseshelled lenses through which I could see sharp eyes like chips of black stone. He was an imposing figure in his gallery-shaped room with its fine desk and leather chairs. But although he seemed to understand English he professed to know nothing whatever about ships smaller than ten thousand tons. However, if I would explain more fully he might be able to put me on to the right department.

I decided that he was of sufficient importance for me to bring in names.

My friend, a Miss Sawyer, had left a very precious diary on board a yacht belonging to Mr Gordon Chester for whom I understood 'Bernardino' acted as agents. It was a diary of a kind she did not wish anyone to read.

Did something move behind his eyes—a change of expression in what seemed to be expressionless? I could not be sure. And he was a fraction slow with his suggestion that I should see his colleague 'Signor Tordero', and even as he made it, changed his mind. On the other hand, he said, it might be better if first I had a word with another gentleman on the floor below . . . But an interpreter would be needed since this gentleman did not speak English . . . There was a young lady on his own staff who was an excellent linguist. He pressed a bell on the desk.

The girl who came in had fuzzy auburn hair and wore patent-leather protecting cuffs over the sleeves of her black, artificial silk frock. He called her Berta. She listened gravely to his instructions and I felt his eyes boring between my shoulder blades as I went to the door with her.

It was a small bare room and the man behind the table, which had nothing on it except a telephone and a wooden pencil with a chewed end, was one of the ugliest I had ever seen.

It was not so much his flat nose and thick lips of the same colour and texture as his leathery, scarred cheeks which made him ugly, as the exuding malevolence of his whole being.

I guessed from the way he put down the telephone at the sight of me that the stone-eyed *Direttore* upstairs had just finished telling him about me, as much about me as was at present known. It was obviously this man's job to find out more. I was pleased with the way things were going. He looked as though he might suit me very well. Suspicion was obviously the mainspring of his mind.

The girl Berta introduced him as 'Signor Cordellese, who will be able to help you perhaps.'

He put on a smile of welcome, sinister in its unnaturalness, and pointed to the hard wooden chair the other side of the table. I took no notice of it. I looked disdainfully round the uncomfortable room.

'Tell him,' I said, 'that if he isn't in a position to tell me whether a personal diary belonging to a guest was found on Mr Gordon Chester's yacht, he is wasting his time and mine. The lady's name—the guest—is Sawyer.'

135

Berta reported what I had said accurately enough, boggling a little over 'Sawyer' with its un-Italian shape. I helped her, 'Saw-yer,' I said. '*Amica*, my best *amica*.' I watched for signs that the name meant something to him, but saw none.

'*La Signorina parla Italiano molto bene*,' he commented.

'What does he say?' I asked.

'That you speak Italian very well,' explained the girl.

'Without offending him, I know a meaningless compliment when I hear one. Three words—one of them happening to mean "friend".'

She conveyed this to him, and he said slowly, in Italian:

'The breasts of the young lady are her own, do you think?'

Because I was on my mental toes I managed to conceal that I had understood. I helped myself in this by sitting down in the chair. It was Berta who looked confused, not recognizing it as a test. She glanced at me covertly and said she was sure they were.

'What's all that?' I asked. 'Has the diary been found?'

She translated my question and added swiftly for his benefit that the yacht in question was on the books of her department. He told her sharply to stick to interpreting.

'Tell her,' he said in reply, 'that we have many yachts on our books and ask her the name of this one.' She repeated it in English.

'*Norse Girl*,' I said at once, and added that Miss Sawyer had introduced me to Mr Gordon Chester (which in a sense she had) and that he would be most put out to know we were having to go to all this trouble to get back her diary.

His thick jaw tightened a little as he listened to the translation of this, and noticeably when he heard that I knew Gordon Chester.

He continued to feel his way.

It might be, he had Berta explain, that Signor Chester's yacht was one of the many for which 'Bernardino' made themselves responsible in their owners' absence but no diary or anything of that kind had been found; he was positive of this because he was responsible for all lost property and kindred matters affecting owners.

In that case, I replied, it meant no one had looked in the drawer next to the bunk in the cabin Miss Sawyer had occupied during the week immediately before Mr Chester had returned to America.

And the quickest way to find it would be for me to go aboard the yacht and look for it myself. Quickest, and the least troublesome for everyone, including the firm of 'Bernardino'.

No doubt, came his reply. But had he not said he was by no means sure *Norse Girl* was in their charge? It would have to be looked up. And if she was, the place where she was lying might make such a plan difficult. She might be anywhere—anywhere. There were many harbours in Italy.

He got up. The *Signorina* would excuse him a moment, please. He would personally look up *Norse Girl* on the registry.

He turned before he went out to ask in halting almost incomprehensible English my name and where I was staying.

I told him. Gill. *Grande Savoie.*

He closed the door carefully after him.

The girl continued to stand by my chair but did not look at me when I glanced up at her.

'Tell me, *Signorina*,' I said, 'who is "Bernardino", if there is such a person?'

She started with a visible nervousness, but I thought it less because I had asked her the question than the fact that I had spoken at all.

I repeated my question. She gulped at me. 'Bernardino?' There was no one of that name now. There once was, of course. It was a company—a limited corporation.

'I really meant,' I explained, 'who is the head man?'

'There are several directors,' she managed to say.

'Who would you suggest,' I asked, 'should be the person for me to see to get what I want in the way I want it?'

'I—I—don't know. I am only in the shipping department —a clerk—a nobody.'

'There seems to be a general attitude of evasiveness. What *is* going on?'

'You're mistaken—'

'Where's that man gone? Who is he talking to?'

If she did not know, she could have made a fair guess; her glance went everywhere but near me.

'If you ask me, ' I went on, 'they've found my friend's diary—and read what's in it.'

' 'It is no concern of mine!' she cried in Italian; I remembered I did not know the language and asked her what she had said.

'Only that I am sure you will receive every satisfaction.'

Here was the same fear which had shown itself in everyone who came within reach of this organization. Angela, Shope, Mizzie, Sammy—they had all shown it in their different ways. To see it again here, was further evidence, if I needed any, that I had come to the right place.

'If they don't produce it,' I said, 'I'll know they have a criminal reason for not doing so.'

She stared at me, shaking her head but incapable of stopping me.

'If they think that by destroying it that'll be the end of it, they're wrong.'

As I reached the last few words the door began to open and by the time I had said them, Cordellese was with us again. He saw the girl's alarm and confusion, and he looked at her until she was forced into translation. She stumbled over it, her eyes pleading with him. He nodded but not in forgiveness. He was confirming knowledge and a logical decision which followed it.

I saw now that there was a subtle change in him; he was a shade less stolid, less self-assured. If he had been of weaker clay even he too might have been afraid.

Something had gone wrong and he in his turn had been brought into danger because of it.

'Well?' I demanded. 'That yacht *is* on your books?'

He needed no translation of this. 'Tell Signorina Gill that if this ship is found to be on our register, a search will be made for the document. But first of all, has she a letter, something in writing from her friend giving her authority to act for her?'

Berta translated it.

No, I had not! And to suggest that I was here without her authority was a gratuitous insult!

He saw my anger and without waiting for Berta to interpret, made a calming gesture with his thick hands.

Please, I must understand he would do everything he could to help. But to find this diary was 'Bernardino's' responsibility—if they were responsible for the yacht.

'Unfortunately,' I said, 'there are other than personal things in it. There is at least one entry which seriously affects another person. Just how seriously Miss Sawyer did not realize until after she left the yacht.'

'*Una altra persona?*'

'An Italian,' I said, 'and obviously it was something very, very indiscreet.'

He drew in his breath slowly. To pursue this further was more than he dared; it would have shown his hand immediately.

But his next question was as revealing as I could wish. He signalled its importance even before he phrased it for the girl to translate and he watched my face intently while I listened to it.

When had I last had contact with Miss Sawyer?

I watched him as closely while my reply reached him.

'Towards the end of last week.'

He sat there trying to work it out. I thought I had him where I wanted him.

He *had* to believe I did not know she was dead; he *had* to believe that if this diary existed it might have something dangerous in it, dangerous if it fell into my or any other person's hands, and he *had* to conclude that the full significance of it would come to me when I heard that Angela Sawyer had been killed.

I stood up at once. I had done what I had come here to do and I must go quickly.

'Please tell him,' I said to the girl, 'that I'll give him an hour to arrange for me to look for the diary. If he hasn't done anything about it by then I shall go straight to the police. I'll wait at the hotel.' I added a word of thanks for her help, and made for the door.

As I closed it I heard his expostulation: '*Signorina! Aspetta*—' and over the sound of his chair scraping noisily as he got to his feet, the beginning of the girl's hurried translation of my exit speech.

Short of running after me and holding me by force, he could not stop me from leaving. He should have done that, of course, but it would take him a few moments to realize it and remedy his slow-wittedness.

So I kept going, fast, my heels making a terrible clatter on the marble stairs. I fled past '*Informazione*' through the wide doorway into the courtyard and across it into the street.

Having stuck my head in the lion's mouth and got it out again I must survive its pounce and reach the bushes from which to twist its tail.

The taxi was where I had left it, thirty yards down *via Gambino*. The driver, hidden behind the pages of *Europeo*, did not see me until I was dragging at the door handle. It seemed an age before he had folded the paper and reached back to give the handle the master's touch it understood and I was able to get in. I told him to take me back to the hotel *subito, subito*! He would have driven like a maniac in any case but to urge him eased my tension a little.

It was natural in the circumstances that I should keep an eye on what went on behind us, and after I had gone through the yes—no, no—yes of whether the small black Fiat bowling along in our rear was really following us the question was settled for me by the way it took the same sudden turn my driver chose, apparently as an afterthought, for we were almost past it when he swung on two wheels into the teeth of on-coming traffic. The little Fiat chased after us. It was still there, pulling up on the other side of the street, when we came to the *Grande Savoie*.

I jumped out and ran into the hotel, asking the concierge to pay off the cab. I made straight for the elevators as fast as I could go without actually running and reached them as a short, squat man came through the revolving doors from the street. He could have been one of the hundreds of people who were staying in the hotel, but there was a very slight uncertainty of purpose about him as he came to a standstill. He wore a light-weight tan suit and a small upturned soft hat of a darker shade. I could not see his face properly since he was against the brilliant daylight which came through the plate-glass windows above and on both sides of the door. He looked round the lobby and then across it towards the elevators at the moment the operator pressed a button and the doors slid together, shutting out my sight of him. He could not have failed to see my yellow figure shining like a beacon in the dark box of the elevator.

I was less alarmed than I expected to find myself. I still felt that as long as I could continue to move a shade faster than anyone coming after me, I needed only a short period of such advantage.

My room looked exactly as I had left it less than an hour ago but I went straight to the wardrobe and felt for the leather case; I took out two spare, loaded magazines and dropped the case out of sight again. I also retrieved the black frock. I emptied my things from the grey handbag into the black one and put the spare magazines in it. But the pistol itself I put in my right-hand jacket pocket, which bulged and sagged with the weight; the distortion, however, was hidden fairly well by the butterfly-wing flap.

The black frock, shaken out and folded lengthways over my arm looked enough like a light top-coat. I paused now only for a quick tidy-up of my face at the dressing-table before putting the dangerous privacy of my room behind me.

The corridor was empty when I stepped out into it and I stood for a second or so before pulling the door shut. As the spring-lock clicked into place the man in the tan suit came round the corner with his hat still on his head. He looked about forty-five, and had a round pink face with a snub nose to match which shone a little from the heat. He was thirty feet away and his hands were in his pockets. He stopped at the sight of me and took his hands out of his pockets. This movement, since they came out empty, slightly reassured me but the corridor still felt like the Gobi Desert. The key of my room was in my handbag and the handbag was under my left arm. I could not get it out under several seconds, while he needed only a fraction of one of them to put a hand back in his pocket and shoot me down. If those were his orders . . .

It seemed better, therefore, to ignore his existence and pretend to be taking a key out of the lock and putting it away in my right-hand pocket. I was thus able to take out my pistol behind the shelter of my body, slip the safety catch and keep the weapon dangling in my hand a little behind my thighs as I turned to face him. It seemed to me he would now have to draw very fast to get ahead of me. I started to walk towards the elevators, which also meant towards him.

His right hand moved. So did mine. I brought the pistol up quickly. But intent on watching my face he did not see it and his hand continued upward, passed his pocket and went to his hat. It froze there, just as he was about to take it off. His glance had dropped from my face to my hands.

'Turn round!' I said in Italian. 'Keep your hands away from your pockets!'

He did not move for a moment. Not a muscle. Then he slowly removed his hat, lowered it—away from his body. He was bald and his pate shone like his button-nose.

He took a deep breath and spoke in a soft voice which to my ear sounded classic New England.

'I'm taking a chance,' he said, 'but I think I can tell you that if my boss could see me now, I'd be out on my ear.' He smiled ruefully at me and looked over his shoulder as though he half-expected to see Mr Haken standing there, raising his eyebrows at him. I realized who he was claiming to be, with that slightly oblique method of introducing himself.

'I'm afraid,' I said, covering surprise, 'I have no previous experience of being followed about by the Federal Bureau of Investigation in little black Fiats. To my eye you don't look the part.'

'Oh?' he said.

'You're not lean enough and your hat is turned up in front.'

His smile broadened appreciatively. 'Maybe that's why I've managed to get by—' His glance went to my pistol again— 'up to now. If you'll let me use a hand to produce

142

the necessary credentials, Miss Gill, I can prove that my name is John Peaslake and that I am indeed a—'

He stopped abruptly. A waiter in a white jacket came round the corner behind him carrying a bottle of champagne in an ice-bucket and two glasses on a small tray. He noticed nothing odd about us; he swerved past the man in the tan suit and said, '*Buon Giorno,*' no doubt in accordance with the hotel's rules for staff deportment.

But he was stopped by a loud cry of 'Hey!' and told in good Italian to take the champagne into the lady's room. He expostulated—the champagne was for *numero quaranta-quatro*—but he found himself being steered towards the door by a pudgy but firm hand on his arm.

I stepped away from the door to the opposite wall, keeping my back to it and the pistol steady behind the edge of my skirt. This man might be who he said he was, but I did not altogether care for the way he was taking command of the situation. He put two one-thousand lire notes on the tray and told the waiter he could easily fetch another bottle for the other people. He was determined beyond contradiction about it, indeed, he took the ice-bucket so that the waiter could fetch out his master-key on the end of its chain. He opened the door with a shrug of amiable resignation, put the tray on the table and came out again, grinning at me. Mr Peaslake also grinned at me, as a man might who had won a neat trick, carried the ice-bucket into the room and at once began opening the champagne.

He used both hands to pour the wine, one to hold the bottle, the other to steady the glasses.

'Shoot if I make a false move,' he said, 'but honest, I'm on the level. We can't talk with the door open.' Or with one of us not even in the room, I thought, but he did not labour the point. I crossed to the open doorway, slowly saying that I didn't understand any of this.

'Usually,' he said, 'people walk out of that place as if they were on top of the world. You didn't. You *ran* out of it. I'm interested.'

'Why?' I pulled the door after me but not to the extent of fully closing it.

'Because you've probably got a reason for being afraid of them which I ought to know about.'

'I'm not in the least afraid of them.'

'Then if I may give you a little advice, you should be. I think you've done something they don't like.'

'Something they don't like?' I asked. 'That respectable business firm of general importers?'

He nodded. 'Don't be fooled by the striped pants set-up. Maybe you met up with a guy in there by name Cordellese, for instance.'

'I met him.'

'Ah! Then you *are* my pigeon.' He seemed pleased.

'Not your dead duck?'

'I don't deal in dead ducks. But Cordellese does. Come on in.'

He held out one of the glasses. His other hand was idle by his side. I gave in, tentatively and with many reservations. I closed the door, approached and took the other glass from the tray. He laughed, then looked at me with a fluffy eyebrow raised. 'Miss Gill, who are you?'

'You know my name—'

'But the concierge didn't tell me who you were working for. Mind you, I didn't ask him, not thinking he'd know . . . You're Scotland Yard, aren't you?'

'Most certainly not!' I said. 'Do I look like it?'

'Yes,' he said.

'Oh dear—'

'If you're not, what are you?'

'I'm here by myself—for my own reasons.'

'Let's hear them.'

'I think first, you'll have to explain yourself a good deal more,' I said.

The lightness went out of his manner and he put down his glass.

'Look, let's not play around. You're a Britisher but you're in a foreign country. You could get into a lot of trouble with the authorities. You'd be surprised how many regulations a girl can run foul of—things she doesn't even know are in the book.'

'Oh!' I said. 'I *am* afraid now.'

'I mean it, Sugar. I'm here with a high-level Washington request for cooperation. I've only to pick up that phone and the Chief of Police himself will start something you won't stop—not easily.'

I shook my head.

'You'd have to wait until after lunch.'

'What's that?' He stared at me.

'Poor Taglioni's indigestion is very bad until he's eaten. It's that kind,' I said.

'Gosh darn it!' Then he laughed. 'All right. I said you were a Britisher, didn't I? You're all the same. I shouldn't have gone heavy on you. I'm slipping.'

'Perhaps it's only that I'm managing to stand up,' I said.

'But not to "Bernardino"—for long. I assure you. If you've crossed that outfit, you—' he made a gesture of impatience. 'All this talk, and nothing being said.' He sat down in an armchair, pushed out his short legs, sipped his champagne and considered me carefully. I remained standing, my handbag still in my left hand, the black frock folded over my arm, the pistol in my right hand.

'Ever heard of Jakus Cicero?'

'Isn't he a sort of Al Capone, modern edition?'

'Was, lady, *was*. He went the way of all flesh at nine-twenty p.m. on third April this year off Pier Thirteen, New York Harbour. He was on his way somewhere else at the time. In a row-boat. But we didn't want him to leave on account of a double murder rap fifteen years old—it would have stuck, though. I personally emptied my gun at him along with two other Feds and half the local Precinct boys who were also present . . . would you care to put that rod away?'

'It won't go off unless I want it to,' I said; 'you were saying—?'

'Okay, okay!'

And he went on to tell me things George had already told me about the Kefauver Committee's efforts to break up the infiltration of American big business by criminal interests. He explained that the word 'Interstate' in the Committee's

145

title fell short of the actual size and scope of the field covered by syndicated crime, which was in fact as international as the United Nations. It had become so, ironically, as a result of the Committee's work, which had blasted great holes in the comfortable darkness of their underworld.

The big shots had discovered, along with other people, that air-travel had made the world smaller, and that in terms of time-space, Europe was not as far from New York as Los Angeles, and had the added advantage of being beyond the reach of both State and Federal law.

'These boys,' he said, 'were for the most part originally emigré Italians, with a strong Sicilian flavour left over from the old Mafia from which they developed. So what do they do when the heat is on? They merely return to the old country, so conveniently also in Europe, and sit here in law-abiding security and by long-distance phone and cable run the only business they know, American crime. Any little thing requiring personal attention can be looked after by subordinate expendables who can be easily replaced. See the picture so far?'

I said I saw the picture so far.

'Sicilians,' I added. 'They tend to dark skins.'

'Very much so. Considerable mixing in of Moorish blood. Why?'

'Nothing important. You were saying?'

'Well now, if one of the crook business men they've got their hooks in,' he continued, 'wants a top-level conference, he has to come over here to have it. It's about the only weakness in the new system. It's one thing for a man with the wrong kind of friends to step into a hotel in New York, go up to a private suite for a talk, and go away again, but it's a bit different if he has to book a passage in a boat or plane, pass through security controls coming and going, and spend time in foreign places he's maybe never been in before with language difficulties, no familiar background to slide away into. Why, he's half the man he is at home and much easier to keep tabs on. That's about the only advantage we seem to have. They stick their necks out. They carry papers back and forth, make these contacts, and one way and

146

another help us quite a bit more than they mean to. We've done a lot of tidying up that way, but all the time we're hoping to get up close to these top-ranking operators-in-exile.'

'But if they are wanted on charges in America—isn't there an extradition agreement?'

'There is. But try to use it. Satisfying an Italian Court that we want some rich and eminent citizen, *Italian* citizen, for drug peddling, vice-rackets, extortion, kidnapping and murder—why that doesn't come easy. Particularly when he's fronted by legitimate business and social respectability. Those things don't help him much at home. But here! No —it's the up-to-date stuff we have to catch them on. *Prove* their criminal activities at the moment. Then the local police can act with us and for us.'

'Look,' I said. 'I've got an urgent date.'

'But, I'm trying to tell you—'

'Yes, I know. But I assure you my business with "Bernardino" is nothing to do with all this.'

'If it isn't, I'll jump into the lake!' he said. ' "Bernardino" is just such a front as I'm talking about—for the biggest outfit of Crime International, Inc., that ever—'

'All the same, I've got a date,' I said.

My conviction that I had already stayed here far too long for safety had become suddenly stronger than any curiosity I might have had about the Federal Bureau of Investigation's worthy and far-flung efforts to preserve the American way of life. I moved towards the door.

'Wait!' Mr Peaslake jumped up. 'Let's cut this short. What's your angle? In three words.'

'In one—personal,' I told him. He shook his head at me; he had such hopes of me, a man becoming desperate in a tough assignment.

'Anything to do with a guy by the name of Chester— Gordon Chester?' he asked.

Although I put my hand on the door knob, I must have shown something.

'Ah!' he said. 'Look, Miss Gill. Chester is the reason I'm here. He led me to this "Bernardino" racket, to Morelli and his hoods and whoever else is hidden in there.'

And now Morelli!

I was in a confusion of conflicting needs again; to get away quickly and yet to stay with this roly-poly little agent with so much knowledge which might fill the gaps in mine. I asked him where I could get in touch with him when I had more time to spare. He frowned at me and said he would get in touch with me here at the hotel. I explained that I might check out at any moment. He had to give in, knowing he would have to trust me to some extent if he wanted any information I might have.

'Box eighty-three, Central Post office,' he said. 'It's cleared every two hours from eight a.m. I'll lose out if I don't get another line pretty soon. The one I had has gone dead—literally. You aren't scared are you?'

The answer came in a small but frightening movement of the door knob, a slow, cautious, exploratory turning of it by someone the other side of the door.

Yes, I was afraid, but I did not say so. I also suppressed a natural impulse to react in a gesture of caution to him. I took my hand away from my side of the knob as if it had become suddenly red hot, gently slid the small bolt above it into place and moved away from the door. Even if they had a key and tried to use it they would not get in. Not for a minute at any rate. I kept my voice down.

'You said just now that a "line" had gone dead on you?' I reverted to this less because I was interested than in order to cover a more urgent effort to think how to get out of this room and the hotel with a whole skin.

'Yes,' he said. 'Gordon Chester himself.'

'What about him?' I looked across at the bathroom door, trying to remember whether it had a communicating door to the next suite, and began to cross to it.

'He's dead.'

That stopped me; I turned and he came close to me. 'What do you know about him?'

'How did he—die?'

'Sudden.'

'When?'

148

'Three hours after he landed in New York from his visit to these parts.'

'How?'

'Of three bullets in the head in an apartment on Fifth Avenue. No flowers by request. Not that we've announced it yet.'

'*Three* bullets?'

'They weren't bothering to make it look like anything it wasn't. A gang killing.'

'They?' I asked tentatively, and I moved to the closet where I changed my shoes for a black pair. He kept close to me.

'Representatives of the big boy over here. God knows who he is, but is he big? Brought up by Jakus himself, I'd say. Same touch, same genius for organization. Left-handed genius if you like—but genius.'

'This Jakus—' I crossed to the bathroom again. He followed, a pace behind.

'Jakus D. Cicero.'

'The one you shot—'

'Me and some others. And a waste of artillery, seemingly. The syndicate's as strong as ever it was.'

'Who is this new man?'

'*You* tell *me*.'

'I haven't the faintest idea,' I said, watching the door on to the corridor which an active imagination assured me was about to be battered down. 'Have you a gun, Mr Peaslake?'

'Yes, Miss Gill. And let's get off this roundabout. It's making me dizzy. *I'm* going to ask the questions from now on!'

'Here?'

'Yes, here—'

'I meant, you have your gun here, with you?'

He touched his side under his left arm. 'What do you think? That I don't know this city can be unhealthy for the curious?'

'It's too late for my date, now,' I said. 'I'm going to take a shower,' and added to quell his impatience, 'I want to think.'

'A shower! *Think!* There's nothing to—'

'Oh, yes there is,' I said, 'chiefly about the unhealthiness of this city and how I'm to keep away from catching something.'

'You know,' he said, 'I think you *are* police of some kind.'

'No comment,' I said, opening the bathroom door.

'I'm betting it *is* Scotland Yard! And them not telling anybody. It's not right! What's *Interpol* for?'

'Has the United States rejoined it?' I asked, and closed the door on him, locking it. I turned on both taps of the bath and the shower as well. Water roared, drowning all other sounds.

There *was* a communicating door to the next room, held by a small bolt; it was not very strong looking. There would be a similar one on the other side, also closed.

I got quickly out of my yellow suit into the black frock, ducked my head briefly under the shower and combed back the result in lank rat-tails. I found a handkerchief in my handbag and with a hair-pin fastened it on top of my head in near enough semblance to a maid's cap, and was ready. I rapped smartly on the communicating door. Nothing happened, no one answered. I put my shoulders against it, braced my feet against the edge of the tub and pushed. The staple holding the bolt on the other side began to give; I felt it going in time to save myself from a fall on the tiled floor, and found myself looking into an untenanted bedroom.

I put the pistol in my handbag and took the yellow suit and the hat with me into the empty room but no farther than the clothes closet, where I hung the suit on a hanger and put the hat on the shelf above it. I might feel death at my heels but I was also aware that this was my only Jacques Fath creation. I scribbled my name and room number on a piece of lining-paper from a drawer and spiked it on the hook of the hanger.

The water was still pouring noisily into the bath and presumably Mr Peaslake was waiting impatiently for me to finish my shower and come out talking. But I could not help that.

I shut the communicating door and wedged a chair

against it; the loose staple was on this side and it might take my pursuers a few moments to work out what had happened. All the moments I could gain added to the narrow margin of safety. I was ready to go.

I pulled the sheets off the big bed, rolled them up with my handbag in the middle and holding the oversize bundle in both arms, fumbled for the handle of the door into the corridor. I got it open, hooked one foot round it and hopped out on the other, pulling the door shut after me. The lock clicked.

I did not look towards my own door as I set off in the opposite direction to the elevators. It took an effort of will not to for I knew with certainty that someone was there. I could almost hear the movement of his head as he looked round sharply and alertly and saw me, saw my back and the white bundle protruding on both sides in front of me, and the cap on my head.

The corridor was terrifyingly long; an inescapable vista of red carpet which would muffle any following footsteps stretched to infinity between walls broken only by blank-faced doors. There seemed to be no turning off it nearer than at its distant end. And there might not be one then, for even a building of the size of the *Grande Savoie* must sooner or later meet the wall dividing it from the next.

Then suddenly there was a break in the succession of doors, a turning to the right and I was round a corner and beginning to breathe again. I hesitated, resisted the thought to step back to it and peer round it with no more than one eye, to see what was happening. I went on more quickly now, and came to a small service elevator of the self-operating kind. I rested on the bundle against the wall beside it, freeing my left hand, and pressed the button. I heard the soft whirr of the machinery and a moment later the elevator stopped the other side of the sliding door. I opened it, tumbled the sheets into it and stepped in after them. I pressed the button marked '2' and during the short two-floor descent, retrieved my handbag, folded the sheets as neatly as I could in the confined space and put them tidily against the wall by the elevator door and continued down to street level, remembering to take the handkerchief off my head.

The elevator came to rest in a concrete-floored luggage reception room opening out into a narrow street at the side of the hotel. There were several *facchini* about, burly men in blue blouses and peaked caps, handling trunks and suitcases and shouting at one another. A uniformed hotel porter presided from a glass-enclosed desk with an open window in front of it. He took less interest in me than if I had been entering.

I wished now that I had taken that look round the corner of the corridor at the man they had sent to find me; the more of them I knew by sight the better.

But I was out of the hotel. That was the main thing.

I found a small draper's shop close by where I bought a red and black flowered headscarf which, knotted under my chin, completed the change in appearance.

It was high time the Field-Marshal heard from me, and in any case this was likely to be my only breathing space before the second round began.

I made for the Central Post Office in *Piazza de Ferrari* by way of the side streets. The day was over-hot and getting hotter.

I went to the *Poste Restante* counter before drafting a message on the chance there might be something by now from George at Cannes, who should have arrived there.

There was a cable and also a second one from the Field-Marshal.

Said George (Copy to the Field-Marshal):

CONCRETE INDICATIONS EVIDENCE YACHT INCIDENT RE-VEALABLE HERE STOP CHESTER IMPORTANTEST WITNESS RUMOURED RETURNING CANNES AND SINCE SUBJECT LIKELY AMENABLE FEMALE INFLUENCE SUGGEST YOU JOIN ME ACK TWO.

The Field-Marshal was having trouble:

BERRINGTON TELEPHONED DEMANDING WHEREABOUTS BE-HALF FATHER ANXIOUS YOUR SAFETY UNABLE REFUSE GAVE

ADDRESS CHEZ FIGGE STOP NORTH COMMITTED TRIAL OLD
BAILEY SEPTEMBER 20 AM CONSIDERING OFFICIAL PRESSURE
TO ASSIGN SMITH THROUGH INTERPOL TO CANNES INQUIRY
ON BASIS STRONG PRESUMPTIVE EVIDENCE CRIME CONNECTED
ANGELA'S HOST SINCE FEDS INVESTIGATING HIM USA STOP
YOUR VIEWS PLEASE STOP COPY TO CANNES FOR INF STOP
ACK ONE.

Assign Smith!

Once again the fluttery, knees-to-water feeling came over
me at the sight of Christopher's name, and it was several
moments before I remembered I was in an Italian post office
a thousand miles away from him. The close reality of his
existence faded only gradually, leaving me unhappy and
lonely. I made an effort to shake it off and read the Field-
Marshal's cable again. What chance should I have with
Christopher here, to go on with my plan, which had begun
promisingly? How effective would I be when my mind
—and heart—were in confusion because of his nearness?
Orthodox methods—I was more and more convinced of it
—would never drive into the open the man who had killed
Angela, or ordered her killing, which was the same thing.

I read the cable a third time and something caught in my
mind like a burr.

The Federal Bureau was investigating Gordon Chester in
America, but *they had not told even Interpol that he was dead.*

I could understand why—at least I thought I could. Mr
Peaslake wanted to avoid spreading the fear of reprisals
amongst the people from whom he was hoping to get information. He had only told me at the last moment, when he
found I was not as afraid as he had expected. He had wanted
to impress me with the predicament Chester's death had
put him in, so that I might help him. But that was not the
point, so much as this:

If the Field-Marshal were told that Gordon Chester was
dead, would he still want to send Christopher out here?

I looked at the thought for a moment.

It was not my secret that the man was dead. No one—
meaning Mr Peaslake—had asked me to keep it.

I pulled a telegraph form from the slit in the box over the desk and drafted a message:

ANGELA'S HOST DIED NEW YORK STOP POSSIBILITY ACTION HERE NOT YET DETERMINED BUT AM DIGGING IN STOP SMITH WOULD ONLY COMPLICATE SITUATION PREFER YOU NOT SEND STOP COPY TWO FOR INF.

But, in fact, I would not send a copy to George; it would put paid to his expectation of Chester's return with revelations, and his next idea might be to join me in Genoa instead of waiting for me to come to him for what was now a useful purpose.

True, he would have difficulty in finding me if I did not want him to, but I could not risk it. I must, *must* have the field to myself for at least the next two days.

I stood at the desk for several minutes considering how I could strengthen the message and finally decided to put at the beginning:

FED BUREAU SAYS . . .

I did this, and took the cable to the dispatch counter. I had done what I could.

It was now fifteen minutes to noon, and astonishingly only three-quarters of an hour since I had walked out of Cordellese's office. I would wait until the hour was up and more before telephoning to him, as I had said I would. Aware of an emptiness in my stomach I crossed the square to the café on the corner of *via Venti Settembre* and at one of the small sidewalk tables in the back row against the wall, ordered an *espresso* and a plate of pastries. I ate four of them without noticeably curing the emptiness and came to the conclusion that it was due less to hunger than to a nervous reaction from thinking about Christopher; since I seemed unable to stop I gave myself up to it and in a few moments was in a worse state of turmoil than ever with the result that the fifth pastry turned to unchewable straw in my mouth.

154

I washed it down with the coffee and at once felt sick.

Then I forgot everything else in an alarming after-thought.

By adding those three words at the beginning of my cable to the Field-Marshal, I had certainly given authority to the information about Chester being dead, but I had also revealed that I was in touch with the Federal Bureau and that my 'digging in' must be an understatement. In short I had destroyed the whole object of the cable and given the Field-Marshal a better reason than any to send Christopher out, and worse still, not to Cannes but to Genoa, here to me! I threw some money on the table and ran back to the post office. There was a small queue at each of the three *Telegrafo* windows and by the time I reached one of them it was nearly twelve o'clock. The cable had been dispatched beyond recall within three minutes of my handing it in.

I had seen something of the Field-Marshal at work. It seemed likely to certainty that before the end of the day Mr Peaslake would receive instructions from Washington to cooperate with a CID man who would be arriving from London in the immediate future . . . I could see it happening. In my mind's eye I even saw Mr Peaslake unlocking his Box 83 over there in the far wall, where a battery of the things were ranged in bronze, each numbered and with a small glass window in the end so that you could see without opening it whether there was anything in it. Yes, there would soon be a pale buff cablegram for Mr Peaslake, wrapped securely in code no doubt, but saying just that . . .

. . . And Christopher would be in this city besieging 'Bernardino' with him and looking for me. No dusty black frock or hair-concealing scarf would hide me from him, who had seen me in every sort of garment and condition from ordered elegance in strapless green satin to bedraggled wetness in next-to-naked swim-suit—with my hair in rat-tails. I might keep out of his way in *via Santa Madre*, but that would mean keeping out of Cordellese's way—Cordellese and Morelli and whoever else I would have to flush out of that 'Bernardino' cover before the big birds began to show.

. . . Four o'clock? Six o'clock? Eight? At which collecting

time would Mr Peaslake unlock his box and find that fatal
message . . .?

I was looking at the big clock hanging from the ceiling in
my full view. Its hands were joined together at the top.
Twelve noon!

I swung round to the banked tiers of PO boxes. Two
people, a man and a woman, were collecting their mail. But
the man was tall and thin and his suit was dark, not tan. I
moved closer. Box 83 was almost exactly in the middle and
there were letters in it, the green and red bordered envelopes
of United States air mail showing clearly.

Time was narrowing. Suppose, before Christopher
arrived, I consolidated myself with Mr Peaslake? Wouldn't
that make throwing me out on my ear a little more difficult?

Someone had left a newspaper on a bench; I appropriated
it and stood pretending to read it but with both eyes on Box
83 a few feet away.

The man who opened it at three minutes past the hour was
not Mr Peaslake but a nondescript, drab-looking individual,
clearly a native of the town; he wore a shiny black suit and
a peak cap, like a chauffeur's. His movements at the box
were easy and accustomed. He put the key in the lock
without fumbling, took out the letters, put them carefully in
his inside pocket without even glancing at them and
slammed the box shut as he stepped away. It was obvious
that he had gone through the operation several times before.
In short, he was part and parcel of Mr Peaslake.

I followed him out of the post office. The same baby Fiat,
or its twin, was at the kerb. He went round to the far door,
opened it and began to slide behind the wheel. I opened the
near door and got in, settling myself on the seat almost
before he did.

'*Il signor Peaslake mi aspetta,*' I said casually. '*Ha una
cigarette, per favore?*'

He had a small lean, lined face with a deep furrow between
wiry eyebrows. He turned to me with a stare of surprise.
Signor Peaslake he began to tell me, had said nothing about
collecting a young woman.

'And why should he?' I asked, and winked as lewdly as I

knew how. And could he spare me a cigarette? I was dying for one.

He shrugged his shoulders after a moment and pulled out a grubby packet of Macedonie and gave me one, taking one for himself. He gave me a light from a flaring wax match and lit his own.

'*Andiamo,*' I said, and we went.

Mr Peaslake had taken off both jacket and shirt and was sitting in singlet and trousers at the open window of a room in a small apartment overlooking the Porto Vecchio. He had binoculars to his eyes trained down on the harbour, supporting his elbow on a table while he made notes on a pad next to a pitcher of red wine in which the remnants of ice cubes fought a losing battle for survival. The binoculars, of course, reminded me of the reed pheasant which had begun it all.

Mr Peaslake was so intent on his spying on whatever it was that he did not hear me until I spoke.

'Angelo asked me to bring your correspondence up with me. He's gone to his lunch.'

He swung round and I handed him the letters and the key Angelo had given me to open the door in case Signor Peaslake was not in.

'Goddam!' he said. 'Have you read them too?'

'Not yet.' I smiled at him with what I hoped was a reassuring expression. He continued to look at me with rounder eyes than ever.

'Your friend Taglioni,' he said, 'swore to me that Angelo was one of the best operatives he had. Perhaps he meant in the double-cross.'

'I'm sorry I had to walk out on you in the hotel,' I began to say. 'But there was someone at my door whom I—'

'*That,*' he said, 'developed. I saw the gentleman. I told him he had the wrong room. His name was Morelli—although he didn't introduce himself and didn't know me, I'm glad to say, from Adam. He said he had just arrived by air from London and was looking up an old friend. He was so sorry. He went away. I turned off the waterfall in your bathroom and came away myself. You studied as a child with Houdini?'

'I want to know,' I said, 'what date Gordon Chester left New York in *Norse Girl*.'

'I give and give and give, do I?' But he nodded at me with grudging admiration. 'I had the same idea myself—about three days late. But I checked.'

'He left the same night this Jakus Cicero was killed?'

'Early hours of the next morning, April fourth. He had to wait for the tide. But not any more for Jakus Cicero. He would have heard the bombardment. *Norse Girl* was quite near enough.'

I sat down, pulled off the headscarf, and put my handbag on the floor. He glanced at it, and asked if I hadn't better open it so as to get the gun out quicker.

'As I told you,' I said, 'I'm here on my own and working alone—trying to, But all the same, I think we both want the same thing.'

'Do you? What do *I* want?'

'You told me. To break up "Bernardino", to find who the "big boy" as you call him, really is, and do something about him. I want to do something about him too.'

'Why?'

I told him. I stuck to the simple facts. I skated over the Field-Marshal and left out Christopher altogether but I included Shope and my visit to the house in Camden Town, and all that happened in it, ending with the 'Bernardino' card on Shope's mantelpiece. I explained that my incentive to action had been Angela's letter, her murder so soon after she had written it, and the arrest of Arthur North.

When I had done he poured me a glass of red wine and refilled his own. I thanked him but did not attempt to drink it. He gulped his down saying that it only made him hotter but soft drinks killed him and the *Genovese* water would obviously do the same for a camel.

'So that's where Morelli went,' he said. 'I think, though, he went and returned by air, probably a private charter plane.'

'Who went with him?' I asked quickly. He shook his head.

158

No one had actually seen Morelli go, it had merely been noted that he was not around from about the middle of last week and had only just reappeared.

'You took on something, didn't you?' he said rhetorically, but he did not question my story, perhaps because his professional instinct told him it was true or maybe because it had so little of practical use for him that there was no point in examining it. If someone in 'Bernardino' had committed a crime, it was only one more added to a long list and the English police did not even believe in it. He had a disappointed look but I would not allow it to discourage me.

'I should very much like to know,' I said hopefully, 'what happened on *Norse Girl* in Cannes harbour, round about the eleventh of June. It set both Angela and Chester Gordon scurrying for home. To their almost simultaneous deaths.'

Mr Peaslake regarded the bottom of his empty glass and after a moment said: 'There was a steward on that yacht, name of Zolski. Stateless person. Came out of a harbourside bar on the rainy night of June twelve and fell down in front of a big blue French autobus that was passing. He was too dead afterwards to say how he came to do such a terrible thing. Harbourside at Cannes, it was . . .'

He shook his head. 'What happened on that damn' boat? Who's to tell us—now? Only the guy who had a secret to keep.'

'Three dead. A big secret.'

'As you say, big. Maybe the count will be four, if this Arthur North goes to the chair—rope, that is. He'll not be saved by any gratuitous confession from the guilty party. A little tough on him, eh?'

'I'm glad you see that.'

'Hell!' he exploded. 'This thing is tough on more little people than you could count non-stop in a month! Nothing goes with these bastards but their own skins, their own cash balances, and their own power-drunk way! Somebody puts a foot wrong. Hit him, bump him, sink him in concrete in Hudson River, blow out his brains in a down-town hotel! A kid's on a racketeer's yacht at the wrong moment. Send a hood all the way to London to squeeze the life out of her. If someone else catches the Law for it—so what?' He wiped his round pink face with the back of his hand. 'I feel like I'm in a jungle, with one bow and a broken arrow. "Smoke 'em out, Peaslake, that's all you've got to do. The State Department, Peaslake, will do the rest." *State Department!*' He glared at the letters where he had tossed them unopened on the table. 'Smoke them out with what? Lists of callers at that goddam fortress in *via Gambino* with its half dozen secret exits? Names of suspected persons? Reports on cargo ships which bring in thirty million cigarettes at a time—for ballast —to load up with every kind of dope they buy in Europe for peanuts and sell for souls back home? *Pfoui!* But you're not interested in that . . . you're here on your own ticket, feudin' . . .'

He stopped, exhausted by his own vehemence.

'But with the same notion, to smoke them out,' I said.

'Them? *Him* you mean, don't you?'

'We keep getting back to that, don't we?'

'I do,' he said with the same positiveness he had shown before. 'There's a dynamism in there no committee or group would give it. Only a leader of the top kind. You've seen it, felt it.'

'The fear of it.'

'That's what I'm talking about. You said it plain enough when you told me about that set-up in London.'

'The rule of Fear.'

'It's their strength. His strength, whoever he is. But it's his weakness, too. If I can catch up with one of his stooges who's in the right stage of fearing I can maybe get him to ease himself of it. By talking. So I hang around, hoping.'

'Which isn't getting you far, you say.'

'It's getting me back to where I was before I started. And 'way before that.' He turned gloomily to the window, picked up the binoculars, and demonstrated in the next breath that he had by no means given me up as a disappointment.

'I suppose you walked into "Bernardino" asking if you could have a few words with your girlfriend's murderer? And Mr Cordellese said sorry, but the gentleman is out just now.' He twisted back suddenly to face me. 'Now *you* tell me for a change!'

I saw something in his eyes, those usually uncomplicated eyes, which explained why he was what he was. I should probably have flinched had I been wanting to hold out on him any longer.

'It wasn't quite as obvious as that,' I said. 'But I did start him thinking I *might* know he had a murderer there . . . may I telephone to him? Do you happen to know the number?'

He put down the binoculars again, his eyes still hard but with expectancy beginning to show in his expression. He gave me the number and I went to the telephone on the top of a low bookcase and dialled. I asked for Signor Cordellese. The instrument clicked and clacked and Mr Peaslake watched me.

'You know what you're doing?' he asked, and I said I thought I did. 'It's supposed to be the beginning of that smoke you were talking about.'

'*Pronto*,' said Cordellese's thick voice, somewhat emasculated by the mechanics of telephony.

'This is Eve Gill,' I said in English, sharply. 'It's more than an hour since you said you'd let me know where that yacht is lying.'

He let out a grunt of what I hoped was surprise at hearing my voice and asked me to '*Aspette, per piacere! Aspette, aspette signorina!*' and I heard him shouting at somebody to fetch Signorina Berta.

'Oh, for heaven's sake, why can't you speak English!' I said crossly.

Mr Peaslake had left the window by now; and gone into a small bedroom. He picked up an extension telephone and covered the mouthpiece with his hand while he listened, sitting on the edge of the bed and facing me through the doorway.

'Mees Gill? Please?'

I recognized the girl's voice in spite of its breathlessness; she must have come down those stairs three at a time.

'I got tired of waiting for that message,' I said. 'What's happening?'

'But it seems—Signor Cordellese assures you that he has been trying to get in touch with you. They—he—says you were not in the hotel—'

'Not in the hotel!' I cried. 'If you ask me this is just one more footling excuse! You people don't want me to find that diary and I am getting very suspicious indeed. There's something behind all this, and I—'

'Please—one moment—' she interrupted. I heard Cordellese demanding impatiently to know what I was saying, and his repeated: '*Dov' è signorina? Dove?*' She came back to me:

'The *Signore* wishes to know where you are now.'

'I'm at this end of the telephone waiting for his answer! Where is *Norse Girl* and how soon can I go aboard her?'

She repeated this to him and his angry, swearing response was only faintly muffled. Mr Peaslake was now registering a lively, almost happy interest. He nodded at me vigorously. The girl Berta sounded near tears:

'The *signore* has not yet been able to trace the yacht on our books. He thinks you must be mistaken.'

'Tell him not to be silly,' I retorted. 'Surely Mr Gordon would know who his ship agents are.'

'Are you sure of the name of the yacht?'

'I read it with my own eyes in letters six inches high on the stern. N-O-R-S-E G-I-R-L, with F.Y.C. under it. Florida Yacht Club, at a guess. Does he *want* me to go to the police and tell them that a private document is being concealed by "Bernardino" for some reason best known to themselves? Illegally. For what must be an illegal reason?'

The mutter of the translation was followed by Cordellese's loud voice as he took the telephone from her.

'*Pazienza, Signorina, pazienza!* Ten minute. You sit, eh? You sit? No move, ten minute? *Ecco, Berta—dica, dica!*'

The girl resumed, explaining that if I would wait where I was for ten minutes, Signor Cordellese would for certain provide me with a satisfactory answer. I was in the hotel? Whereabouts in the hotel? In the lounge? In my room? Where please, so that I could be found quickly?

'I will ring you back in ten minutes,' I said and put down

162

the receiver in its cradle. Mr Peaslake did the same with his, synchronizing the break in the connection.

'Smoke!' he said. 'They're buzzing all right!' He came out of the bedroom.

'What's this stuff you've started? This diary. What diary?'

'A diary which doesn't exist. But Angela *might* have kept one, might have put something in it about the thing which had frightened her, and *might* have left it behind on the yacht. They'll have to accept that.'

'And the big secret may be in it?' He grinned at me. 'And they think you may get hold of it.'

'They can stop that by taking *Norse Girl* apart and making sure it isn't there. In fact, they're probably hard at work on that already. But after that they cannot be sure how much I know already of what is supposed to be in the diary, or what I will think and do when I hear Angela has been killed.'

'I get it,' he said.

'And I've tried to build myself up with them as a character who turns naturally to house-top shouting on the slightest excuse.'

'You've sure thought it out.' Mr Peaslake pursed his small mouth in concentration. 'By the way,' he said, '*Norse Girl* is on their books.'

'I know. And lying at Portofino. But I'm saving that up for the next puff.'

He came up to me and put a hand on my shoulder, a hot hand through the thin material of my frock, and said quietly: 'As I see it, you're using *yourself* for the smoke. Putting yourself in the same spot as the others were in—Gordon, Miss Sawyer, Zolski the steward. Now that's all very fine and dandy in theory but—'

The door opened without warning and a tall, lean young man with a snap-brim fedora on a sculptor's model's head stepped into the room and immediately began to back out again.

'Sorry, folks,' he said. 'Sorry indeed.'

My heart tried to pick up the beat it had slipped, not because he was so good-looking but because henceforth any

163

door opening suddenly would be a thing of which to be justifiably nervous.

Mr Peaslake took his hand from my shoulder and growled at the young man to quit being funny and come in and shut the door, Bill, for God's sake.

'This is the smoke we were looking for,' he added.

'Smoke—' said the young man.

'Good morning,' I said.

'She doesn't always look like hell that way,' Mr Peaslake explained. 'It's only her hair.'

'Usually wears a wig?'

It was all very light-hearted and although some sort of relief would be welcome, I could do without this. However, I said I should like to know who this 'Bill' was, since he could not possibly be another Federal Agent looking this time, as he did, so exactly like one. He exchanged a quick, subtle glance with Mr Peaslake who nodded slightly.

'I am afraid I am,' he told me, and smiled engagingly.

'Out of Hollywood,' remarked Mr Peaslake. 'He'll never get on . . . and don't *stand* there, Bill. Get you over to the *Savoie* and see what cooks. There's likely to be a posse on its way there, six-shooters and all. Looking for her.' He pointed at me with his pudgy forefinger. 'Bill' began moving towards the door again.

'What do I do? Shoot it out?'

'You keep your handsome face out of view and count faces, marking down in your little book any new ones—or nice cosy, well-documented finger-pointed old ones from back home. Morelli will probably be in charge, or even Cordellese himself . . . No, not Cordellese. He may wait in for a telephone call.'

''Bye,' said the young man; his eyes, which were a translucent green, the colour of deep water against a pale sea bed, smiled at me in recognition. I was accepted, I belonged, I was almost a Federal Agent myself. He closed the door and I heard his feet going quickly down the stairs.

'You're quite right,' I heard myself saying to Mr Peaslake. 'He is handsome.'

'For God's sake,' he implored, 'never let on.'

'I certainly won't.'

'And now what?' He was frowning a little.

'Another five minutes, then I call them again. I think it's important to do exactly what I say I'm going to do, in things like this. It sets up an expectancy, nervous expectancy. Then you change to being unpredictable. It's very shaking.'

'Things like this . . . have there been many?'

'Not quite like this. "Bill"—what?'

'Cabot. Yes, actually a Cabot. Working for a living. Keeper in a snake farm would be safer and better paid. I want to say, Eve—if you don't mind our American trick of first names first—you may know what you're doing—deliberately sticking out your neck, but I'm not sure that I can okay it. Not unless I can figure some way of hiding you really safe, and—'

I stopped him there. I said that if I detected the slightest sign that he was making himself responsible for me, I should be off faster than the wind.

'I'm sorry,' I said, 'but I mean it. Also, you yourself made the point that the essence of their success is the respectable front they are working behind. They'll think twice about doing anything to spoil it—they'll try other ways of stopping me than—direct ones.'

'Maybe, maybe!' His retreat was hasty, and I feared that it was merely tactical and temporary.

'I wish,' I said, 'I didn't get hungry so often. I want my lunch. I want a large lunch.'

'There's nothing here,' he apologized. 'There's a *Trattoria* on the corner where I go sometimes.'

'Which means I shall have to find somewhere else.'

I caught sight of myself in a small mirror over the bookcase and shuddered, and wondered at Bill Cabot's friendliness before leaving just now, but it might well have been because he was leaving.

'They haven't spotted us yet,' Mr Peaslake was saying. 'They're so set they don't even look, knowing no one can touch them. But you're right we mustn't be linked up. Even if they haven't placed you yet, they know you.'

165

'Not looking like this.' I turned away from the reflection of the dankly hanging rat-tails.

'There's quite a difference,' he admitted.

'But not enough to rely on.' I knew I had to put up stronger defences against his inevitable desire to protect me, although he couldn't do much about it without risking his own anonymity. There were still three minutes to go.

'This Jakus Cicero—' I began.

'That was the best day's work that Law Enforcement ever did.'

'I'm sure it was. Of course you checked over all the people closely associated with him for someone who could have taken over from him?'

'Checked and rechecked. But he was always so deep in the background there could have been room for two or three aides sitting in there with him we need never have known about. Some first lieutenant ready to step into the captain's shoes when he'd gone. As I said before, there's the old Cicero technique as clear as daylight, and several of his original mob. Morelli and Cordellese, for instance. And a stuttering gorilla called Bogsie Hart.'

'Could it be Morelli himself?'

He shook his head.

'No, it's someone with a hell of a good brain. Morelli's a jumped-up hood who'll never be anything else even if he does wear dark neckties these days.'

'The universal principle of silk purses out of sows' ears.'

'Jakus recognized it. He kept the sows' ears as sows' ears. Mind you he began as one himself. Did plenty of the rough work, and even when he was silked up he wasn't above doing a killing himself—if the guy was big enough to rate the honour or Jakus needed it to consolidate. The big shots have to, sometimes.'

I asked how such a killing would do that.

'Stoked the fear that kept him on top. How long does King-Wolf last when some young Pretender finds his fangs are worn?'

I had seen that the jungle analogy was a good one even before there had been an expert Peaslake to illustrate it.

166

'And he had competitors?'

'Other King-Wolves looking for new hunting grounds for their packs.'

'Could one of *them* have taken over?'

'Not and kept the Jakus pattern, nor so many of the original pack. A new king from outside wouldn't have trusted them. He'd have imported his own.'

'The political necessity for a boss crook to do his own killing sometimes,' I said. 'Could that have arisen—recently?'

'You're shrewd,' he said. 'It wasn't in my mind until you told me about Miss Sawyer. The steward seemed small fry stuff, and Chester was killed in New York.' He looked at me sideways like a sparrow with its feathers fluffed out. 'You're thinking the late night passenger to the Channel port might have been King-Wolf himself. King-Wolf the Second. Could be, could be.'

'I was thinking,' I said, 'that if he'd only recently inherited from Jakus Cicero, he might have decided that the situation, whatever it was, would be an opportunity to "consolidate". To go all the way to England to kill a girl. It would be quite a risky, showy thing to do?'

'I'm ahead of you,' Mr Peaslake replied. 'And now what have you done? Made the risk worse for him and the "show" part of it can go on for a long time without a curtain—if you'll excuse all the metaphors.'

In short, although neither of us said it, the new man's political necessity to kill again was now more urgent than ever.

'I'm glad you agree with me,' I said.

'I agree with you,' Mr Peaslake was frowning again, 'but I can't say I like it.' I was glad to see that he didn't know what to do about it. The ten minutes was now up and I dialled the 'Bernardino' number. Mr Peaslake went to the extension in the bedroom.

From the minutes it took to get through to Cordellese and again the wait while Berta was fetched to interpret, it was satisfactory to deduce that he had been confident his messengers would not fail a second time to find me at the hotel.

The more shocked and angry he was, the better, and he sounded both when he repeated my name.

'Tell Signor Cordellese,' I said to the girl, 'that I have positive information *Norse Girl* is on "Bernardino's" books.'

He took several seconds to work out the reply which the girl ultimately gave me. Yes, it had just this moment been established that this was so. But it was remarkable that Signorina Gill should have found it out in no less time—without the benefit of internal information.

'Who says I didn't have that benefit?' I asked, and Mr Peaslake nodded approval at me through the doorway. 'A firm like "Bernardino",' I added, 'has a lot of employees. Most of them underpaid.'

'No!' She choked on it. 'No! He will think—think that—'

'That *you* told me? Then tell him that I said it's common knowledge that *Norse Girl* is at Portofino.'

I heard her translate this, and the man's ready swearing. He recovered himself but spoke loudly enough for the mouthpiece she was holding to pick it up.

'Tell the *vacca* that my representative is on his way to her now—that everything has been arranged!'

She relayed this to me, but without calling me a cow.

'I'm glad to hear it,' I said, 'but if he doesn't show up in the next few minutes, I shan't be here. I'm going out to lunch.' And I rang off, Mr Peaslake putting down his receiver simultaneously as before. I said it seemed odd, if Cordellese was one of the original Jakus Cicero lot, that he had no English.

'He's one of Jakus's home-town pals from Palermo. He's never been to the States as far as we know. They've made him responsible for security here on the assumption that it is only a local consideration. You're showing them it isn't. I think he's likely to lose the job.'

I picked up the scarf and tied it over my head, found my handbag.

He protested at these signs of departure.

'I'm doing what I said—going out to lunch.'

'You'll be right back, afterwards?'

'I can't say exactly when I'll be back.'

'I don't like—'

'You worry about "Bernardino",' I said. 'I'll keep up the

smoke, you watch the buzzing. There'll be more. After lunch I'm going to have heard about Angela. My suspicions will become specific.' I was at the door. So was he, trying to block my way.

'But if I want you in a hurry,' he fought on.

'It's more likely I'll want *you* in a hurry.'

'You haven't even got the phone number—'

'But I have. It's on the dial.'

He gave up, shaking his head, stood aside and—

'If you were Scotland Yard, like I hoped at first,' he said, 'cooperation with us would come before a private war.'

I chose one of the small semi-underground restaurants on the edge of the *Calata Callaneo*. My hunger turned out to have been a genuine one. I filled myself with *osso buco* after *datteri marinare*, and put a *zabaglione* on top for good measure; it was not as good as the kind I made myself, but it was fair enough.

I went slowly in a somnolent daze into *via Santa Madre*'s airless crevasse and climbed the smelly stairs to my lair. The fat proprietor was in such a deep siesta, his head on the desk, that he did not hear me pass him.

I locked the door, opened the window, pulled the shutters together, took off my shoes and the frock for which I felt nothing but gratitude, forgiving it all its drabness, and resisted a strong impulse to brush some attractiveness back into my hair. The less I interfered with it, the more effective remained its disguise. I transferred the pistol from my handbag to under the pillow, knowing that the 'Bernardino' search for me was by now widening and increasing in earnestness with every passing minute.

All the same I must sleep a little, for a short half-hour at least, and I lay down on the bed which had seldom, I felt, been used for such a purpose. Nevertheless it welcomed me with its best comfort and I slept for a solid, undreaming two hours, drugged by food and heat and legitimate exhaustion.

I awoke thick-tongued, headachy and full of self-condemnation. It was more than three hours since Cordellese had last heard my voice, the voice which must drive him and his masters into a frenzy of impatient uncertainty, and that was too long, particularly if, as I calculated, the London papers of Sunday and Monday's *Daily Mail* had reached the local bookstalls.

I took a deep breath of resolve and washed my face in the water from the toilet table pitcher and an even deeper one before rinsing out my mouth with that in the carafe.

Slightly refreshed, I dressed, put the pistol back in my handbag and went down the stairs. The fat man was also awake now; he nodded at me with a yawn and I slipped into the concealing stream of people climbing the hill to *Piazza di Ferrari*. I was about to ask for a *Daily Mail* when I was saved the thirty-five lire and the slight risk of being seen with an English paper by catching sight of a copy of it folded in the rack between the *Corriere* and *Il Populo*.

Angela's name came out at me from the right-hand headline.

I turned away quickly and made for the nearest *Telefono* sign, which was hanging outside a man's hat shop. I bought some *gettone* from the assistant and shut myself in the box. I called Mr Peaslake first. Bill Cabot answered. John was out, he said, but he had left instructions that I must be held on to the moment I reappeared. Bill Cabot had a wheedling note in his voice by which in other circumstances I should have been delighted, up to a point, of course, to be wheedled.

'This is not reappearing,' I told him. 'This is asking if anything has happened.'

'Plenty,' he said. 'You come on over and I'll tell you about it. John says I should have seen you in some yellow outfit he's crazy on. Maybe you're wearing it now.'

'It's in the wardrobe of room forty-four at the *Savoie*,' I said. 'I'd be very grateful if you could pick it up and look after it for me. There's a hat too. But I was wearing it this morning as a kind of bull-fighter's cloak. It still is one, even if I'm not in it. You'd have to fetch it without being seen—and followed.'

'It's important?'

'Yes.'

'I'll do what I can.'

'They're still waiting for me?'

'Until half an hour ago they were at every door, back, front and side; in the lobby, leaning up against the telephone booths and riding the elevators till their stomachs must have been sore. I've got two more names in my little book and a sight of another guy I feel I ought to know but don't . . . My, what haven't you done to them! John has just left to go see the Capo to get some collateral action.'

I was alarmed.

'What sort of collateral action?'

'He thinks he'd like to have Morelli in the cooler—he's wanted for murder in Culver City or some place. John wants to make a test case of it to see how the extradition system comes off in these parts. Also he thought a move like that would increase the heat you've turned on—from another quarter as it were.'

I thought for a moment.

'Morelli was with the others who came looking for me?'

'He was.'

'What time did he arrive?'

'Twelve thirty-eight.'

'Where did he go?'

'Straight up to your room, knocked on the door, then opened it with a master key. He was in there about three minutes.'

'All right,' I said. 'I agree with Mr Peaslake but I think the heat—and smoke—should continue to come mostly from me.'

'John wasn't going to figure personally. Our security must have absolute priority if we're to go on working.'

'All right,' I said again. 'I think I know what to do.'

'I bet you do. You married?' he asked.

'No, and—if you'll excuse me, I must go now.'

'Going to be?'

This was an inappropriate subject but I said: 'One day.'

'But not got a ring yet?'

'Not yet.' I wished I could feel as light-hearted as I sounded.

'Get you one first thing,' he said. 'Come on over.'

'I'm too busy to leave here for a while,' I said.

'Where's *here*?' His tone was urgent.

'I'll call you again,' I said, and hung up.

It seemed to me that I could use this Morelli development as a further build-up of tension and save up Angela for next time.

The priority with which I was now given rights of connection when I asked the 'Bernardino' switchboard for Signor Cordellese was very encouraging. I had a pleasing picture of the whole organization waiting on tip-toe for my call while I was sleeping through the hot afternoon.

But I was not put through to Cordellese. Instead I was met by an American with an uneducated roughness in his voice unnaturally softened by a slight stutter.

'Y-you Gill?' it said. 'What the h-hell's bin keepin' you?'

'I asked to speak to Mr Cordellese,' I said, 'and I don't care for bad language.'

I heard him grunt.

'Mr Cordellese ain't here. I'm dealin' with the c-case.'

'And who are you?' I demanded. Who, indeed? *The* one? Couldn't be. Not yet.

'Th-that's not important. Let's get to business, lady. We bin expectin' you'd call b-back before this.'

'I am so sorry,' I said sweetly. 'But something happened to delay me. A sneak-thief got into my hotel room this morning. These police here are *so* slow. And *so* many photographs in their files. But he's been identified and they're quite positive they know who he is—in fact they've probably caught him already.'

'Well can you beat it! But now, let's you and me talk turkey, Miss Gill. About this diary you say your friend—'

'A nasty-looking little squirt of a man,' I went on, 'who is wanted in America for all sorts of crimes.'

'Is that s-so?' He was abruptly aware of what I was saying.

'And the strange thing is, they've a notion he's employed by your firm. I don't like to think so myself, because it would mean something very funny indeed is going on, wouldn't it? His name seems to be "Morelli".'

172

'Morelli? No one here of that n-name—'

'You mean if he's a crook, he'd be using a false name?'

'That's s-so, indeed.'

'But I don't think he is,' I changed my tone abruptly. 'You people know perfectly well who he is! You sent him over to my hotel to see what he could find out about me—if not worse!'

'For land's sake, Miss G-Gill!'

'Furthermore, I think you've found the diary and discovered something in it of concern—great concern to someone in your firm!'

'That's im-m-impossible!'

'Is it? If you have men like Morelli there, who else mayn't you have of the same kind and more so.'

His stutter increased.

'Th-that's-a-a-a l-libellous s-statement! This c-corporation's bin here a hundred y-years!'

'With the same personnel?' I asked.

'L-look now, Miss G-Gill—I can c-clear this up r-right away.' I could see him wiping perspiration from his face. 'You come an' see us, or w-we—I'll m-meet you any place you say—*n-now*.'

'I can't do that,' I said, 'until I've spoken to Miss Sawyer. I've put through a call. I must ask her what she wants me to do about this. After all, it's her affair.'

He started to say something, stopped and pulled himself together. 'You w-want to call me—I'll be here—' he said. 'W-waiting.'

But he might well be the only one of them who would be. The others, to a man, would be out hunting again, and Cordellese as one of the few who had actually seen me, most actively.

I went quickly back to *via Santa Madre*, locked myself in my room and lying on the bed—there was nowhere to sit, even if there had been room for a chair—waited for the light thrown by the slatted shutters in golden bars on the wall to dim and vanish.

I pressed Mr Peaslake's bell and waited impatiently. It had

been a nervy journey from *via Santa Madre* although I had followed the uneven in-and-out of the harbour line all the way as being an unlikely quarter for Cordellese to be covering except thinly. Also I had had to spend time doing what I could to make sure this apartment was in fact not 'blown', or that if it was, the greater priority of finding me had called for every man they had, including any routine watch they might be keeping on less immediate dangers.

I rang the bell again with a long pressure on the button. Why I should have imagined with such certainty that one of them would be in . . . I tried the handle again, but it did not yield as it had this morning, when Angelo had been expected back with the mail. Probably they used a signal amongst themselves which . . .

The door opened, and Bill Cabot stood there. He opened it wider.

'Thank God!' he said as though he had never expected to see me again and I went past him into the living-room looking for Mr Peaslake. 'John's still down at the *Questura*—' He followed me into the room. 'The Morelli play looks like being a flop.'

'Does it?' But I could not bring myself to care, not for the moment. Indeed the sight of an open dress box containing my yellow suit neatly folded, with the small hat at one end, seemed far more important. I took out the suit, asking Bill Cabot if he could find me a hanger. 'I was just going to look for one,' he said, a little aggrieved, as though I had accused him of negligence.

'I am most grateful,' I told him.

'Don't give it a thought.'

'But I *do*. It's my very best suit. And it's useful to know it's where I can get at it easily.'

He brought a hanger from the bedroom, took the suit from me and arranged it expertly on the hanger, looking for and finding the loops inside the waist of the skirt as if lady's maiding was his second profession.

'You know,' I said, 'I had put you down as unmarried.'

'Don't cross me off. I'm not married.' As he saw the point, he laughed, but without bravado. 'That doesn't mean I have led an entirely sheltered life.' He carried the suit on its hanger into the bedroom, and I followed him with the hat.

'When Mr Peaslake and the policemen from the Eighth Precinct shot Jakus Cicero off Pier Thirteen,' I said, 'did they recover the body?'

His arm, half raised to hang the suit in the wardrobe, froze momentarily, then completed its action. He took the hat from me, put it on the shelf, closed the wardrobe and turned to look at me.

'You switch subjects uncommon fast.'

'Did they?' I repeated.

He paused, but very briefly.

'They did.'

'You hesitated?'

'Because it wasn't for the best part of three weeks before it showed. There's quite a tide, with contrary undercurrents and so on.'

'Oh—' But I kept after it, this beautiful answer. 'It was identified?'

'Yep.' He continued to look at me. 'You've a thought, have you?'

'I have. And there was no doubt at all in the identification?'

'None.'

I tried to see into his mind, to see to what extent the thought was meeting suspicions of his own, however new.

'There was a wallet in the pocket of his jacket, with at least three bits of paper in it which could only have been in *his* wallet, and a driving licence in his name.'

I seized on this.

'You mean he wasn't identified by his—by the features?'

'Three weeks in the water, bumping around. No.'

'Fingerprints?'

He shook his head slowly and I could see the dawning in his eyes of something which although far from enthusiasm for a fresh belief might be slight doubt about an old one.

'No fingerprints,' he said. 'But then Jakus Cicero didn't have any—had them removed by plastic surgery, quite early in his career. For business reasons.'

'Where *is* Mr Peaslake?' I was impatient now in an urge to settle this—this possibility. Yes, it had reached that. Possibility. A wallet in a jacket pocket of a fingerprintless corpse unrecognizable after three weeks' buffeting in a tidal harbour.

'That three weeks' interval,' I pursued. 'Didn't that seem exceptional?'

'It can't have,' he said, 'though I must say it does now —now that you . . .' He made an effort not to believe what he wanted to believe, and which would fit into the present picture so very well. 'It doesn't make sense. There must have been a dozen bullets in him at that range!'

'What was the range?'

'I'm not sure, but—look, I wasn't on the case.'

'Suppose there were only two or three in him, and not in dangerous places?'

He shook his head. There had been expert pistol shots amongst those boys.

'It was night, wasn't it? And *Norse Girl* was there. Mr Peaslake said so. He also said that she was close enough for Gordon Chester to have heard the shots. He would have known what they meant.'

'I don't see—' Bill Cabot struggled with it.

'But you do,' I chased after him. 'You see, as I do, that it would be the sort of secret, perhaps the only secret, which would *have* to be kept. At all costs—up to murder. And at a moment when it was vital for him to re-establish himself with his organization—his transplanted organization.'

Bill Cabot sat down but went on looking at me.

'You'd sell a refrigerator to an Eskimo.' He glanced at his watch. 'But you'll never this side of Paradise sell this to John Peaslake. Never.'

'Who, outside the organization, knew the secret?' I demanded. 'I'll tell you. Gordon Chester, the steward Zolski, and by some accident, Angela Sawyer. Suppose she wandered into the wrong cabin, and found someone she didn't know was aboard—whom no one knew was aboard?'

'Go on,' he said, 'why not add that it was someone with his arm all bandaged up and maybe a leg.'

176

'All right,' I agreed. 'Add that. And that in an unguarded moment, Gordon Chester used that someone's real name. Oh, it could have happened in a dozen ways! Jakus Cicero was on the ship and so was she.'

'If Chester had that sort of cargo, why go all social and have girls aboard?'

'Could have been an effort to act as if he hadn't—and it backfired on him.'

He got up and came close to me; he was taller than I had realized. He put a hand under my chin, tilted my head upwards and stared into my eyes. It made me feel a little silly, as though I were a child who had just demanded of a grown-up to be reassured that fairies, of course, existed.

'You certainly don't pull your punches, do you?' He spoke slowly. 'We'll see what John says about it. He has a way of making guesses look awfully foolish.' He released my chin and I moved away.

'I can't help that,' I said. 'I shall still have a feeling that the man who must do something about this himself—as he did before—is Jakus Cicero.'

'You mean about you?'

'Could be.'

There was a moment's silence, then he became suddenly active, reaching for his jacket and saying:

'You stay here? I'm fetching John! I want to hear you argued out of this crazy notion.'

'Why not call him up?'

'And let the *Questura* telephone monitors know we've gone nuts?'

He muttered 'Jakus Cicero!' under his breath as he made for the door. I reached it at the same time to ask him what the chances were of successful extradition if the guess turned out to be right. He paused and shook his head.

'Slim—assuming we could persuade them to arrest him in the first place. But Washington would go to town on it.'

'It would be different in England?' I suggested.

'And on the moon—if we were there.'

He added that he would be right back with John, and

repeated his injunction that I must not stir out of here. 'Promise, eh?'

I promised, and he went down the stairs.

But it was a promise I could not and did not keep. It was not my fault. The telephone began to ring.

I hesitated before answering it but was decided by realizing that Bill Cabot was supposed to be here, holding the fort, and but for me would be still doing so.

I picked up the receiver and as much by instinct as the effect of environment, used the customary Italian, '*Pronto!*' instead of an English equivalent. I nearly dropped the instrument.

Christopher's voice was immediately recognizable through the mush of background noise.

'Mr Peaslake?'

'*Pronto?*' I said again, in a squeak which I was not putting on.

'*Vorrei parlare col* Signor Peaslake,' he said slowly with a painful English accent.

'Signor Peaslake *e uscita*,' I told him, now squeaking deliberately in disguise. '*Il Signore ritornera a casa fra un' mezz'ora. Chi parla?*'

'Half an hour? *Grazie.*'

'*Chi parla?*' I asked again.

'*Non fa niente . . . grazie.*' He rang off.

I put down the receiver slowly, telling myself with extreme firmness that this was not a moment to lose my head but to use it, use it sensibly, coolly, and to effect.

But I was finding that the possibility of Christopher's arrival on the scene had been as nothing to the fact of it, now that I had to face it. Christopher . . . My mouth was drier than even after that fifth pastry this morning . . .

Time had suddenly run out on me . . .

I looked at my watch. Nearly eight o'clock . . .

Could I assume that the firm of 'Bernardino' was on overtime tonight, those members of it who had fallen down on the priority job of finding a girl in a yellow suit? Had someone banged his fist on a desk and decreed that there must be no pause in the search, day *and* night?

I had given that someone enough cause, hadn't I?

And was this the moment, premature and forced on me though it was, to burn my boats?

It looked like it.

'All right,' I said aloud. 'Let's get on with it.'

I went quickly into the bedroom and set about my hair with Mr Peaslake's brushes, furiously, grudging the minutes even on this, now that I had made the decision . . .

As for the Field-Marshal, that master of campaigns, that snake in the grass, he must have ordered Christopher out here at least twenty-four hours before sending me that cable asking for my views on such a step! And what was more, he had played my hand rather than George's, believing that Christopher would do better in Genoa than in Cannes. My reply, my unnecessary reply, with its news of Chester's death must have done a great deal to guide him to that decision.

What else *could* I do but burn my boats?

I changed into the yellow suit, put on the grey feather hat and flung into the wardrobe the black frock with its cloying smell of the '*Albergo*'; I ran out of the apartment and down into the street.

The courtyard gates of the house in *via Gambino* were still open and lights showed in several windows on the first floor. But the big black door under the portico was shut; its huge iron studs, close-set except where a barred and shuttered peephole at eye-level in the centre interrupted their even ranks, added to its air of bristling impregnability. A modern bell-push, a white spot in the centre of a circular brass plate in the stone beside it, seemed a feeble means of getting it open, but since it was the only likely one I used it. The very smallness of the act of pressing it increased my sense of finality. This touch of my finger must set in motion an inevitable chain of cause and effect which could bring about only one of two results in the end; either the destruction of the man who sheltered behind the strength of this door and the violence of his evil, or my own.

The sudden slight rattle at the peephole was like an explosion to my waiting ears.

There was a glimmer of a face beyond the grille, and a pair of eyes. I mustered all my wits.

'*Ch-chi è?*' came out through the bars in a thick stutter.

'Good evening,' I said.

'Who the h-hell—'

'Gill is the name.'

Bolts thudded back and hinges creaked. The door opened a quarter of its way. There was no light in the foyer beyond it.

'C-come right in, Miss Gill. We bin w-waitin' for you.' He had heavy shoulders, not much neck and a smaller head than one would expect. His face in the half-light was difficult to see in detail. 'C-come right in,' he repeated hospitably.

'I haven't time,' I said. 'I've only called to leave a message. I have a taxi waiting.'

A thick arm came out of the dark bulk of his body and at the end of it a grasping hand from which I stepped back a pace. I affected not to have seen it or understood its purpose.

'I'm not coming in. I don't think it would be wise. Not after what has happened to Miss Sawyer. I happen to have seen the papers.'

The door opened wider and the lumpy figure came closer, both arms curving towards me.

'No!' I said, moving backwards. 'I'm in a hurry. I want something done about this business, but it's no good trying here. I don't trust those policemen. I prefer our kind. Anyway, the whole thing will take a bit of thinking over. I'm going back to England right away—tell Jakus Cicero that, please.'

'Tell—*what did you say?*' He stopped as if something had hit him between the eyes.

'Of course, it's giving him time to run away,' I went on, 'but he wouldn't get very far. Once our people began to go after him.'

His movement towards me quickened. I lifted my hand and let him see the pistol in it. He stopped, gaping at me.

'Wh-who are you—?'

'You know who I am. I'm just a girl who thinks there may be another story behind the murder of a friend.'

'You come in here—wid a r-rod—'

'Rod? Oh, you mean this? You can buy these across the counter in Italy, like a hat or a pair of shoes. Don't *move*! I've been shown how to work it—' I began to walk backwards away from the door— 'Don't forget to tell Mr Cicero everything I said. And how glad I am I found Mr Chester's yacht at Portofino *yesterday*, before ever I came near this nest of crooks and murderers . . . No, Bogsie, *no!*'

I put a bullet into the door six inches to his right as he started forward towards me. He stopped again, and even in the dim light I could see his consternation, but whether at my shot or my knowledge of his nickname, I could not tell. As the sound of the pistol echoed and re-echoed round the courtyard, I cried out that I hadn't known it went off as easily as that! And hastily I put the Neptune centrepiece between me and the door and the lighted first-floor windows above it. I did not think they would be able to see me from them, even in the yellow suit. The statue was between Bogsie and myself and it was only ten yards or so to the gateway. I turned and ran like a hare for it, and got through it and round the corner of the arch without anything worse happening than a shouted question from one of the windows. The essence of attack is surprise. But again it would be a matter of only that small half-jump ahead of them.

I had warned the cab-driver I should possibly be in a hurry when I returned, and he had his motor running. If he had heard the shot over the noise of it—to the extent that the sound could have escaped the confining walls of the building—he must have attributed a less dramatic cause for it. We started off without comment from him.

I had paid him off and within something under three minutes of my farewell to 'Bernardino' I was in welcome sight of the car, which I had left at the corner of *via Gambino* and *piazza Volterra*.

But a great deal of the welcome of it vanished when I saw that a man was standing on the sidewalk looking at the car with his hat pushed back from his straight and altogether too clever forehead. He was tall, but not as tall as Bill Cabot, and his suit was grey, not tan, like Mr Peaslake's, and his

181

name was neither Cabot nor Peaslake. It was Christopher Smith.

Fortunately his back was half-turned to me, for it was another two yards before my shocked brain could call upon my feet to stop in a slithering stumble. I side-stepped hastily into the nearest doorway.

Until this moment things had been moving according to plan. My timing of the length of twilight had been accurate; the darkness in which I hoped to leave the city had fallen during the last fifteen minutes or so. But I had not been very clever in choosing that particular spot to park, under the brightest street lamp in Genoa, or so it looked to me, staring in horror at the slender figure standing under it within a foot of my means of departure.

He stood there without a sign of any decision to leave. I watched him light a cigarette and put his hands in his pockets to consider the situation. I could hear his thoughts as though he were shouting them aloud.

He merely had to wait until I turned up if he wanted to make contact with me. If he wanted—and it was abundantly obvious that he did want. The mere fact that he had recognized the car proved it, proved that the Field-Marshal had deserted me.

He must have told Christopher the whole story of my share in this business even to a description of the Bristol.

But the seconds were becoming minutes and the minutes would see the completion of every effort to prevent my leaving Genoa. The platform, for instance, at which the Rome–Calais express would pause on its northward run must already be crowding up with 'Bernardino' representatives, already smarting from frustration. Others would be deploying to guard the exit roads . . .

Christopher walked round the car, tried the door on the passenger side, found that it was not locked, opened it and got in. He closed the door with a gentle snap and all I could see of him was the slight glow of his cigarette.

That settled it.

I took a deep breath, summoned all my reserves, and walked at a normal pace to the driver's door and got in, affecting not to become aware of him until I was actually behind the wheel.

'Oh, hello!' I made it as casual as I could.

'Hello!' he said, with equal lack of emphasis.

I pressed the starter. He should have waited *outside* the car. I moved quickly into third gear, turned the corner, crossed the *Piazza* into *via XX Settembre* and went up it, making a poor show of smooth driving. I was lucky with the lights at the first crossing. The wide circle of the *Piazza di Ferrari* welcomed me at the top. Christopher maintained a relaxed and extremely irritating silence.

'Clever of you,' I said, 'picking out this car.'

'I happened to pass that way. They don't make so many Bristols that you would expect to see more than two or three in this part of Italy. And fewer than that with British number plates.' His tone was as empty of significance as his previous silence.

'And this particular colour,' he added.

I should be screaming hysterically if this went on for long.

'May I ask,' he inquired mildly, 'where we are going?'

I was glad to detect a faint uncertainty behind his casualness.

'Ah, of course!' I said. 'You must have been on your way to *via Gambino*.'

'I had half an hour to kill,' he admitted. 'I thought I'd take a look at the place. It seems to be of great interest to a number of people.'

He knew perfectly well that if I was not in fact wholly responsible for starting the great interest, I had had a considerable hand in it.'

'Yes,' I said, 'the FBI for instance—as of course you know.'

I caught his slight nod—and his lack of surprise. He might not have found Mr Peaslake yet but he had certainly been in touch with the Field-Marshal since he arrived here; only from my cable mentioning the FBI could anyone have been aware that I knew of the Bureau's interest.

What *hadn't* the Field-Marshal told him about my part in this? Precious little. It looked as though the only thing left to me was my basic plan and purpose. Nobody had taken that away from me—yet.

I found I was breathing more easily and the effort to drive tidily became less conscious. I had lost a point or two, but gained, momentarily, an important one.

Uncomfortable as it was for my heart, to be with Christopher like this, a near-stranger who would have been completely one but for the active dislike he felt towards me, it was emerging as a piece of good fortune; while he was sitting here by my side, he could not be talking to, or rather listening to Mr Peaslake and Bill Cabot, who would find him a ready ally in stopping what I was at this very moment in the midst of doing. But how long he would be content to sit here was another matter. I was beginning to realize he wanted something from me. I did not know what it might be but it could take him quite a while if I was careful.

The lights of the big ships in the New Port were bright below the wide road which led to the entrance of the *autostrada* for Turin and Milan. I put on a little speed. The toll-gate where I must stop to buy a ticket for the privilege of using the *autostrada* might be a danger in that Jakus Cicero's efficiency surely included some sort of control on what was the city's only main route northwards; transportation of illegal goods was part of 'Bernardino's' business and at least representation of a kind must be ready at hand at such a key point.

I wanted to get past it before they had time to reinforce it.

'May I ask again where we're going?' he said.

'Are you too busy to drive a little way with me? It's a lovely night.'

'I have to make one or two contacts fairly soon.'

'Mr Peaslake is having a session with the local chief of police. He may not be back for a while.'

'You are certainly in touch.'

'More than I want to be.'

'Really?'

I did not rise to the sarcasm, so little but noticeable, which I had never before met in him. But it was horrible to feel that I had put it there.

Oh God, I cried in my heart, *make him stop hating me!* Aloud and involuntarily I said: 'Damn the Field-Marshal!'

'Seconded,' he remarked, 'but I didn't think you felt like that about him.'

'Was he heavy-handed with you?' Sympathy swamped my futile attempt at the impersonal.

'No,' he said, surprised. 'How should he be?'

'Oh, then he—' I stopped abruptly.

'"Then he", what?' But I did not dare add anything.

'I realize,' he went on, 'that he may have had more to go on than merely your misguided efforts to find Angela was murdered for some other reason by some other person.'

'Thank you.'

'Sarcasm doesn't suit you.'

'Neither of us,' I muttered.

'What?'

'You were saying you thought he had more to go on.'

'I began to feel that a chap like that doesn't often go off at half-cock, and less so when he knows he is emotionally concerned. There has to be something more to it.'

Was this what he wanted from me, some piece of unrevealed evidence? Why hadn't he asked the Field-Marshal for it?

However, that would have to wait a moment; I had changed my mind about going out via Milan, Como and the Swiss route, not because I was afraid of what might be waiting for me at the toll-gate but because I realized suddenly that when I came to buy the *autostrada* ticket I would have to say how far I wanted to go on it. Not only would it sound a very long way to a man who was anxious 'to make one or two contacts fairly soon' in Genoa but it would also tell him that I was leaving in a hurry. I did not want him to ask me why.

I pulled the car back into the straight in the middle of a right-bearing turn towards the toll-gate. The swerve threw him against me, and for a moment his shoulder was hard against mine, and he put out an instinctive, steadying hand briefly on my knee.

'What happened?' His voice was startled.

'We were nearly in each other's arms.' But he chose, rightly, to ignore it and I explained that I had mistaken the road.

'The road to where?'

'If you're busy,' I said, moving my foot to the brake, 'you had better take a bus back into the town. I would take you myself but I'm in a hurry.'

'About what?'

'I think we agreed to go our own ways.'

'Surely only in the personal sense?'

Would I always say the wrong thing; never think clearly when I was with him? I said quickly that I was referring to the question to which he had one answer and I another.

'I have been ordered to investigate this other possibility. I need help from everybody.'

'Did he tell you to ask me for it?'

' "He"?'

'The Field-Marshal.'

'I keep saying—' he was less casual now— 'Lord Orme is not in a position to tell me what to do.'

This time I managed to keep a hold on my tongue.

. . . The Field-Marshal was not in a position to tell Christopher what to do?

I moved my foot back to the accelerator; the uneven cobbles of *via Giacomo Buranello* which would eventually become the coast road along the Italian Riviera made even the Bristol bounce noisily. I took a moment to reflect. When the surface improved a little I said:

'To have got here so soon on this "other possibility" you must have had orders from pretty high up.'

'High enough—an Assistant Commissioner by name of Wilson. Lowly detective-inspectors from borough divisions do not argue with such. They obey—and like it.'

'A man called Wilson said you were to ask *me* for help?'

'Oh, he'd been briefed by the Commissioner, I daresay, who had been got at by your Field-Marshal. And, of course, it wasn't said in so many words that I should get in touch with you. Only that you were here, in such and such a car, address probably one of the big hotels, and that you were a friend of Angela Sawyer's who knew a bit about the background. As if I didn't know that already. But it was a broad enough hint. Naturally I took it, and here I am, my pride swallowed, waiting for anything you care to tell me.'

I did not have to ask him which pride he had swallowed, private or professional; it would take more than a broad hint from an Assistant-Commissioner to make him have anything to do with me again as a young woman.

But there were compensations, particularly the clear indication that the Field-Marshal had steered a skilful course in getting his own way without causing me more hurt with Christopher. He had contrived not only to keep behind the scenes in forcing Christopher into an investigation in which he did not believe but also he had arranged things so that it was left to me to choose how little or how much Christopher should learn of my share in turning the fight against him.

Finally the Field-Marshal had not allowed him to discover who was to succeed the retiring Commissioner.

'I think I've managed,' Christopher was saying, 'to get myself back to something near an open mind, helped considerably by a bogey on which the AC based his view that we should take a look at this, the worst bogey in a policeman's bad dreams—Wrongful Arrest.'

'A bogey,' I said, 'which has been haunting me too.'

'*You* don't arrest people.'

'But you do.'

He gave me a quick sideways glance, and then looked ahead again.

'Interfering in a man's career,' I added, 'is a reprehensible thing in anyone. In a woman, unforgivable. You can't tell me that more emphatically than I tell myself.'

I did not really expect him to say anything to that and he did not.

'I'll try to help you, of course,' I said.

'Thank you. Shall we stop—is that a café we're coming to?' On firmer ground his tone was brisk and confidently objective.

'But I was going on to say—' I drove past the café—'that there is really nothing I can tell you about the London end you don't already know, except—and it makes no difference that I can see—the story of what happened in the house in Pawley Street, Shope's sort of home. The truth is, it didn't reach the Field-Marshal from Turnbull, as he let you think, but from me.'

'You!' The briskness was more pronounced but the objectivity less confident. 'That means you had just come from Pawley Road when I ran into you fetching your bag!'

'And I didn't go to Aunt Florence's for the night as I allowed you to believe, but to Grosvenor Square. Also I was there earlier in the evening. When you were seeing Douglas in the library I was upstairs.'

'Douglas—' he muttered.

'The Field-Marshal if you prefer it—'

'I don't care to prefer him by any name. Go on. You were the dear little nigger in the woodpile all through! Tell me more.'

'And the dear little nigger listened in to your conversation on the intercom, and hid under the stairs when you left, so that she could follow Shope to Camden Town, and so see his near-kidnapping by Sammy, meet Mizzie, find the "Bernardino" card on Shope's mantelpiece, take it back to the Field-Marshal and one way and another try to destroy your case against Arthur North. By the way, how is Arthur North?'

He did not reply and I felt rather than saw the bitter set of his mouth. Dear little nigger . . . how he loathed her.

'And what's been going on here?' he asked finally. I pulled myself together.

'John Peaslake is up-to-date on that part of it.'

'He's fortunate in having your confidence.'

'*How* could I argue with you?' I flared at him. 'You had made up your obstinate mind!'

'The evidence did that. But let's not get heated—'

'I'm not heated!'

'No,' he said, his tone infinitely distant. 'I beg your pardon.'

There was a moment's silence. A signpost in front of me read, 'Sestri, Savona, Ventimiglia'. There was a bus stop just beyond it the other side of the road with two or three people standing at it. I slowed down.

'So I'm to refer to Peaslake for further information?' he said.

'He has a fuller picture than I can give you.'

'The dull police mind is not untuned at times to the more subtle nuances of atmosphere,' he said a little pompously. 'There's a feeling in the air of something having happened. If you can spare a moment to satisfy my professional needs —if it's something important—'

'Important? Yes, I think so. The name "Jakus Cicero" has come up.'

'Jakus Cicero?' There was surprise in his voice. 'He's dead—been dead these three months.'

'That's what John Peaslake wants to believe. But there's a young man called Cabot working with him who may be in doubt about it. He's very good-looking but don't let that prejudice you.'

I drew up opposite the bus stop and waited for him to get out. He did not immediately do so, pausing to light another cigarette.

'Jakus Cicero was one of the most successful and dangerous criminals of this half century,' he said. 'The New York and Kansas City police gave celebration dinners and I think Peaslake was the name of one of the FBI people who got a medal.'

He opened the door and closed it, keeping his hand on it.

'I'll call you at the *Savoie* in the morning.'

'That reminds me,' I said, 'I should be very grateful if you could collect a suitcase of mine there—and a small hat box. The room is paid for until Saturday.'

'Oh,' he said and his eyes were sharply on me, trying to see my face in the darkness of the car. 'What do I do with the suitcase and the hat box?'

'Bring them back to London with you—if it's not too much trouble. I'll pick them up sometime from the porter at Terry House. In accordance with custom.'

'You must have good reasons for not collecting them from the hotel yourself.'

'Good enough reasons.'

'Don't let me frighten you away.'

'My courage is not what it was.'

'I don't awfully like you,' he said quietly, 'but I won't eat you.'

'And I hate you,' I replied with the same serenity, 'but in point of fact I was thinking of Jakus Cicero.'

'But he—'

'I know. They've had celebration dinners. I think they were premature. Goodbye, Christopher.'

'I don't understand,' he said and for a moment he seemed to have forgotten to be distant.

'It's probably better that you shouldn't,' I told him and let in the clutch.

In the driving mirror I saw him move a pace towards the people waiting under the street lamp at the bus stop but he changed his mind at the sight of a private car travelling citywards; he stood firmly in the middle of the road and flagged it. It stopped, he spoke briefly to the driver, and got into it. He had not once looked back.

So that was that . . .

I came down firmly on the accelerator. Through my tears I could just see the dashboard clock . . . Twelve minutes to ten. The road would now edge the sea all the way, endlessly cornering the high hills which came steeply down to it and adding driving time to the journey. But I could expect to cross the frontier into France at about two o'clock; I might, of course, pause for a few hours' sleep at San Remo but although national boundaries meant little to the 'Bernardino' people, there would be comfort, however spurious, in knowing that once I was the other side of Ventimiglia I should be out of Italy. The possibility, however, that I would collapse before I could make it seemed likely.

As it turned out, however, I seemed to gain strength as Genoa receded, and although it was nearer half-past two when I passed through the Customs at the border and three by the time I drove down the empty main street of Mentone, with the sky behind me already light with the coming day, I was still reasonably fresh.

The night porter at the small *Hôtel des Palmes* found a room for me, and I undressed without the fumbling of real exhaustion. I sat up in bed and cleaned the pistol as best I could without the proper things; I replaced the used shell and put the weapon under my pillow. I was as sure as I could be of anything that I had not been followed, but that was no excuse to relax normal precautions.

My mind was active yet pleasantly detached for a moment.

I looked at the situation as it now was and thought that I could say I had succeeded in presenting Jakus Cicero with quite a convincing picture of a young woman whose little knowledge was a dangerous thing for him and whose high-handed behaviour was an insult to a man of his reputation, his precious and hard-won reputation. To this I could add a reasonable hope he would see in her a conceited belief that she could decide alone what to do about him. It would be assuring him he had time to deal with her. He would certainly have discovered where to find her, and easily.

When the clerk at the *Savoie* had asked me for my home address in order to fill in the *fiche*, I had taken the trouble to write it down myself in a bold and legible schoolgirl hand.

In short, I had shown Jakus Cicero a second Angela. My fright now was perhaps less than hers had been at this corresponding moment but only because where she had in ignorance fallen into peril, I had put myself in it deliberately.

I would not risk using the return ticket for the somewhat noticeable Le Touquet-Lympne air passage, but would go in by the longer and least convenient route for Suffolk, the Dunkirk-Newhaven auto-carrier. This would add nearly twelve hours to my journey, but I stood a good chance of not being seen by those who might be set to watch for me at the more obvious crossing places. Furthermore, to arrive *after* Jakus Cicero would put me at a slight advantage in that if he hurried to Kessingland, and I thought he would, and found that I had not arrived, he might begin to worry, and worrying lose the fine edge of his alertness.

In fact I would dawdle home. Saturday would be about the right day, first thing on Saturday. Sunday was the sort of day to begin trying to forget unpleasant things . . .

Unpleasant. Did one have to be half asleep to achieve such understatement?

CHAPTER 8

I found my Uncle Harvey Gill, Baronet, asleep under the blue azalea he had brought home when he returned in '33 from Tibet and the last of his famous explorations in that then mysterious country. At this time of year, however, there was no way of telling that the azalea was blue or by his present relaxed position flat on his back that Uncle Harvey had ever been more active than in supervising the mowing of the two acres of lawn, which like a smooth green lake surrounded the pale stone masses of Pakenhurst Grange.

The Bristol, dusty but discreet, stood in the drive the other side of the azalea thicket and out of sight of the house. Having made sure that the grass was dry and would not stain my already so ill-used yellow suit, I sat down close to my sleeping uncle, glad to be at rest on a substance as solid and stationary as the ground. I stretched my legs cautiously; I did not want to start badly by disturbing his siesta. Success —it was not much I was asking him to do—would depend on his keeping quiet about it, in other words, not telling his wife, whose distrust of my most innocent intentions was as constant as his own life-long feud with Father, his younger and only brother. His affection for me came perhaps from an uneasy conscience due to this feud, but it was undeniably genuine and certainly I reciprocated it.

The bees droned, a distant cuckoo stumbled in its late-season call, and the clock of Pakenhurst church struck four, slowly, as if careful not to wake the Squire. I watched his broad tropics-yellow face with its deep lines and thought how alike, apart from his colour, he was to Father and yet how different; they were brothers in nothing save blood.

After a moment, his eyes opened, focused gradually on me, then closed again.

'What does he want?' he asked.

'Nothing. It's me wanting something.'

He opened his eyes and smiled at me cordially.

'Grammar,' he said. 'What?'

'Uncle Harvey, you've heard of Lord Orme.'

'Who hasn't? But in point of fact we were at Harrow together and I met him later when I was Governor and he came out with some Military Mission or other. A big pot these days—or was. Retirement halves a man if it doesn't quarter him. Well?'

I told him what I wanted him to do. He listened without interruption. At the end—and it wasn't long, since I only went as far as was necessary in telling him that I was helping the police in something quite important—he asked if Father knew about it. I said he did not, naturally. He wouldn't approve at all. This pleased Uncle Harvey very much.

'All right,' he said. 'Glad to oblige. I suppose Orme really will know what I'm talking about?'

'He will. He knows all the rest of it.'

'Like to know it myself.'

'Not now. But you shall the moment it's possible. If you'll take it on trust for now?'

'Of course.' He sat up and looked at me more closely, shaking his head. 'I don't know how Rupert did it. Must have been almost entirely dear Margaret's work.'

My mother had died when I was a baby. There was a story that Uncle Harvey had come in second when the brothers ran the same race; it would account for the feud. But that had not been my fault, and he was a just man.

'Come on, then.'

He did not need to be reminded that Lady Gill would be best left in ignorance of my visit, and without further talk he led me by a roundabout route through shrubberies and a sunken garden to the stables.

He opened a door and I climbed a narrow wooden stair-way after him into the pigeon loft, where I had spent so many happy hours when I was a child. There were still a great many pigeons, and for all the difference I could see, they might have been their own ancestors.

Uncle Harvey talked to them for a minute or two and they talked back in a very friendly fashion, one of them perching on his shoulder with its soft head in his ear. He had saved himself and whole expeditions several times with his pigeons. Presently he said:

'I think John Bailey is the chap for you. He's in love with Pink-Eye Jennifer.'

'Could I—would it be possible to take two, in case of accidents?'

'What accidents?'

'Don't people shoot them sometimes, not knowing they're different from ordinary pigeons?'

He nodded, reluctant to admit it. 'The Prince Regent is in love with her too. Mutually stimulating, if they're away from her together.'

He took a small basket from a shelf and put two pigeons in it. I thought I recognized which was the Prince Regent; he had a high white stock round his neck, contrasting noticeably with his otherwise mauve-grey habit. John Bailey had a more plebeian look.

'How long before you'll use them?' Uncle Harvey asked.

I said I thought within twenty-four hours at the latest.

'In that case only a little water and a grain or two of corn.'

He gave me a handful of grain from a bin. 'Put it in your pocket.'

This reminded me of something else. I asked if Cousin James was at home but it seemed he wasn't; when last heard of he had been buying a Geiger-counter in Valparaiso before disappearing into the mountains with it. I explained about clothes—about Jacques Fath and how different were the purposes for which he had created this suit from those I was engaged upon. Said Uncle Harvey:

'She's playing bridge in the west wing, and James's rooms are the other end of the house. I expect we can manage it.'

He put the grain in an ex-mustard tin, jammed down the

lid firmly, put it in the basket with the two pigeons and as a final preparation, threw a switch by the side of the inner door of the trap; warning bells would tell him a pigeon had entered the trap, sounding simultaneously over his bed, in his study and loudly in the porch at the front of the house. They would persist until the door of the trap was opened.

We left the stables and by another and equally well-covered route he took me into the house by a side door and up to James's room.

Once again the yellow suit found itself hanging in a strange wardrobe. I equipped myself with a pair of well-worn jeans with a Texan maker's name in the waistband, a dark blue cotton sweater and a pair of black rubber soled shoes only half a size too big for me. I also borrowed a haversack, a flashlamp and field-glasses, small ones but powerful.

Five minutes later I backed to where I could turn the car without ruining lawn or flower-bed and with an encouraging wave to Uncle Harvey, set out for Kessingland fifty miles to the east.

But before reaching the open country of the coastal belt I turned north-east by small roads so that I could enter the final stage of my approach from the safer direction of Yarmouth, rather than by the trunk road from London by which normally I should arrive home.

Even so, I took the car no farther than a lock-up shed at the back of the Blue Boar at Swathling Parva, a little fishing village five miles up the coast from Kessingland and nearly six from Marsh House.

I chose the Boar rather than the Fox and Crown, remembering that it had recently changed hands and the new publican and his wife would not know me. They were friendly to a girl whose idea of a holiday was to tramp the country by herself, and after a meal of cold meat and salad the woman made me up a packet of sandwiches, hard-boiled eggs and oranges which I put in the haversack, which already contained the pistol with its spare clips and the field-glasses. I also added a few things I should need from my handbag, so that I could leave it in the car.

It was now half-past seven. I slung the haversack over my shoulder and, carrying the pigeon basket, slipped away by the back door into a lane leading to the marshes. If I kept the sea on my left and followed the main dyke I should soon come to familiar surroundings.

After an hour's walk, I saw a recognizable hillock which rose slightly above the marsh and knew that I was nearing our own land; away to the south I could just see the thin masthead of *Peacock* where she lay at her moorings in the backwater. The house itself was hidden by the higher ground projecting into the marshes which followed the outward curve of the intervening coast, but it was there, and I was almost home.

The sky was clear and therefore still full of daylight; dusk, however, was shadowing the earth and night would soon be upon it. But for my needs it must be fully come, so I found a patch of bracken still warm from the heat of the day, and lay down in it to sleep. I did not bother to set myself a time to wake knowing that the fall in temperature would ensure that I did, and at about the hour when I should be able to move without fear of being seen or heard if I moved carefully.

I sat up, a little stiff, my clothes damp with salty dew. The sky was black, the stars invisible and I knew the marsh mist had risen even above the little hill. I looked at my watch with the aid of the flashlamp and learned with satisfaction that it was nearly three o'clock. I had about an hour in hand before the false dawn would begin; it would not see anybody stirring although there was a remote chance that Father might wake up very early, as he so often did, and take it into his head to go for a walk in his wheelchair to get up an appetite for breakfast. But even so, that would not be before five o'clock and in fact nearer six.

I fished in the haversack for a sandwich, ate it, and smoked half a cigarette before making a move.

My eyes, always good at night vision, became accustomed to the darkness and I did not have to use the flashlamp once I had found the cart track which connected the Home

Farm with the Kessingland road and continued through the woods, which eventually thinned as the gardens of Marsh House began. I was making comfortable progress along it until I fell headlong over a sheep which had chosen the cool of that particular spot in which to spend the night. It grunted in that peeved way they have and crashed away noisily into the undergrowth. But my concern was for the pigeon basket, which jerked out of my hand and bounced and rolled away in front of me in the darkness. Horror-stricken I waited for the whirr of escaping wings. But the lid had held and I retrieved it thankfully. I whispered to the panicking inmates with an attempt at Uncle Harvey's cooing tones, but undeceived they continued to protest for a long minute.

Hereafter I would carry them even more carefully with arm bent and elbow flexing to every unevenness of movement. I started off again, at which they stopped scolding rather abruptly. Fearing they might be injured, I shone the flashlamp briefly through the small, barred airhole in the basket's side. Bright beads of eyes shone back at me, malevolent in their lack of expression. John Bailey and the Prince Regent might not care for me any more but our paths had crossed and they must necessarily put up with me while we were together. Like Christopher in Genoa . . .

I wondered later whether there might not have been an altogether different end to this business if I had not fallen over that sheep. Otherwise, should I have found the caravan hidden in the trees on the edge of this particular track?

Anyone else in the household coming on it would not have realized its significance, would have assumed reasonably that it was another example when permission to camp had not been sought, either from bad manners or more probably because the remoteness of these parts and the thinness of population suggested that to find the owner of the land would be as difficult as it was unnecessary. Their defence would have been simple and credible; they weren't doing any harm were they, either to crops or livestock, parking in a wood all this way from anywhere? And they would have been allowed to stay there, and the fact that they were no more innocent holiday caravanners than the

Field-Marshal had been an innocent bird-watcher would have been lost. Indeed, they were less so, for at least there had been a reed pheasant to support his claim, whereas from the conversation I now overheard, coming at me with a curious muffled quality from the pitch darkness of the trees, it was clear that these people were there for reasons which included neither right by law nor natural inclination.

It sounded as though they were talking in a cupboard with the door shut, an effect which puzzled me for a minute or so.

'I tell you,' said the woman, 'I *heard* it!'

'Damn you, I heard it too—' A man, and less assured than he would like her to think. 'Whatever it was, it's gone.'

'I *know* it was a wild cat! They have them in these places. I read in the paper! They're like tigers and leopards and things! For God's sake let's have the light on!'

I stood at the side of the track perhaps fifteen feet from a caravan which I could feel rather than see; also I could smell, very faintly, an oily, metally sort of smell as of a car, somewhere to the left of the voices.

A rectangle of light suddenly flashed into existence about six feet from the ground immediately in front of me; it was bright only because of the extreme darkness, actually a green curtain masked it but threw no shaft which would be visible at any distance.

'But why did you have to choose a *wood*?' the woman demanded.

'I told you. See without being seen.'

'I don't like any of this—I've liked it less and less, and now—'

'Don't start that again!' His tone was harsh.

'How do you know this will be the last time—how?'

'Because I know—'

'They found you again the very moment you were telling me you'd done with them! What's to stop them—ever? . . . *What was that?*'

'What was what, for crissake?'

'I heard something scratching at the steps!'

'Let it scratch. The door's shut.'

'This is driving me mad! Look—can't I stay in a pub somewhere and wait for you? *Please*—Sammy?'

That name, anxiously cried in the night, and with it recognition of the girl's voice—the shock was such that I was very glad I had put the pigeon basket on the ground; to have dropped it a second time would for a certainty have driven all memory of Pink-Eye Jennifer from the birds' minds.

'When I go from here,' he said heavily, 'I shan't have time to waste collecting you from some bloody pub.'

'Oh—this Jones!' said Mizzie, obscenely.

Jones! The same pattern . . .

I held my breath.

Mizzie began to bemoan her ill-luck. Nothing ever went right for her. On form, Sammy would not let her grizzle long before he hit her. I began to move quietly towards where the towing-car ought to be.

'Why don't you tell me the truth?' Mizzie demanded. 'What has he got on you?' The bedsprings creaked. 'Don't you trust me, darling?'

'No,' he said.

'Then why in hell did you bring me along!' Scratching came more easily to her than caresses.

'For company—I thought. And for dressing the stage—I'd hoped, but chiefly because I was a bloody fool!'

My hands found the car. I was tempted to use the flash-lamp but left it where it was in the leg pocket of my jeans. A medium-sized Standard? Its paintwork, snce there was no glimmer at all from it, was either black or dark blue. I explored for the number plate and was glad to find that it was die-stamped and readable with the fingertips, a simple combination of letters and numerals which I memorized.

Mizzie went on with her mixture of cajolery and complaint. Sammy told her that he'd take his belt to her in a minute. 'And I will too—d'you hear!'

'And so will the whole neighbourhood if you try any such crude thing!'

'Who's going to yell with her loud mouth full of sock!' He must have put his hand over her face for she began whining like an animal; the bedsprings twanged as she fought him.

'Will you stop getting at me!' he demanded, 'or do I have to give it to you?'

Apparently she surrendered, for when she finished gasping for breath, she did not speak.

In the meantime I had a better idea than remembering the car's number, and used the noise they were making to open the hood of the car. I groped for the distributor head, unclipped it, took out the rotor-arm and slipped it in my hip-pocket. I replaced the head and lowered the hood gently. They were now too quiet for me to risk pressing it down on its catch, so I left it unfastened. Sammy would not be suspicious of so small an irregularity and might only remember it after fruitless efforts to get the motor to run.

'Sammy—how long do you think it'll be?' Mizzie asked, timidly now.

He said it all depended. She did not ask him on what. Thus encouraged he told her.

'Like I said yesterday, on when she shows up. It won't be long after that.'

'I can't get it out of my mind she's the one that came that night.'

'So you've said before.'

'Does Jones think so?'

'Was I fool enough to tell him about her?' Sammy asked derisively. 'The way she walked in and out under my nose? You talk as if I was a dope like Shopie-boy.'

There was a pause.

'What'll he do to her?' Mizzie asked.

'I don't know and you don't know.'

'I'm only worried for you—if anything goes wrong.'

'With him it doesn't go wrong.'

'All the same—'

'Oh, for God's sake!'

She giggled unexpectedly. Sammy asked irritably, 'Now what?'

'I was thinking what it'll be like, having him in here with us.'

'What's going to be so funny about it?'

'Only one bed.'

This time he really hit her.

She cried out but it was neither loudly nor in anything but pleasurable pain.

'I was just having a game,' she said.

'As long as you play it with me—'

'Yes, darling.'

The light in the window went out, the bedsprings grumbled a little, and that seemed to be the end of it. I went carefully back to the track and the pigeon basket. It was satisfactory to have put the car out of action before hearing about Mr Jones's plan to use the caravan for his getaway; not only did it show my instincts were working properly but also it would have been difficult, in the restored quiet, to fidget about getting the hood open and so on without reawakening Mizzie's fear of noises in the night. Sammy might have beaten her again but he might also have been forced to investigate.

The rotor-arm dug knobbily into my right hip as I moved but I was happy to feel it there, knowing that practically any piece of an ignition system can be improvised, but not that one.

The final two hundred yards provided neither obstacle nor interest. I came to the edge of the east lawn as the first tinge of grey light made it just possible to distinguish the individual tiles of the roof. The wall of the house was still dark, however, and the french windows of the Long Room slightly darker squares in it. They would be open since Father slept there in his built-in bunk between the stone fireplace and the inner wall, his wheelchair, the hand-operated one, by his bedside.

I made a circuit of the lawn rather than risk a direct crossing of it; apart from the danger of waking him he would notice my footprints in the dew when presently he wheeled himself out to look at the day.

I passed through the archway into the courtyard on the south side of the house and kept close to the wall as I made for the coach-house. One of the windows of the kitchen quarters had been left slightly open for the in-and-out going of Mary's restless marmalade cat.

I felt under the stone by the main doors of the coach-house for the key of the small door beside them. I opened it, put back the key and went into the pitch darkness, easing the spring lock into its staple so that it should not click as I pulled the door shut after me.

Although it might have been safe to use the flashlamp now, I decided I did not need it, since the space where my Lagonda usually stood between Father's Daimler and Charlie's small Austin museum piece would be wide enough for me to cross to the spiral iron staircase in the far left-hand corner without error of direction.

I stepped out confidently—and caught my shin a violent blow on the fender of a car.

I smothered a cry of pain but the pigeons chirped crossly as I jerked to the shock.

I stood back, rubbing my shin furiously with my free hand; my first thought, when the worst agony subsided and allowed me to think at all, was that the repairers at Norwich had sent back the Lagonda sooner than they had promised. Then I felt very strongly that it was *not* the Lagonda; I got out the flashlamp. It was a car I had never seen before, a new Vauxhall. The place seemed to be alive with strange cars. I wondered angrily who could have chosen to visit us at this extremely inconvenient moment. I cursed them— him or her, or maybe a whole damned family—and made a quick examination.

The first thing I noticed was the sizeable plaque, a 'Drive Yourself' car-hire firm, screwed to the dash. This might explain why I had not recognized the car but it did nothing to identify the person or persons who had arrived in it. The glove compartment was empty and so were the side-pockets. A carelessly folded map of East Anglia lay on the back seat, but it looked as though it had been thrown rather than consulted there; also the carpet below it was clean whereas cigarette butts were scattered on the floor in front; those under the driver's seat were crushed but below the passenger seat they were more or less whole and none had lipstick on them. Added up, it looked as though there was only one unwelcome guest, a man—unless a woman who did not use make-up. All I could hope was that he or she was not one of Father's disreputable adventurer friends whom he had taken advantage of my absence to encourage. There was trouble enough without that.

I switched off the torch, rubbed my shin again, and feeling my way along the car reached the staircase and climbed up into the old hay loft. Here was a second staircase by which one came to a narrow attic with sharply sloping walls of which the floor was the open cemetery of a thousand million flies. Their dry corpses crunched like sand under my feet as I went gingerly across the uncertain boards with a hand outstretched for the small perpendicular ladder in the centre. I found it and putting down the basket made sure that it was steady in its ancient brackets. The narrow trap-door at the top was very stiff on its hinges and took all my strength to push it upwards.

I retrieved the pigeons, carried them up with me, lowered the trap-door and I was in the tiny compartment which housed the works of the coach-house clock. On three sides of the machinery there was an eighteen-inch space; passage along the fourth side was barred by the spindle of the hands protruding from the body of the clock to pierce the wooden wall behind the clock-face. The gentle whirring was a softer sound than in the old days before the clock was converted to electricity; but it was enough to obliterate most of any external noises I might otherwise have heard.

Its height above ground, however, outweighed this disadvantage; from here I should be able to see the house and three-quarters of its gardens, and also, most necessarily, the approaches to it both from heath and marsh. Even a portion of those from the north would be visible, although the woods masked most of them except here and there where the direction of the track by which I had come in happened to coincide with my line of sight.

Having made sure that the cracks and chinks in the elm weatherboarding allowed a sufficiency of spy-holes—for now rather than later was the time to enlarge them if I had to—I sat down with the pigeon basket at my feet and my back against the opposite side, a position which called for physical patience and narrow hips. As I lowered myself I felt the rotor-arm in my hip-pocket break into at least two pieces, which I took to be a good omen.

I unpacked the haversack, found places for the various things on the supporting battens of the clock and gave my mind to devising a way to get rid of Father's guest. Everything I could think of, however, entailed putting in an appearance on the scene, and the foolishness of that even in such a good cause was all too obvious. It looked as though the guest would have to take his chance with the rest of us when Mr Jones showed himself.

The day began as a thousand days before it.

At seven-fifteen Mary opened the back door on to the courtyard and put the old cannon-ball against it to prevent it swinging shut—the cannon-ball which had come through the west wall of the Long Room during Thomas Cromwell's priest-hunt and his local commander's visit to what he mistakenly thought was a monastery.

The marmalade cat appeared a moment later, stretched in the early sunshine and went in again. Over the sound of the clock I could hear occasionally the voices of Mary and the maids, the clatter of the stove being stoked. I thought I heard one of the dogs barking in the yard of the Home Farm. The last shreds of mist blew away in the light breeze.

At three minutes past eight Father in his pyjamas wheeled himself out of the Long Room, looked at the sky, crossed the lawn to the main rose-bed, inspected it, lit a cigarette, climbed out of the chair and bending stiffly on his wooden leg, blew smoke at the aphids for a moment or two, then threw the cigarette angrily at them and wheeled himself back into the house to dress.

The parlour maid, Ellen, one of the prettiest we had ever had, came out of the garden door with Father's breakfast table, opened it under his favourite cedar tree on the edge of the lawn, spread the white cloth and retired to emerge again a moment later pushing the trolley. She laid the table, the silver winking in the sun, put Father's *Times* on the side plate and returned to the house.

Father in a duck suit as white as his hair, which made his square face look rather redder than in fact it was, wheeled himself once again through the french windows and made for the breakfast table as Ellen brought out the coffee and bacon and eggs. She served him neatly, chatting away to him with fine unconcern for his uncertain temper at this hour. I had sometimes wondered at her temerity but it was now at least partially explained when she turned to go. Father was picking up *The Times* at that moment, but he was evidently on the alert for he reached out with the other hand and smacked her bottom. Her giggle was inaudible to me, but its existence was evident. She swung away with a flirt of her hips and went back to the house.

I was wondering what further if minor revelations in the daily and beloved routine of my home I should witness with this unique opportunity for observing it, when an unexpected one drove away all pleasure in it, leaving me breathless and infinitely alarmed.

A man came out of the garden door almost as Ellen entered it. He was carrying one of the folding wood-and-canvas chairs with one hand and had a cup and saucer in the other. For a short moment I had thought it was Charlie Berrington; there were the same very wide, heavily-built shoulders and the leaning-forward head, but he was shorter and his hair many shades darker, quite black in fact, and much smoother. Also, Charlie had not a light grey suit with a loose, long jacket.

. . . A black-haired man with a dark face, so dark that he might have Moorish blood in him . . . as Sicilians often have . . .

I pressed my forehead hard and hurtingly against the rough wood above the crack and shut my eyes tight against what I was seeing. But neither the pain nor the star-spattered darkness of closed lids could destroy the fact and truth of what I had seen.

Here was Jakus Cicero . . . sitting down with my Father as a guest with his host.

I had imagined several ways in which he might come to Marsh House; creeping across the heath in darkness, perhaps, to break into the house with expert skill and silence and seeking me out, or coming in disguise by daylight, hiding and watching, waiting for his opportunity. But this —this open arrival in a car which now stood in my Lagonda's space, this easy, casual friendly arrival—this was frighteningly different.

I dragged the pigeon basket close to the largest crack I could find in the weather boarding, opened the lid sufficiently to get my hand inside and grasped one of the birds firmly across its back to confine its wings while I pulled it out. I thrust it through the crack and it took off with a noisy flurry. I pushed the second one after it and the thing was done with only one peck at the base of my thumb, which was actually bleeding.

The two pigeons came together in a matter of seconds, and I watched them anxiously as they went in and out of my view, climbing in widening circles above the house and garden.

Then at the top of the fourth circle they turned as one bird, their under-wings flashing together, and flew westwards with a speed and purpose of flight which set my anxiety at rest.

In a little over an hour from now Uncle Harvey would be telling the Field-Marshal where Jakus Cicero could be found, which meant telling, also, the whole police force of the country, Interpol, and the Federal Bureau of Investigation.

And that, of course, included telling Christopher in Genoa, who together with Mr Peaslake and Bill Cabot might or might not by now have decided to believe that Jakus Cicero could be found anywhere at all in the living flesh. But what the effect on Christopher would be I seemed at this moment unable to care. It surprised me a little, but even that slight emotion did not last.

I edged my way back to where I could see the lawn. Jakus Cicero was drinking coffee and Father was laughing cheerfully about something. Laughing . . .

A movement below me caught my eye and I shifted slightly to be able to look more directly downwards.

Charlie was standing on the far side of the courtyard. He wore his usual faded blue cotton sweater and trousers and tattered rope sandals; his short hair was thick and curly on his big head. I enjoyed the large, familiar comforting sight of him for a brief moment; then the pleasure went abruptly. I realized that he was staring at the sky in the direction in which the pigeons had gone. He must have watched them out of sight before he turned his head slowly and shading his eyes with his hand looked up at the clock tower, straight up at it. I pulled back my face in alarm before I realized that he could not possibly see me through the narrow chink, particularly with the light against him.

Clairvoyance was not necessary to read his mind.

Pigeons in the clock tower were extremely unusual. Homing-pigeons in the clock tower came under the heading of phenomena.

When he had stopped staring, he would come across the courtyard towards me and disappear from view as he entered the door below, but only for a moment, and if I did not open the trap for him, he would open it for himself. I began to shiver even in the warm stuffiness; to explain anything however slightly out of the ordinary to Charlie was at the best of times a matter of planned diplomacy, but to be caught in here by him, in circumstances such as these—

I stopped shivering.

He had begun to move not towards the coach-house door but to the arch, as though to join the breakfast table. But again I was wrong. When he reached the arch he paused, and slowly, showing as little of his face as possible, peered round it.

Jakus Cicero had pulled out a large cigar case and offered it across the table. The field-glasses showed me the ornamental gold corner pieces of its crocodile leather. Father took a cigar, unashamedly sniffed it, crackled it at his ear and nodded appreciatively. Each lit up with the engrossed care of connoisseurs.

At last Charlie turned and came back into the courtyard. This time I was quite happy to see him coming towards the coach-house. The angle sharpened and he passed out of sight immediately below me without once glancing upwards, a precaution I appreciated as a care not to alarm the unknown enemy in the clock-tower.

I slid round to the trap-door, preparing my greeting. 'Good morning,' I would say, 'Charlie, dear. I'm home you see.' Then I would go on quickly with something about badly needing his help because the police could not possibly be here for at least an hour and a half if not longer.

I dropped the trap-door, unable to believe my ears.

Loud above the hum of the clock I was hearing the explosive uproar of a motor, unmistakably that of his ancient Austin. I got back to the spy-hole in time to see the little car swing into view out of the coach-house, turn sharply in the courtyard, and gathering speed, set off down the drive to the road across the heath, the road to the turnpike and its choice of directions to distant places.

I shifted slightly to be able to see the lawn again. Jakus Cicero's face was turned towards me, towards the courtyard and the decreasing sound.

His alertness was slightly, but only slightly, unnatural; the cigar poised in his hand halfway to his mouth spoke of constant watchfulness suddenly brought forth from its hiding place behind his relaxed air. Father seemed quite unaware of its significance, although he had not missed the man's curiosity and now explained the noise to him.

The watchfulness withdrew, the cigar went to the mouth.

And Charlie continued to drive blithely away from me at this the one moment in months and years when I felt I really needed him. I moved back to the position from which I could see the heath road—and stared in open-mouthed surprise at its complete emptiness.

I could see at least a mile of it with all its curves, but nowhere in them was there any sign of the car. Yet I thought I could still hear it faintly above the sound of the clock. I put the field-glasses to my eyes to check on what I thought must be an optical illusion. It was not. The only possible explanation, and it seemed quite senseless, must be that he had left the road and was driving about the heath between the gorse thickets.

What *was* he up to? Then suddenly it made sense—I thought. I could soon check if the guess was right, and in any case this was something I had already decided to attend to.

The *tête-à-tête* at the breakfast table still showed no sign of ending and it was as good a moment as any. I made a quiet but rapid descent to the coach-house below. Only the door opposite the Austin's stand was open so I was shielded from any chance observation from the kitchen windows. I saw now that the Daimler was jacked-up on blocks with its wheels off, and remembered Charlie's intention to fit new springs. As a means of escape it was out of the question . . .

I unfastened the hood of our guest's hired car and took off the distributor head. My guess was wrong. The rotor-arm was still in place and I was back with my bewilderment. If Charlie was not hiding the Austin, what *was* he doing with it?

I took out the rotor-arm, put it in my hip-pocket on top of the bits of the first one and lowered the Vauxhall's hood.

I climbed up to the clock-tower again and made another effort to clear up the mystery. I looked at my watch. On my guess that pigeons averaged fifty miles an hour on a homeward flight, John Bailey and the Prince Regent still had half the way to go. Add five minutes for Uncle Harvey to discover their return, another five minutes for him to begin the telephone call, five more to get through to Scotland Yard—always assuming that the Field-Marshal was going there first thing every day—it might still be an hour or more before I could expect to see anything remotely resembling a police car on that empty ribbon of road. Had I been too cautious in believing that Jakus Cicero would come to Marsh House? If I had gone straight to Grosvenor Square yesterday with my story of all that happened in Genoa, wouldn't the Field-Marshal have seen enough likelihood that the man would come after me, and prepare his forces? Or at least to have alerted the local police? Superintendent William Bull would have played with everything he had, being a good friend as well as a most efficient officer . . .

Father had finished the cigar but apparently he had not yet run out of conversation. He was talking and talking. In the normal way of things, he would have started off by now in his motor-chair for a morning's tinkering aboard *Peacock* or a tour of the estate or some other of his numerous and incessant ploys.

Jakus Cicero, however, seemed to have him charmed silly. Charm, of course, would be in his armoury; indeed after his gun and his strangler's hands, it might well have served as the most potent weapon in his rise to eminence in his particular world.

Not that he had used it in Angela's case, or was planning to use it mine . . .

He was looking at his wrist-watch, not merely with a glance but for a long moment as though making calculations. Was he more worried than he seemed by the fact that I was taking longer to reach home than he estimated?

An aspect of this now occurred to me which I had not foreseen; I had been expecting him to lie in wait under cover, where his conviction that the game was in his hands would keep impatience quiet. But out in the open like this, playing a part, his nerves could be very taut for all his toughness of mind and will. They might suddenly, under strain, set him smelling danger. He was in my trap, but it was not sprung. He might abruptly get up and walk out of it.

The likelihood was almost more alarming than the physical presence of the man himself.

Was I strong enough to do the bold thing, the only certain thing which would keep him here for the next hour? I told myself very quickly that I was not. Let him sit there awaiting a fate which would come to him without any further effort on my part.

But at the moment I made up my mind to this he stopped sitting there. He stood up abruptly, made a stiff-legged circuit of the table and sat down again.

210

I saw it as one of the most eloquent demonstrations of inner tension I could have asked for, and it pushed me straight back into a desperate feeling that I must do something to ease that tension.

The only thing in the world which would do that was my arrival . . .

If I arrived—and in innocence? Could I play it for that hour . . . plus?

Latterly's van was just what I needed. It came into the courtyard as I reached the bottom of the spiral staircase.

I waited until Mary had taken the packages from Mr Latterly and he was back at the wheel. Then I stepped out of the coach-house and kept the van between the kitchen windows and myself as it completed its turn and moved towards the drive. Mr Latterly saw me, of course, but there was no harm in that; he touched his hat and I returned the greeting.

It was years since I had climbed the ivy of the north wall but its growth had kept pace with mine, or at least to the extent that its ancient branches had become thicker and its hold on the wall even more tenacious. It supported me very well. But it was as dusty and dirt-purveying as ever, and I reached my bedroom window in a fine state of mess and dishevelment.

I stood up on the sill, clinging to the cross-piece of the window-frame, pulled up the lower half of the window and had to crouch dangerously before I could ease myself in.

The sight of myself in the long dressing-mirror was something of a shock, but in my obsession I could not allow myself more than a few minutes to clean up. I stripped as I made for the bathroom and was under the shower in a matter of moments.

But I was no sooner there than I began worrying whether that blue linen skirt was in the closet where I thought it was. Had I sent it to the wash? I couldn't remember, and the failure put me in a new dither. Dripping water I ran back to the bedroom and tore open the closet. The skirt—the skirt with

211

two seam pockets hidden in its fullness, was there.

My hair was full of twigs and heaven knew what; a comb was poor substitute for a shampoo, but that was all I had time for.

Stockings—no. The white sandals were the quickest to put on. I chose a white piqué blouse and spent a short two minutes putting my face in order.

I decided against carrying anything in my hands, even a small handbag. It would help me to look more innocent, more unprepared.

They had put him in the Blue Room. He must have made his own bed, for it was tidily covered and Ellen would still be doing the downstairs rooms. His luggage consisted of a small leather and canvas overnight bag which was on the floor by the side of the chest of drawers in which his things had been neatly put away; two expensive silk shirts, one plain cream, the other in a small black stripe, two pairs of socks, a change of underwear and a mushroom-pink tie without a maker's label. The bag was too small to have held an extra suit but all the same I looked in the wardrobe to make sure. I also stood on a chair to see if there was anything on top of it. There wasn't. But as I was about to leave the room the bed caught my eye again. It was true that I could not have put words to my conception of Jakus Cicero, but I felt there was something out of picture about a person with a way of life and attitude towards his fellow man such as his who would make his own bed in a house where there were servants to make it for him.

It was not a strong feeling, but it was enough to send me back into the room to run my hands under the mattress. I found the revolver without great surprise.

It was a .38 short-barrelled Webley. I stood holding it a moment and then on the same principle as the rotor-arms, took out the shells and dropped them out of the window into the herbaceous border below.

The fact that he was not carrying the gun on him seemed significant; for some reason he was not relying on it for what he had come to do. It worried me a little. Nevertheless, I felt I had won another point. I put the revolver under the mattress again.

I went down the main staircase. Ellen was using the electric sweeper in the morning-room and did not hear me. I came to the Long Room, cool and glimmering with the polished surfaces of old furniture, and moved across it to the french window and a view of the lawn, shining green in the sunshine and at its far edge under the dark cedar, the table. Ellen had cleared away the breakfast things in the meantime, but the two men were still seated at it.

I stepped out on to the flagstones and with a throat tightened by nervousness to the point where I had to force my breathing, I began to walk across the lawn. Father's back was towards me and Jakus Cicero would be the first to know that I had come home.

It seemed a hundred years and only after I had walked for endless miles that he raised his head, glossy with a close helmet of the blackest hair, and saw me.

All my senses were alert to catch his first reaction to read every subtle thought in his eyes, the satisfaction with himself for his planning, the certainty of impending triumph . . . and the thought to kill.

But sharply as I watched I could perceive none of these things. His eyes were so dark that he would never fail to hide his inner mind; his mouth was lipless in the swarthy skin, with no lines at its corners to deepen and betray emotion. Below the unparted hair was a wide, intelligent brow but the thick black eyebrows, straight and joined over his hook nose, and which did not rise even fractionally as he looked at me, spoke of a ready and primitive anger.

I managed to keep moving, and to greet Father almost naturally when in the next moment he became aware of me and turned his head.

'So you're back,' he said. 'I thought it was old Latterly.'

He was perceptibly sheepish under his matter-of-factness, remembering the state of things between us when we had last been together; he was clearly glad he was not alone. He waved an introductory hand.

'My daughter, Eve. Eve—Major Penshanger. Don't think you've met.'

The man stood up and held out his hand. I took it briefly. Major Penshanger! Had I been less frightened I might have laughed. *Penshanger!* It did not even sound like a real name —I had certainly never heard of it before. I took a little heart—just a little. Perhaps after all he was stupider than his legend made him out to be.

'No,' I said, 'we haven't met.'

I waited to hear his voice, with the heavy vowels and clipped words of a Sicilian's English, probably with a nasal overlay of Chicagoese. Father, however, continued to speak.

'The Major—' there was the faintest note of warning— 'is our new Chief Constable.'

'How nice,' I heard myself say, losing Major Penshanger's face in a sudden mist of confusion. *Chief Constable?* Was the man crazy, to come here in such an incredible guise, which only a gullible old silly like Father would believe? A small twinge of uncertainty, almost like a pain, shot through my preconception.

He spoke.

'But we have a mutual friend, have we not?' His voice, and this was the greatest surprise of all, was soft, and his accent of the pure Irish-English such as only a native Irishman could have. I tried not to stare at him, my mouth slack.

'What's that—*who*?' Father demanded. 'Not that fella Smith?'

'A fella called Orme,' said Major Penshanger, smiling at me with coal-black eyes—when they are not blue or any of the lighter colours, Irish eyes can be as dark as the darkness of skin and hair. Was not the south-west corner of County Cork known as 'Spain'?

All this, strange as it was, could be feasible. *But where, then, was Jakus Cicero?*

'Orme?' muttered Father, 'never heard of him,' and added that the Major was staying a couple of days with us. 'Taking a look round the county, putting himself in the picture. Don't much care for policemen as a rule. Nosy bastards.

214

But then you're not a policeman in the usual sense. Eve, of course, doesn't mind 'em.' He scowled at me with the false courage of belief that I was going to forgive him.

'I was going to marry one,' I said idiotically, 'but Father threw him in the creek.'

I tried to keep my head from turning to look about me, behind me—in all the directions from which attack might come.

Where was he? *Where?*

Father pulled on a wheel of his chair and swung himself about.

'I'm going to show the Major over *Peacock.*'

'She's not strictly speaking part of the county,' I said. 'You mustn't waste his time.'

'I think, if you don't mind, Commodore, I should like to have a talk with your daughter. The woman's angle you know.'

I was glad he seemed to want a word with me as much as I wanted one with him. Father's china-blue eyes were suspicious.

'Don't let her stuff you up with nonsense,' he said. 'She thinks practically everything a man does is a crime. I've got a lot to do—sextant to clean—see you at lunch.' He set off across the lawn at a fast clip towards the veranda round the corner where his motor-chair was parked. He stopped once to shout back at me to get up two bottles of the Roderer '47.

And I was alone with our new Chief Constable. I did not look at him but at the corner round which Father had disappeared.

A thought was filling the vacuum of my mind. Jakus Cicero could be a well-educated, linguistic sort of Italian. It was all very fine to have regarded him as a kind of evil force, but evil often has face and tongue and other human characteristics. Why couldn't I have taken the trouble to ask Mr Peaslake or Bill Cabot more about him as a *person?* My throat was going tight again . . . Jakus Cicero also could claim that Orme was a mutual acquaintance. Angela could have talked of her 'Uncle', and there was Shope's visit to Grosvenor Square . . . My confusion was greater than ever,

215

and fear lurked closely. Why was he so silent now, why were his eyes so intently and undeviatingly on me?

I forced words out.

'I have a telephone call to make—I'll be right back—' The voice did not seem like mine, nor the legs on which I began to walk away from him. The french windows were in the very far distance, the grass of the lawn was suddenly knee-high. Telephone . . . telephone—must get to it—only way I could check up, and if he was genuine, warn the Field-Marshal that my announcement via Uncle Harvey had been premature and that he must move very quietly lest he—

Oh God! The man was following me!

I thrust my hands deep into my skirt pockets and turned to face him. I coughed my paralysed larynx into life.

'I said I wouldn't be a moment, Major Penshanger.'

'I should feel easier,' he said, 'if we could have our talk at once.'

'And I should feel easier,' I retorted, 'if I knew you were comfortably smoking your cigar out here while I get rid of one or two chores—didn't Superintendent Ball tell you I like to have my own way?'

'Don't you mean Bull? Superintendent William Bull?'

'Ah, yes,' I said. 'Bull. And so many letters after his name . . .'

'Indeed there are. Order of the British Empire, Distinguished Service Cross, and the Military Cross. He referred to you as the most beautiful little devil of a girl in East Suffolk—yes, he did that.'

I had a moment to think while the staccato sound of Father's motor-chair filled the quiet morning. It lessened as he drove off towards the main dyke track to the creek.

'What has happened to Anderson?' I asked.

'Anderson?' He was puzzled. 'Oh yes. Colonel Alderton resigned about three weeks ago—ill health.'

'The trouble was,' I said, 'you looked too much like someone else, or rather what I've been imagining he would look like . . .'

It was my knees, nothing else but my knees, the looseness

of them suddenly, which made me sway like that. He caught me by both elbows.

'Lord Orme sent you?'

'To take a look here. It was some sort of help he was thinking you'd be wanting.'

I straightened up and stood on my own feet again and continued towards the Long Room. He kept by my side, walking stiffly in the same awkward way he had shown when he made that circuit of the table and had broken my patience. I realized now that he might not have been as worked up as I had thought. I was beginning to feel angry, and not only from reaction. I had cause for it.

'The Field-Marshal,' I said, 'is entitled to put two and two together. But he shouldn't have gone off half-cock—to use his own vernacular. He's upset everything—everything!'

'He has, has he? And in what way?'

'You've got to leave here at once!'

'I have, have I? My instructions are otherwise, Miss Gill. Quite otherwise.'

'There's a man here—somewhere near—waiting for a chance to come out of cover. He won't move as long as there's anyone about he can't account for.'

'What kind of a man would that be?' he asked with interest, but I thought he knew perfectly well what I was talking about.

I went ahead of him through the french windows and hurried to the telephone extension by the side of Father's bunk, saying that his instructions would have to be changed. 'This man has a lot at stake and he's capable of running a big risk. But we can't take even a small one that he may smell the trap and walk out of it.'

I had the receiver to my ear, waiting for the voice of the local exchange. They were taking their time. Major Penshanger stood quietly a pace or so behind me.

I jiggled the bar impatiently. 'Hello?' I said. 'Hello—exchange?' But they went on shucking peas or whatever they were doing. It was a little nightmarish, the sort of thing you dreamed about—the house burning down and the operator failing to notice your signal on her board.

217

I put down the receiver slowly.

'This line is dead,' I said.

'It is, indeed?' He sounded concerned. 'You think may-be—'

'Yes,' I said. 'Cut.'

'That's right, so it is,' said Sammy's voice from the region of the door. 'Don't move anybody, don't move. Don't even turn round.'

We did not move. I did not want to. It would have been too difficult until I could breathe again. *Now what?*

Sammy had come closer but remained behind us.

'Out,' he said. 'Get out. Through that window. *Out!* The girl first. If you don't make a start, sir, I shall shoot you. It's got a silencer, if you'd care to look round.'

Major Penshanger looked round and then followed me out on to the flagstones. I waited for him to come level with me.

'Take one of those chairs, sir, for the lady.'

The Major picked one up, a fellow to the one I had earlier watched him carry out when he joined Father. Sammy continued to issue orders.

We were to go and sit ourselves at the table, taking it nice and easy and natural you might say, and not to try running away or anything like that as there'd be a gun on us all the time—we would count on that.

I did not doubt him. Sammy was competent enough when it came to action of this sort. I said as much to the Major as we began to walk side by side across the open lawn towards the table.

He was taking the situation quietly so far. He looked over his shoulder.

'He's not behind us—'

'Someone has to lock Mary and the girls in the cellar.'

I had no sooner said it than there was a short scream in the house—from Ellen, I thought it must be. Sammy was at his game of frightening young women; I hoped he would not progress to his favourite one of knocking them about.

'I'd like to get my hands on him,' Major Penshanger commented '—and I will. All the same, he doesn't look

218

much in spite of the gun and that handkerchief over his face.'

'He's not *the* one. Sammy helps prepare the way on these occasions. I don't know his other name. You wait.'

'I don't think I will.' He seemed to be working himself up.

'I think you'd better,' I said. 'Look over there, to your left—and that's not Number One, either.'

A thin man in black wearing a wide-brimmed black hat pulled down to hide the upper part of his face was leaning against the trunk of an oleander on the edge of the lawn. He had a long-barrelled automatic pistol in his right hand.

I added—having difficulty with my breathing—that I was fairly certain he must be a man called Morelli, whose voice was all I so far knew of him. 'Even so, he doesn't talk much.'

'What do they think they're playing at!' It was a statement of anger rather than a question.

Morelli was affecting a bored casualness, but he watched us like a lynx from under his hat.

'I hadn't expected to see him here,' I said, 'but I suppose Sammy alone wouldn't be a good enough witness. Not being on the inside—'

I was aware of gratitude to Major Penshanger for his admirable calm. He was making it possible for me to pretend outwardly at least that I was still in control of my senses. We were still some way from the table. I had to put effort into walking steadily. Luckily the Major was going slowly; his gait had a bear-like roll.

'If there's a chance—' he began.

'Please—there isn't, not yet—'

'I was going to say, a chance to hear just what you've brought home with you, it might help me in dealing with this.'

'The Field-Marshal didn't tell you?'

'No,' he said.

How could I be expected to put together a coherent story at a moment like this?

We were at the table at last. I sat down with immense relief in the chair he unfolded for me. He went round the table and sat down himself. Morelli had not stirred except to keep his pistol on us. It was an easy shooting distance but we were out of range of his ears if we kept our voices down.

'What exactly did the Field-Marshal tell you?'

'He asked that I should personally come over and keep an eye open. He said he thought you had been trailing your coat.'

'A yellow suit—as a red cloak. Is that all he said?'

'And that someone rather dangerous might come after you.'

'Did he give him a name?'

'No.'

'Jakus Cicero,' I said.

'A crook of some kind?'

I was looking at him, but now I looked more closely. It seemed odd that there should be anyone in the world who had not heard of Jakus Cicero. But then I had become obsessed with him. And as Father had pointed out, Chief Constables are not always recruited from professional policemen—and although unlikely, there might even be policemen also who had never heard of him.

'A crook?' I said. 'Yes. But chiefly the murderer of Angela Sawyer. You'll have heard of her.'

'Lord Orme's niece! But I thought—'

'That Arthur North did it? So does everyone. But in fact he didn't. This Jakus Cicero was responsible. Personally. She was a particular friend of mine. I let him know I knew he did it—and that I could prove it.'

'If you have proof, for the Lord's sake don't hang on to it—tell me what and where it is. We may not both get out of this—and if I may say so, if one of us does it's more likely to be me—' Major Penshanger took out his crocodile cigar case and chose a cigar with commendably steady fingers. 'If the Law is to mean anything—'

He found a box of matches in another pocket and lit the cigar, moving it round in his mouth so that it should burn evenly, but his eyes remained on me, insistent and compelling, even through the eddying smoke of the cigar. A single-minded man, to pursue an abstraction in the midst of mortal reality . . .

'If the Law is to mean anything,' I began, 'the Law will have to—'

I stopped in mid-sentence.

The movement was over there to my left . . .

Christopher, still in the clothes he had been wearing in Genoa, came through the arch. Immediately after him walked Sammy with a green handkerchief covering the lower half of his face and a pistol in his hand, a smaller pistol than that favoured by Morelli. Christopher's hands were raised and his expression was perceptibly bleak even at thirty yards' distance. This was an arrival for which I had not nerved myself.

'Oh God! What have I done?' I said it aloud.

But Major Penshanger was too occupied with the scene to ask what I meant.

Sammy ordered Christopher towards Morelli, and they passed some ten yards or so behind me. I did not look round or speak, but I watched Major Penshanger watching him. He certainly did not know who he was, for the slight frown, which made his heavy eyebrows point up together in the middle, had no recognition behind it.

'He rang the door bell,' I heard Sammy announce loudly, as though Morelli was deaf. 'Says he's a police officer. Could be. They come all kinds and sizes over here. Rustic type. Came on a bicycle. Don't ask me why he's not in uniform. Says he's inquiring about some smuggler or other believed to be in these parts.'

Morelli's silence dispelled my last doubt about his identity; he had taken a long time to open his mouth in Shope's room that night.

There was a faint clicking sound, then Sammy's voice again, as loudly as before:

'These are good enough passport for me—and here's his warrant card. Look at that, for crissake! All the way from the big city! W'adyaknow!' Sammy's movie-gangster idiom was as typical of his subordinate rank as a lance-corporal's stripe.

The clinking sounded again, followed by two successive clicks.

I would not look round. I had had enough of seeing Christopher in his bad moments and he knowing that I was seeing. Never again, even if for the best of all reasons it might be the last I ever saw of him in this life.

But I jerked round convulsively at the sound of the sharp thud and the choked groan which came swiftly after it. Christopher, his wrists handcuffed behind a copper-beech sapling near Morelli's oleander, dropped forward with hanging head, his knees buckling so that he slid slowly downwards into a distorted sitting position. Sammy stood over him with reversed gun, eyeing him intently, gauging the extent of his unconsciousness. Morelli, however, was still watching us at the table. Sammy turned away towards the house without hitting Christopher again. You did not overdo a thing like that—not with a policeman.

'I cannot believe,' Major Penshanger was picking up his interrupted thread with surprising pertinacity, 'that he would go to all this trouble and danger on the mere chance that you had proof.'

I turned back to him . . .

And it was at this exact moment I realized that something very odd indeed had happened. It had happened under my nose—and I had not noticed. For a moment, however, I could not focus it properly, and I was silent for several seconds. This bothered Major Penshanger, for he repeated that if I had proof I must say so—now, quickly, before the situation changed for the worse, as he felt it must do.

'There is the diary—' I said. 'Angela's diary.'

'Ah!' he said, and the way that small exclamation came from his invisible lips confirmed why Morelli had let him put a hand inside his jacket for his cigar-case without immediately shooting him.

It had not mattered in the least to Morelli whether Major Penshanger brought out a cigar-case or a gun.

So I said, 'There is a diary,' instead of what I had been on the very brink of saying: 'He *thinks* there is a diary.' And Jakus Cicero said, 'Ah!' being glad to hear that one of his

222

reasons for coming after me had been substantiated. I could have spoken his next words for him:

'Where is this diary?'

But for that cigar-case I should never have doubted his right to ask it. He had prepared the way to it boldly and cleverly.

'In a safe place,' was the best answer I could find on the spur of the moment, sharp as it was.

'They'll find it!' he said, under his breath, leaning forward, staring at me. 'You've brought it back with you?'

I nodded the lie. Here was time, but was there enough of it?

'You've hidden it?'

I crossed my fingers in the secrecy of my pocket and nodded again.

'For God's sake, girl, *where*?'

'There's no safety for it in telling you. Not while you're in their hands.'

'Do you think I propose to stay in their hands—or let you stay in them?' he added quickly. '*Where is that diary hidden?*'

'I'm frightened,' I said, 'but I think I can trust myself not to talk—'

'Brave words—'

'—but only because no one else knows. No one here, that is.'

He was on it like a trout at a fly.

'Someone else does know, then?'

'I can't stand this waiting!' I cried, and looked about me wildly. I did not think Morelli would shoot me for that sort of movement, or indeed for practically any other I made at this point. Morelli, in fact, was a stage prop as far as this scene was concerned. His master was playing in it and his master was more than the chief actor; he was author, director and impresario as well. That I knew it, however, neither he or his master yet realized. But how long I could hide it from them was another matter.

'Listen to me!' Jakus Cicero sounded very angry indeed, 'you talk big, but you've bitten off a great deal more than you can chew—and I think you're beginning to realize it. If you're not a complete fool you'll see that the more people on the right side of the law who know where—'

I looked up at him, twisting my face in agony of panic.

'If you've a way of getting us out of this,' I said desperately, 'please, *please* do something about it!'

'I can't do anything about it as long as you persist in this obstinate stupidity! I've a plan, but I can't use it if I haven't the means.'

'What means?'

'The diary, Miss Gill.' He stood up, the better to force my attention. Morelli remained languid and impassive; indeed, his pistol-point did not seem as alert as it had been. The play had an entertainment value, perhaps. 'The diary,' said Jakus Cicero again. 'I propose to bargain with these men over that diary, and in such a way that although this Jakus Cicero may get his hands on it, it will be too late.'

'But,' I said, 'I think you should also know that the real danger to him is not proof that he killed Angela but the revelation of his identity. He's supposed to be dead, you see.'

He snapped his fingers impatiently. 'Let's get back to the diary,' he said, 'and realize that you haven't all day to—'

I never knew what the rest of it was to have been. Sammy once again interrupted, this time with his voice from the french windows, loud enough to reach not only Morelli but also, I now realized, Jakus Cicero at the table.

'If she had any kind of gun out there with her she hasn't brought it home. Maybe she scared herself with it and ditched it some place.'

I looked round briefly while he was speaking. He was there on the lawn behind me, his pistol stuck in the top of his trousers. Christopher's drooping head moved as though he was aware of Sammy's voice, if only as a meaningless sound.

It was Morelli, however, in whom I was most interested in that moment before I had to face Jakus Cicero again. He had not left his position at the tree, but he was no longer leaning against it and his negligent air had given place to

224

alert and indeed critical attention to what was happening between his master and me. There were larger issues than the whereabouts of the pistol with which I had missed Bogsie at two paces.

He gestured to Sammy to go away, and Sammy shrugged and went towards the archway. I was remembering my conversation with Mr Peaslake about king-wolves . . .

Morelli had been expecting, had been given to expect, a straightforward show-down with me which was to have been followed by immediate action. But nothing had happened —except a lot of talk he couldn't hear. *Why* all the talk? Something wrong? Was the Big Shot slipping? Things lately had shown the possibility of it.

I lowered my voice to a point where Morelli could not possibly hear me and returned Jakus Cicero's stare. It was a big chance to take but I thought it worth while.

'You're a silly fool if you think I've gone to all the trouble of getting you here just to hand over the proof you killed Angela Sawyer merely because you say you're someone else.' And I laughed derisively in his face.

He got to his feet with a stumbling jerk which upset his chair and stood looking down at me in a choleric fury, his dark face plum-purple with the pressure of it.

If he was trying to say something, he failed, and I hoped that Morelli, who was not in danger himself from his master's rage, would be freer even than I, the object of it, to appreciate his consternation.

Quite possibly, I thought, this is my last moment. I looked it coldly in the eye, which was all there was left for me to do and continued, somehow, to talk.

'You've come here to kill me, of course, as you killed her. You'll get a certain amount of satisfaction out of it but I wonder how much reputation? I might add that there isn't a diary and never was one—'

He was moving round the table and I was getting to my feet as I was speaking, words which meant nothing to him and little more to me. I squared my shoulders and kept my hands in my pockets. I did not expect him to be put out by this defiant attitude but it might look effective to Morelli, whom I could see now that I began to back away from Jakus Cicero's slow advance. The pistol-point was lower than ever. This was beyond guns, even for a gunman, and he had almost forgotten the trigger within the curl of his forefinger; a girl might be about to die but the circumstances of her death were more important to him than the fact of it. Jakus Cicero was on trial; Napoleon had returned in a bid to keep his empire. Was he fit to keep it? Morelli watched with half-hidden eyes which would miss nothing of this, neither in its physical nor in its political implications.

I backed slowly. Jakus Cicero followed, his intention crystallized in cooling rage, but as yet moving no faster. I told myself not to be deceived by that lumbering walk, the right leg seeming a little stiff in its hip-joint. One leap and he would close the gap and because I dared not turn to run and still defy him for Morelli's benefit, he could reach and crush me to the ground in a single movement. His hands would be round my throat in the same instant. My choice of moment must be timed to that fraction of a second when he gathered himself for the final forward lunge.

Three . . . four . . . five paces backwards on a diagonal line across the lawn, with the courtyard arch twenty yards or more behind me . . . Morelli at his tree was now at right angles to me . . . Christopher's head was moving with more life as though he was summoning his will to drag him back to consciousness; I hoped with all my heart that it would elude him a minute or so longer . . . Morelli took no notice of him—he knew he could not play any part with his wrists secured behind the sapling like that.

But Jakus Cicero, without taking his eyes from me or pausing in his advance, snapped at Morelli in Italian to 'watch that policeman.'

Because his jackal showed no reaction to his order he repeated it with greater emphasis and added, 'Do something about him!' Morelli's head turned slightly but what he saw did not disturb him, and certainly not to the extent of missing any detail of the killing he had been brought all this way to see.

I found another trump in my hand which I had almost forgotten. I had hidden it so carefully from them. I called out: '*Ecco qualche cosa di nuovo! Teme la polizia, il famoso Jakus Cicero! Per dire la verità, ha paura anche di me, una semplice ragazza!*' I put into it all the derision of which I was capable.

I expected it to release the spring at last and set him at me—not the insult that he was frightened of a policeman and even of me, a helpless female, but the discovery that I could speak Italian and had therefore fooled them even more than he thought. But it did not. Instead he stopped short, breathing fast, as though he had been running. I stopped also, in keeping with defiance.

'Who are you?' he asked under his breath. 'Who the hell are you?'

I answered him in Italian that if he wanted it in a nutshell, it could be said that I was the end of him.

This was surely the signal for his leap, the immediate proof that on the other hand he was the end of me.

But still it did not come.

And yet the desire for it—the urgent, violent need for it —was in every line of the man.

Then I realized the truth . . .

He dared not make it for fear that it would fail.

Why? Because he was physically incapable of it! That awkwardness in his movements, the getting up from the breakfast table to walk around it, stiffly, the drag of his right leg . . . Mr Peaslake had deserved some part of his medal after all.

Morelli watched and waited, and even in this moment was realizing that what he and the rest of the pack had suspected, was indeed true. The old wolf could stand within reach of his kill, and yet could not make it.

But because he could not did not mean that I would be spared. He might have lost his kingship through me, but I was still the enemy and must not live. Morelli would take over that responsibility—now.

So then, as I saw his pistol-point begin to move, I raised my hand in my pocket and fired. The bullet passed close to Jakus Cicero and he flinched with a simultaneous and instinctive movement of his hand towards an underarm holster which was not there, his eyes on the black tear in my skirt. He had not realized in the shock of the thing that I had hit Morelli, and where I had meant to hit him.

The man had swung about, his pistol jumping out of his hand and falling near Christopher's feet. He clutched his right shoulder with a yelp, the first sound I had heard him utter. At the same moment I set off at a run for the pistol; he still had a good hand if he recovered sufficiently to use it. I heard Jakus Cicero moving behind me, but I found no terror in it. Morelli was in fact recovering. Blind to the danger that I might shoot him again he made a dive for the pistol. I had my own out and levelled but Christopher, conscious enough to see him coming, kicked out with more luck than aim and caught him in the face. He gave a squealing gasp and staggered backwards, turned and made for the far corner of the lawn and the track through the woods. I scooped up the pistol and kept going, flung myself into the bushes behind Christopher and sat up on my knees. But Jakus Cicero, if he had started after me at all, had changed his mind for a surer plan and veered towards the french windows. He was within a few feet of them and there would have been time and enough to shoot him down. But I thought I could count on that movement of his hand for the gun he had disdained to carry.

In the meantime there was Sammy to consider. He would have heard the single pistol shot, but I could not assume that he would believe it had been my execution and continue to guard the other side of the house. He might come back again to see what was happening.

I watched the archway for his reappearance while I crawled up behind Christopher. He was pulling at his wrists, puzzled as to why he could not free them. He was still very dazed.

'Key,' I said.

'*Eve!*' It was more a groan than a word.

'Which pocket—quickly—'

He groaned again and strained at his wrists. The archway remained empty; I put down Morelli's pistol, and transferring my own from right hand to left and back again, tried to search his pockets.

'Ticket pocket—' he mumbled, 'inside right—'

I felt for it, meeting a pipe and something which might be a packet of cigarettes.

'Higher—top of lining—'

I found the small pocket and the key in it and unlocked one side of the handcuffs. He did not wait for me to unlock the other, but shifted his arms forward with the things dangling from one wrist. He grunted with pain. I pulled his arms back again, unlocked the other cuff and held on to his hands.

'Don't let them see you're free,' I said.

'Oh God—Eve?'

'I'm here. You've had a bang on the head . . . keep still.'

'Heard shooting—' His voice had more energy in it. 'God's sake give up trying to handle this by yourself . . . must telephone—' He pulled at his hands. I hung on to them.

'Telephone isn't working—' I told him.

'Should be by now—eyes acting up—double vision. Oh damn and blast!' But he stopped trying to get his hands away from me and I was able to release them. He clasped his fingers and from the front would seem to be still hand-cuffed. I put the handcuffs in his jacket pocket and picked up the pistols again.

'He'll be back any moment,' I said.

'Jakus Cicero?' There was no sarcasm in it. 'Brute at the table with you? Talked with Peaslake—you knew what you were about after all . . . Sorry, *Eve?*'

'I'm still here.'

'Should have listened—first place—sorry—'

'Why on earth did they let you come alone!' I said violently. 'Wouldn't they listen?'

'Didn't consult.'

'But the Field-Marshal—'

'What could he do? Not Lord Almighty.'

The archway still revealed nothing of Sammy, and the french window was a dark slit in which nothing moved. I kept my eyes on it, crouching behind Christopher and hidden by him.

'But he's Commissioner of Police—' I said, 'or designate.'

Christopher jerked as though I had stuck a pin in him.

'What—*what* d'you say?'

His head dropped and his arms went slack. In a moment of heart-breaking terror I thought he was dead. But in the next I realized that he had only passed out again, as though the bruised brain had taken refuge from the activity which he was forcing on it. I swallowed with a dry mouth.

At that moment I saw Jakus Cicero in the french window, or rather, a few inches of him—his left shoulder, a portion of his thigh and his left foot. He stood there examining the lawn and its surrounding garden. A momentary glitter of metal told me he had the revolver in his right hand.

Then, at last, Sammy appeared in the archway. He also was holding his pistol. Neither could see the other, and would not unless one of them moved out on to the lawn.

Sammy was obviously puzzled; indeed he took an involuntary half-pace backwards and surveyed the lawn from the same place as Charlie had chosen when I was watching him from the clock-tower. He had reason to be puzzled. The policeman slumped at the foot of the sapling was the only thing which matched what he had been expecting to see. Morelli, no longer leaning against his tree, had completely disappeared. There was no one at the table, and the chair from which Jakus Cicero had been exercising his masterful command of the situation was lying on its side on the grass . . . and there had been but one single shot. It would have perplexed anyone, and I was not surprised that Sammy should stay safely where he was while he tried to add it up.

I also tried to add it up from my point of view with a slight advantage over him, over them both. I could see them but they could not see me. I had two pistols—as indeed had they between them—but both mine were loaded. I did not know whether Jakus Cicero had discovered that his was not, or if he had, whether he had been able to rectify the matter with spare ammunition I had not happened upon when I had searched the Blue Room. And I did not know how far away or how close the Law might be at this critical moment.

The only thing I did know was that Jakus Cicero's intention to kill me, based on absolute necessity and unshaken by the surprise of my resistance to it, still governed and controlled him.

Neither man moved, as if each waited for something to guide him in the line of action suited to his need, Sammy to decide where he stood in relation to his own skin, Jakus Cicero in terms of his necessity to kill.

The brief seconds followed one another and I found myself counting them.

Christopher stirred slightly, and afraid that he might move his arms forward I put my knee across his hands, holding them to the ground.

A full minute passed before Sammy finally made up his mind, presumably on the basis that the shot had in fact been my end—although not the one he had been led to expect—and that the absence of his bosses meant they were hiding my body somewhere—again, perhaps, a change from the original plan. But reassured by the quietness, he came out of the archway and began to walk slowly with pistol ready along the path by the side of the house; he could face the lawn all the time, having the protection of the wall on his immediate left. He was wearing rubber soles and moved silently on the flagstones. I watched with interest, for he would come unheard upon Jakus Cicero in the window. It would be somewhat of a surprise to both of them, but more so to Sammy; he would have to guess again about what had happened. Would Jakus Cicero tell him? Whether he chose to or not, Sammy might feel even more uncertain about the wisdom of staying with a plan which had gone wrong.

But when he was only a few yards short of the window he cautiously left the path for the lawn itself and thus had his back to Jakus Cicero when he came into his view. I saw that his diagonal course towards the far corner of the lawn would bring him to the woods and the track where his caravan was hidden. He would be able to help Morelli start the un-startable car, if Morelli's wound had allowed him to get that far.

It looked as though Jakus Cicero was content to let Sammy go, for he was making no effort to stop him. Then I realized his silence hid a purpose. Sammy was providing him with an admirable decoy. If nothing happened to Sammy it was reasonable to assume that I was not around, that I had run away while the running was good.

Even as I saw the point, Jakus Cicero spoke a name sharply: 'Murdoch!' it sounded like, and Sammy spun about with his pistol up. Jakus Cicero came out of the window with a more definite limp than ever, and joined him, holding the revolver at an innocuous angle. I could not hear what they were saying, but I guessed the import of it; Sammy looked swiftly round the lawn as though to reassure himself. Then the savage emphasis with which his master now began to talk to him drew all his attention. I caught a phrase in Jakus Cicero's rising voice: '. . . a thousand of your pounds, alive—five hundred dead . . .'

He made a movement with his left hand, an encircling movement, and gestured towards the archway. Sammy seemed doubtful, and was punished for it with a short spate of even more emphatic words. If he thought he was going to be allowed to walk out of this now, he was much mistaken. His ginger head wagged from side to side in an 'okay, okay' surrender.

In a moment they would part in the search for me.

I was in temptation . . .

Against the alternative of keeping quiet until the police arrived, making sure that Christopher conformed to what these men imagined to be his condition, even to handcuffing him again should it be wiser to leave him and find a better hiding-place—against this I had an opportunity to bring the thing to an immediate curtain. The objectives for which I had been working had never been clearer to me than in this moment of doubt. They arranged themselves in silent words— '*Catch her murderer and stop Christopher making a terrible mistake.*'

I could not look at the morality of it, or judge it in that way. It might be expediency, or even cheating on a scale for which I should one day have to pay an awful price.

Perhaps I did not stop to think at all but simply saw instinctively a chance of putting things right—even to the extent of easing my own conscience about that deceitful moment when I had let Christopher fire off those warning shots which had sent *Peacock* scurrying . . . It was such a chance and I took it.

I removed my knee from Christopher's hands, pushed his right arm forward with my own inside it close to his hip, and with Morelli's pistol aimed carefully at the fleshy part of Sammy's right thigh. I pulled the trigger.

Three things happened together.

Sammy gave a leap into the air and fell down, losing his pistol, which slid along the grass to his right. He made a cawing noise as he rolled over and tried vainly to get to his feet again as more fear than pain possessed him.

Christopher was jerked back into nearly complete consciousness by the burst of the explosion within six inches of his ear, and his head came up on his shoulders and stayed up.

And Jakus Cicero, momentarily thrown off balance by Sammy's fall and also hampered by his own difficulty in moving quickly, was a little slow to throw himself on the ground. But he got down all right with his gun still in his hand and his body in line with the angle of fire, which told me he knew where the shot had come from. He began to raise his gun. His head rose an inch or so with it so that he could get his eye to the sights. The only target he could see was Christopher, who was muttering that his eyes were still playing him up. And what was happening . . .

If I shot first, and I could, for I was on my knees with pistol already aimed, there was only one place I could hit Jakus Cicero if I were to stop him. But it would also mean his death. I had never killed anyone in my life and in that timeless moment I knew that I never would, that I had not the courage for it.

There was only one way out of it. The desperate gamble of the cartridges in the herbaceous border. But it was one which only I could take. That, and the difficulty he might have in hitting a moving target.

In the fraction of a second left to me I thrust Morelli's pistol into Christopher's hand, picked up my own, and ran like a hare in and out of the bushes on a zig-zag course towards the north corner of the house.

Ten, twenty, twenty-five yards, but the crack of the shot did not sound, no bullet pursued me. I changed direction for the solid if narrow trunk of one of the three copper beeches we had planted on my tenth birthday, caught it in the crook of my left arm and swung myself to a standstill behind it.

Jakus Cicero was crawling towards the pistol Sammy had dropped. He still had six feet to go and I had time to aim. The bullet ploughed into the turf a few inches from his head. To make sure he understood it I put another in almost exactly the same place. He stopped and lay still like a death-feigning spider, a black spider. Sammy had begun to drag himself towards the archway, oblivious of everything except the wound in his leg and the urgent need to get away. I saw no reason to stop him.

I looked back at Christopher. He was standing up, his feet apart, swaying. He had heard my two shots, of course, but I did not think he knew that they had come from me; he was rubbing his eyes with the back of his hand. He still held Morelli's pistol in the other, but I doubted if he was more than just beginning to realize it was there.

I was right. He peered at the still figure of Jakus Cicero and Sammy's slightly more active one, and from them with noticeable bewilderment to the pistol in his hand. But he tightened his grasp on it and began to move unsteadily forward on to the lawn.

He picked up Sammy's gun, nearly falling down as he did so, and put it in his pocket. He raised his voice at Sammy, ordering him to stay where he was. Sammy turned over and lay staring at him glassily. He told Jakus Cicero to get up. 'Or did I wing you too? . . .'

I drew a deep breath of infinite relief.

He had accepted the evidence of his eyes against the doubts in his confused mind. The chance had come off. I had lowered the curtain.

234

The man rose clumsily to his feet, watching the pistol. Christopher called my name:

'Eve!' It was the third time, but his anxiety to have me answer him was no less. I dropped my notion to leave the scene by way of the bushes.

'Yes, Christopher—' I put my pistol in its unobvious pocket, hoped he would not notice the blackened hole in the skirt before I had time to change it, and came out from behind the copper beech.

He did not look round while I was approaching, his eyes on his prisoners. I stood to his left, a little behind him.

'You're not hurt or anything?'

I told him that I was all right.

His shoulders moved.

'Come where I can see you.' It was a naked avowal—if I dared believe it. I moved to where he could see me without endangering his control.

Jakus Cicero had not uttered a word. His dark face was set in a blankness which hid the fear and the hatred consuming him. His eyes were fixed on me, opaque and terrible in their expressionless stare. I turned away from them, and was reassured. While Christopher could look at me like that hatred would not hurt me. He smiled at me and sighed, and himself reassured, was able to revert to Jakus Cicero, whom he addressed by name, telling him he was under arrest for being found in possession of a lethal weapon and that anything he said might be used in evidence. It was a safe enough charge for the moment.

Thereafter things were without reality for me. Even the abrupt appearance of Charlie carrying a shotgun, and men in dark uniforms, any number of them, ringing the lawn and moving in upon it with intent faces. Amongst them was Billy Bull himself, his silver stars gleaming on his shoulder straps. But nothing at the moment could distract me from the greater reality of Christopher's smile; it remained there, indestructible under the resumed watchfulness of his expression.

He handed Morelli's pistol to Charlie, who was nearest him, and reaching into his pocket for the handcuffs stepped

235

up to Jakus Cicero. But Billy Bull saw his unsteadiness and took them from him. They were put on the thick dark wrists and two policemen led the man away. Billy Bull had said something to Christopher but my ears did not take it in. His uncertainty on his feet was increasing. I reached him first and caught him as his knees gave way. He was too heavy for me, of course, and I did no more than break his fall, so that we came down together in a heap. But my arms were round him and I held his head against my breast.

'More of a crack than I thought,' he said. 'It's you?'

'Yes—it's me.'

'Good,' he whispered, and again: 'Good.'

Then he laughed softly as he had failed to laugh a week ago, when I held him like this on the beach after Charlie had pulled him out of the creek. It was a rueful but unashamed laugh—at himself. I wanted to cry. He had come a long way since then.

'Get a stretcher,' said Billy Bull and a policeman hurried away. The faces looked down at us but I cannot say I saw them clearly. Except Charlie's. Charlie was frowning.

'Please,' I said, 'please, Charlie—'

'All right,' he said, 'if you want him.'

'You know I do!'

'You've never been sure you—'

I cut across the argument: 'And where were you all this time?'

He gestured at Christopher: 'He wanted me to telephone Billy Bull—nearest police—'

'That's right,' Christopher muttered. 'Line was cut—'

'—out on the heath. Been mending it. He came in, to take a look at things for himself—' He shook his head at the result. 'How could we know you'd arrived?'

'You saw my pigeons—'

'*Your* pigeons? I thought—' Charlie stopped.

I never really found out what he thought about the pigeons for there was a bustling at the archway and the Field-Marshal appeared, escorted by more policemen, several of them with silver on the peaks of their caps. Douglas himself was in a dark suit, wore an unnatural bowler hat and carried a tightly rolled umbrella. He was like a thundercloud descending on us.

'*Pigeons!*' he said, as though he was joining in the conversation he had not heard. 'What's the matter with the telephone! Why couldn't you telephone! He might have killed you!'

That was true enough. In fact, it had been the main idea, as he well knew and which probably explained his anger.

'They cut the line out on the heath,' Charlie began again. 'Smith told me to mend it, so I—'

'I'm not talking about *this* telephone!' the Field-Marshal bawled. 'You—Eve—you should have got in touch the moment you landed—hell and damnation! I'd have believed *you*.' But the lightning which flashed in his eyes was obscured by the tears in them. However, one could see he would make a tartar of a Commissioner—it was in all their expressions, even in Billy Bull's, who is afraid of no man. Douglas turned his thunder upon Christopher, who did not hear it.

'And as for you, Smith, your message was as blatant a piece of insubordination as I ever met—is he hurt?'

'Only a little,' I said. 'Mostly concussion I think. But it won't do him any good to have you shouting at him. What message?'

'Telling Scotland Yard he couldn't wait for them to make up their minds about—' He broke off and demanded who had taken Jakus Cicero. 'Smith?'

'Who else?' I said it loudly. It was something which they—and Christopher—must never question.

'That's right,' said Billy Bull and took Morelli's pistol from Charlie. 'Where did he get this? It's not regulation. Sam Murdoch's?'

'No,' I said and told them where I thought they could find Morelli. A bunch of them started off at a run, Charlie leading because he knew the way.

I heard Father's motor-chair before I saw it but I could do nothing to save him from the shock of what he would see when he came off the dyke path and in sight of the lawn.

It would take him weeks to get over it. All these policemen. But their numbers quelled the outbreak of indignation which was his first reaction. Even Christopher Smith being put on a stretcher with me closer to him than anybody, in fact with my arms more or less round him still, failed to arouse him to more than a scowl of recognition. I had never seen him taken so unawares. 'Heard gun-fire—' He revved up the motor to cover his efforts towards an outburst. 'What —what the hell is this all about?' was the best he could manage.

'Our new Chief Constable,' I told him, 'turned out to be someone else.' And with that he would have to be content until I could find the right moment for a fuller story, preferably with a good dinner and a bottle and a half of claret inside him.

I introduced him to the Field-Marshal as a diversion.

'Seem to have heard of you,' said Father, reassured by the fact that he did not appear to be a policeman. 'Are they *sure* he isn't the new Chief Constable?'

'Quite sure,' said the Field-Marshal.

'Lot of damn' fools, generally wrong about everything. Can you drink champagne mid-morning? Proper time for it.'

'To my mind the best time for it.'

Douglas walked beside the motor-chair to the Long Room while I waited with Billy Bull for the ambulance to come.

I sat on the grass and held Christopher's hand. He was coming out of the dizzy spell and saw no reason for being cosseted.

Billy Bull, who had already stamped fiercely on my attempt to have Christopher put to bed here, told him that the sooner they did an X-ray of his skull the better.

'I've got a head like iron,' he protested.

The parts of it which aren't wood, I thought, but that was no way to begin a life-long association with a man, even to let oneself think such a comment.

I must learn to be a nice girl if I was to be a good wife.

When the ambulance arrived he refused to let me come to the hospital with him.

'You've had enough of this, one way and another. Just

stop, will you. *Stop*. If you understand what that means . . . darling,' he added.

Billy Bull promised to telephone.

'*I*,' said Christopher firmly, 'will telephone.'

If I had not kissed him temporarily goodbye, he would not have thought of it for himself. It would probably always be like that, although possibly I might with time and a little skill develop that side of him. However, I could not have everything.

Billy Bull grinned at the kiss. Nobody seemed really to mind that I had chosen at last, although I thought Charlie would continue to have reservations.

I watched the ambulance out of sight round the curve of the drive and hurried to the kitchen. Mary and the two girls were busy telling each her own version of the outrageous attack on them, how dark had been the cellar, how near sudden death. All three were telling it together. For the first and only time in my knowledge Mary had yielded the handle of the big black teapot to another; Angus was keeping their cups full, the stern correctness of his bottle-green uniform softened by a ministering air. They were in good hands, and I could go straight to my room to change my skirt. There were going to be a terrible lot of questions in any case, but why add to them with one about singed bullet holes in my pocket?

I unloaded and cleaned the pistol before putting it away in the bureau drawer—without its leather case, which would still be lying on top of the wardrobe in the *Savoie* . . .

Had Christopher stayed in Genoa long enough to pick up my bags? Was George still waiting for me in Cannes? And where was Mr Peaslake? Had he resisted the pressure of belief that Jakus Cicero was alive, and remained a terrier at the rat hole of the house in *via Gambino*? Would Jakus Cicero be extradited or stand trial for Angela's murder, with Morelli and Sammy by his side in dock—or one of them, the other having turned Queen's evidence? Sammy, for instance?

And Arthur North? They mustn't hold him a minute longer . . . but having charged him with murder they would have to take him before a magistrate to be discharged, without a stain on his character and so on. It could be done immediately however—must be done immediately. Had the Field-Marshal remembered the poor wretched young man?

And Mizzie? I had completely forgotten her. She was a silly girl, nothing worse. I might be able to make them understand that.

And the Bristol to be returned to the Field-Marshal . . . and Figge to be written to and told the story.

My evidence would . . . Oh, dear heavens, yes—evidence . . . I was going to be one of the witnesses . . .

Stop, he had said. How could I stop?

I hurried downstairs. I had far greater need of that champagne than either of them. Besides I must toast my love.